Georgiana and the Wolf

Georgiana and the Wolf

Jane Austen's
Pride and Prejudice
Continues

Marsha Altman

Laughing Man Publications

Previous Works

The Darcys and the Bingleys
The Plight of the Darcy Brothers
Mr. Darcy's Great Escape
The Ballad of Grégoire Darcy
The Knights of Derbyshire

Short Story Collections

Other Tales: Stories from the Ballad of Grégoire Darcy
The Road to Pemberley

Dedication

I was mostly busy working on the series when I was in school, so I submitted part of this book to my current class. The professor told me it was "junk" and if I didn't submit something else, he would flunk me.

Thanks, Professor, for giving me the courage to ignore your opinions.

Introduction

Welcome to the sixth book in our series! If you're new, you're in luck – the events of previous books don't matter a lot in this one.

I started writing these books for fun and posting them online in 2006. By what is now known as book 5 (*The Knights of Derbyshire*), my writing was massively popular and besieged with comments. I was very proud of myself. I was also very tired of writing about England. I had at this point a fair idea of where I wanted the series to go as a whole (and that it was going to be a ten-book series), but I felt I earned a break. "If I want to write a murder mystery set in France, I should write a murder mystery in France. Everyone can just deal." I wouldn't say I was young and naïve, but I was definitely young.

This is the only stand-alone book in the series, though some prior knowledge of the universe will serve to move the plot along for you. After this we return to

England-based wacky shenanigans and occasional murders.

I am not including a family tree, so enjoy not having to reference it.

Marsha Altman
New York, NY
2012

PROLOGUE

Inspector Robert Audley turned to the mortician and said with annoyance, "You are aware that the body should not have been moved until my approval?"

Monsieur Lambert was an elderly gentleman, and so was excused to sit in the corner of his dusty workshop. "*Oui.* But Inspector, you were not called when this body was found. You were not called for another day."

Audley frowned. "That is true," he said as he looked at the body again, uncovered partially by his own actions. The corpse of a man named Simon Roux was in a state of ready decomposition, now three days old. Monsieur Roux had been found by a shepherd at dawn, already stiff by the description of the local guard. That information was all he had to pinpoint a time of death—probably sometime in the early morning, while it was still dark, or the body would have stunk then as it did now. Only the mortician's chemicals under his nose prevented Audley from being overwhelmed.

The inspector probed the wound on the dead man's neck. He had died quickly after his wounds, as no one survived a slash to the throat, much less three. "These marks – "

"Claws. Definitely."

"I agree," Audley said. "Not a blade, certainly, but have you ever seen three claw marks so evenly spaced?" He took a measurement of one with his forefinger and thumb, and then checked the next, and then the last. "That is very rare on an animal wound. Also, strange that the animal would merely kill him with one swipe and then leave the body so intact otherwise."

Old Man Lambert said quietly, "It is odd, yes, Inspector. I have never seen anything like this before. Perhaps this is why you were called."

"Perhaps." Audley took a final look at the messy, bearded face of Simon Roux. By reputation, he was a gambler who worked the fields in season and made his living by selling firewood the rest of the year. He was also known to be good with a blade – or at least a hatchet – and one had been found on him, unused, at the scene of the crime. Inspector Audley had barely been in town two hours, and he already had the impression that the man had not been well liked, at least by the female populace. "Were you called to the scene or was the body delivered here by your assistant?"

"I was called, Inspector."

"I will need a list of everyone present, even women and children, when you arrived. Was the marquis there?"

"*Non*, Inspector. He remained uninvolved until the ... rumors ... started spreading."

This was when Inspector Audley had been summoned, by special request of the Marquis, and rode from Paris immediately. Normally he did not like to be approached about a case from a suspect, but apparently the nobility still held more sway than they were supposed to, because Audley had been pulled off a significant strangler case on the docks to attend to this murder in the wilderness with a startling order from above.

Of course, logically, the Marquis was not a suspect. He had no known reason to kill Simon Roux, no real association with the man. If there were any connections, it was hidden – but Inspector Audley would find it out. That was his profession and his duty, even to a man like Simon Roux.

~~~

The meeting with the marquis took place earlier than he expected, until he reminded himself that the country noblemen often ate earlier than city folk.

He knew very well that the marquis would want to parade him about at dinner to show that he had brought in (undoubtedly, at his own expense) this superior inspector to investigate the brutal crime. Inspector Audley was not bothered by it, as it would give him a terrific meal and a chance to see the local people in action, from the servants to the marquis himself.

His appointment with the marquis took place precisely at four, when the inspector was often accustomed to taking tea. To his surprise, he was not left to stand before the noble, but instead offered a seat and a rather wide selection of flavored teas. "I heard, Inspector, that you are of English descent."

"Yes," Audley said. "My father was an officer. He retired here."

"In Paris?"

"Valognes," he said, making his selection quickly and waving off the servant with sugar cubes. He wanted to preserve his teeth. "He still lives there with my mother and sister."

"But you are the famed inspector of Paris." The marquis was not quite what Audley had expected, not an ostentatious noble of old, trying to flatter him openly. He was a quieter man, more intense and serious, almost frightening with his pointed nose and long black hair. All the inspector really knew of him at the moment was that he was a widower.

"Hardly," Audley said humbly. "My lord, I am afraid I must of course begin with the most basic inquiry – "

"Of course," said the marquis. "I was asleep that night. I went to bed very late, being distracted by a new book. I will not deny that I frequently take walks along my lands in the early morning. I enjoy the morning mist, especially this time of year." He sipped his tea. "Do you have a conclusion as to the time of death?"

Audley knew the man was clever, and also guessed that the marquis could likely tell if he was withholding information. "Early morning, but likely, very early. Perhaps one or two hours past midnight."

"Then I was asleep," the marquis said. "I do not know this man – he has been identified as Monsieur Roux?"

"Simon Roux, yes."

"I know of him only by reputation. He came to the village a few years ago, after the war, and never fully settled himself. He remained unmarried and was apparently a known womanizer. You know the type, surely?"

"I do." War brought out the best – and worst – in men. Many were left scarred by it, unable to find their place in this new

France, whatever it was to be. "Have you any idea of the foundation of these rumors concerning yourself and Monsieur Roux?"

"None whatsoever. It came as a shock to me, but what good free countryman is not ready and eager to discredit a noble? Even by stooping so low as to start rumors about ... werewolves, or whatever this nonsense is." He paused. "You know, it was not even a full moon the night of his death."

"So you are aware of such legends?"

"Such are the things told to a child, especially one who lives so close to the woods. Wolves, vampires, witches – that sort of nonsense. I thought we got rid of that nonsense with the revolution, but apparently, not so."

"But somehow, someone started the rumor that you were seen running through the woods that night – or, someone with a wolf's head was seen in the woods wearing your clothing. Am I correct?"

"You are."

Audley made a note in his book. "Have you done an inventory of your wardrobe since the event?"

"No. I had not thought to do so until people seemed to be – taking these ridiculous rumors seriously." He smiled, and Audley could not help but notice his teeth were very pointy. "But – in the dead of night, I imagine one would only have to acquire one splendid coat to give the effect of appearing as me."

"True, but I would appreciate it if you would do the inventory as soon as possible, perhaps even before dinner. If a servant can be rooted out, it will make our lives much easier."

"Of course. It will be done." The marquis rose. "If there are no other pressing questions, I must prepare for dinner. You have joined us on a very special evening, Inspector Audley."

"I have?" Audley said, rising with him.

"Yes. My bride – my *intended* bride – is joining us with her companion. She is studying in a seminary for English women very near here."

"Very convenient." The inspector could not help but look at the marquis and be reminded that this man was in his forties and a widower, and a seminary girl could hardly be more than twenty.

"We are very distant relations. Our families arranged the match two years ago – hers in England, mine here – but I would not agree to it until I saw her and we felt it was a good match ourselves. So she came to study in the seminary, but five miles from here, and I have arranged that she may occasionally visit."

"Her name?"

"Lady Heather Littlefield. You shall be introduced tonight, of course." He made motions to leave, and Inspector Audley bowed.

Something struck him. "My Lord – "

The marquis stopped in the doorway and politely turned around. "Yes."

"You said she had a companion?"

"Yes, her friend from school, who accompanies her so she is not alone while travelling and making calls. I apologize – her name escapes me now. I am quite a bad host." He snapped his fingers. "Ah yes. I remember it."

The inspector readied his pen again. "Yes?"

"I believe it is – Miss Georgiana Bingley."

CHAPTER 1

Dinner was a desperately calculated affair. The nobility of the Restoration – descendents of nobles clever enough to hide during the Revolution – were ready and eager to resume the traditional lifestyle of the idly rich, but not as ready to suffer the consequences of doing so. It brought to Inspector Audley's mind the great Greek temples he had read of, and then the false attempts to recreate them during the Renaissance – wooden facades over interiors, stone over buildings, all looking ridiculous and out-of-place. He put those thoughts aside when the bell rang, as he was escorted in by a server and shown his proper spot at the long table. His business was not idle musings but serious considerations if he was to solve a murder, and he had yet to even identify any serious suspects.

There was some chattering in the hallway as the other guests assembled, standing behind their chairs – local magistrates, invited relatives, other people he would quickly identify and take note of in his book later. The marquis made his entrance, a somewhat modest one for a noble (the inspector had been privy to a few). The grandest thing about him was the woman on his arm, a foreign girl clearly lost in a sea of unfamiliar faces. Her gown was a beautiful crème color, and her style of blond hair so carefully wrapped up would have given her away as the marquis's English fiancée, if her presentation did not.

"Lady Littlefield," the marquis proudly announced, as if he were the servant introducing the guest. Lady Littlefield curtseyed shyly and took her place an appropriate distance away from him at the table. She was English after all, and weren't they so careful of such things as propriety? The inspector watched her, but not too harshly, having no intention of frightening her off if she happened to catch his gaze. He focused instead mainly on the marquis, who continued without her to his station at the head of the table with great delight. It was not in his clothing that he was ostentatious, or his speech, but there could be no mistake that pride shimmered across his exterior. *Pride for his successful catch of a bride, or his upcoming marriage, or the money it would bring?* Audley already knew it would bring quite a good deal of money. He had been able to ascertain that from the chatter of the other guests while they waited for the bell. How much, he was unsure, and the marquis's own finances would have to be taken into account. Certainly *that* situation and the plot against him – if there was one to do with the murder of Simon Roux – had to be interconnected.

There was one more guest. She made every attempt to enter quietly and no one took much notice of her, except the inspector, because it was his business to do observe everyone carefully. When he caught a proper look at her, he could not understand why she did not attract more attention. The girl – no, a woman, perhaps nineteen or twenty years old – was also dressed in the English fashion, though far more modestly and in an insignificant earthy brown gown that brought nothing to the eye, enhancing her own invisibility, or desire for it. She sat next to her schoolmate even more quietly than she had entered the room. Audley assumed this was the Miss Bingley, mentioned so briefly by the marquis – he seemed to forget her as easily as everyone else.

But the inspector did not. She had rather striking red hair, half-hidden by an unnecessary cap, probably because of the oddness of the cut, which was far too short for a proper lady, who was expected to pin up her long hair every day. Illogical really, now that he thought about it – her idea seemed much more sensible, if inappropriate, but no one seemed to care. Her friendship with Lady Littlefield was obvious. They occasionally exchanged quiet whispers in English, which was the only time in the entire course of dinner that Audley saw a genuine smile on Lady Littlefield's face. So the lady did not feel comfortable with her betrothed, and brought along a close companion for support – or perhaps it was just that she was shy or liked to gossip with someone. Either possibility was feasible.

"Ladies and gentlemen," the marquis said, raising his glass for attention, "I am pleased to introduce to you, if you have not met him, Inspector Robert Audley, the famed inspector of Paris, who is here to see justice done for the unfortunately deceased huntsman, at my behest. Welcome, sir!"

At his behest. And Mr. Roux wasn't a huntsman. You didn't know him at all, did you? "Thank you," Audley said, rising to bow to their clapping, "but I am hardly 'the famed inspector.'" *But I was called in to solve the case of a man that the marquis doesn't care about. Or, I am called in to save his reputation.* "His Grace is very generous in his compliments."

"Don't be modest, young man," said Lord Rousseau, a neighboring count of considerable wealth – and girth. "I recognize your name from the papers. You solved the church murders. Someone knocking off the poor, taking sanctuary there. Turned out to be a priest, did it not?"

"I was fortunate. The killer left a wealth of clues. One needs only to find them."

"The inspector is modest," the marquis said, "while he scopes us all out like a vulture to his prey." This was greeted by hearty laughter, which Audley thought it prudent to join as he took his seat.

"I have no suspects at the moment," he said evenly.

"But clues?"

"Some."

Rousseau was still interested, mainly because his wife seemed to be encouraging him. "And what would those be, unearthed so quick since your arrival?"

Audley smiled. It put people at ease. "I am not at liberty to divulge them."

"Let us not pester my guest," said the marquis, notably emphasizing *my* again. "If you wish an interrogation, I am sure the inspector would be happy to oblige you, but not while he is eating."

More laughter, and then the conversation turned to other topics, for which the inspector was grateful.

~~~

Inspector Audley was delayed in joining the others for the after dinner entertainment by a servant, who wished to ask him about a relative in Paris who worked on the docks. He quickly answered that no, he had not heard of him being among the dead. The servant bowed thankfully, and he finally entered the large sitting room, where he found all eyes on him.

"Inspector, I would request that you indulge us in a party game," the marquis said, appearing to his right.

"And what sort of game is this?"

"Your favorite type – an investigation. It seems Sir DuBois has been murdered!"

Sir DuBois, a thin man in his forties, was sitting in the center of the room. He put down his goblet on the stand, dramatically grabbed his throat, and slumped into his chair, one eye half-open to watch the proceedings as the others giggled in amusement.

"And I suppose," Audley said, watching their faces, "that I am to guess the murderer? What are the rules of this game, precisely?"

"I, as the master of the game, will explain them," the marquis said. "First of all, you may discount the servants, or we would be up all night. It was someone in this room. Second, there is no motive – one person was merely good enough to volunteer, and Sir DuBois was good enough to volunteer to be murdered."

Sir DuBois had problems stifling his chuckle.

"You may ask me about any evidence you wish to discover. You may interview anyone in the room about what they might have seen, and they may not lie – unless they are the murderer. Do you find this suitable?"

"Very," said Audley. Without hesitation, he immediately walked over to the stand and picked up the goblet, which he smelled. It contained ordinary wine. Willing to play along with the scenario, he tipped his last finger in and tasted a drop on his tongue. "Do I detect poison?"

"Yes."

"Fast-acting or slow? Surely you know that poisons are specifically designed to act on the body so that the person responds at a certain time after ingestion."

"Of course," said the marquis. "Very fast. He must have drunk the poison in the last five minutes."

"So, something akin to cyanide. Very well. It is easy enough to obtain." Audley set the goblet down and looked around the room. There were four people at the card table, engaged in a game of whist. "I will inquire of you all – did anyone rise for any reason in the last five minutes?"

Lady Rousseau giggled and said, "No, Inspector."

"Then I must rule out all four participants." He turned around and looked at Lord Rousseau, who was on the couch with his own glass in hand and his feet upon a footrest. "I must also rule out His Lordship."

"Why should you do that?" Rousseau said, almost offended. "I am quite close to Sir DuBois – certainly close enough to poison his drink."

"But you are facing him. Even if he was distracted, or called up from his seat long enough, how long would it take you to get up from your current position, slip something in his drink, and return to your position without being noticed? For the sake of argument, I will time it." He withdrew his pocket watch. "If you would, my Lord."

Rousseau realized he was serious, and with a nod from the marquis, set down his glass, took down his feet, got up, and walked over to the stand with the goblet, put his hand over the goblet, and then did the reverse of all of his actions. He was a broad, lumbering man, and when he was finally finished, Audley announced, "Nearly a minute. Forty-nine seconds, to be precise. Far too long to go unnoticed. Did anyone in this room notice it? I recall the rules of the game are that only the murderer is allowed to lie."

There was a chorus of denials.

"Very well then. That leaves only three." He turned to the marquis. "Sir, where were you during the past five minutes?"

"Inspector, you will recall, I am the master of this game."

"And I will also recall that you never once mentioned that the master cannot be the murderer." He studied the marquis very carefully. As simple and amusing as the game seemed to be, he knew the marquis did nothing lightly, and would not put himself into suspicion for anything, especially because he was the only suspect on the current list, even if it required more nocturnal activities than normal nobles participated in. "But it is, of course, not you." He turned away without an explanation. "That leaves Lady Littlefield and Miss Bingley. And, as you said, there is no motive, so I do not need to begin to speculate if either of them wished to kill Sir DuBois. So I must only consider the circumstances and use my investigative abilities." He decided to approach Lady Littlefield, who smiled shyly as she rose.

She had been sitting at the pianoforte, as if she was intending to play soon. There was even a sheet book in front of her, but it was still unopened. He bowed politely and said to her, "Lady Littlefield, are you the murderer?"

"You will recall once again, the murderer may lie," said the marquis from behind.

"Yes," Audley countered, his gaze never wavering from the lady, "but lying does not mean one is telling the truth. Often there is a quickening of the heartbeat – which I am not now close enough to hear – or rapid blinking of the eyes when lying. That I *can* see, and though she is nervous by my stare and my questioning, I ask again – Lady Littlefield, are you the murderer?"

"No," she said quietly.

"She is not lying," he pronounced. "That leaves only one suspect: Miss Bingley." The woman in question was by the bookcase, holding up a book. "You will notice two things. One, she is standing while reading, something people rarely do. Second, she is nearly halfway through her book, but she did not bring it with her, because there is an empty slot right behind her on the bookshelf. Either she is a very quick reader or wished to appear engaged in an activity. And she is close enough to poison the drink."

Miss Bingley turned to him for the first time, closing her book, and curtseyed, rather impudently, he thought. "Congratulations, Inspector. You have caught me."

There was a round of clapping and raising of glasses to the inspector, who was grateful for it. He did not seek their praise, but he had been offered information that gave him questions – and questions were the beginning of the search for answers.

Why wasn't the marquis willing to play the murderer? And why was Miss Bingley willing?

~~~

The inspector's work was just beginning as the guests left. He only had time to scribble a few names and notes of the evening in his book before he headed upstairs to meet the butler, Monsieur Durand, who was awaiting him as the marquis said the final good-byes to his guests. "You will see," said Durand as he escorted him into the private chambers of the count. Old wealth was in every fixture, every tapestry, every false pillar, but Audley could sense a sort of darkness here. Maybe it was the dust of a house not being in use for almost two generations, metaphorical instead of literal, but the place seemed *old* in every sense of the word. He was escorted to the wardrobe full of coats, vests, shirts – everything a marquis or count or duke would need for every occasion, a shop with no bill.

"Here," said Mr. Durand, indicating the empty hanger.

"There was something here that was removed recently? Like a coat?"

"I do not know, Inspector Audley, to be sure, but the valet knows the marquis's wardrobe extremely well. He had a very grand red waistcoat with silver buttons, and there was certainly not an empty hanger here. We put those in a special box."

"When did he wear it last?"

"I do not know, sir. Not since I have worked here."

"How long have you worked here, Monsieur Durand?"

"Five months."

Audley raised his eyebrows. "Five months?" It was a short amount of time for a man in so great a position. Even though Mr. Durand was old and wizened, he must have proved his mettle on smaller jobs, surely?

"Yes, Inspector Audley. I previously worked for the Count de LaFebre in his southern estate, but he passed away recently."

"But the marquis has been living here since the Restoration. Who was your predecessor?"

"I met him only once. A Mr. Arnold. I do not know his location now, if you wish to find him."

"Who else would know?"

"No one," Durand said. "I was hired amidst a massive change of staff at the time. There is no one here now from when Mr. Arnold was butler."

"Why did he change his staff?"

"I don't know, sir."

Audley made a note of it. "So this was – October?"

"Late October, Inspector."

He nodded. "Is anything else missing? Jewelry? A watch? Artwork?"

"Nothing that we have discovered. We will continue the inventory, but we have exhausted all of the major possibilities."

Audley paced the floor in front of the wardrobe. *Doesn't creak*, he noted. "Tell me – is there anyone here who would have issue with the marquis?"

"Of the staff?"

"Yes. How does he treat them?" He stopped his pacing and gave Durand a reassuring look. "You have my word that I will keep your confidence." He knew Durand was in the marquis's confidence, and if there would be any admission, it would only be slight. "I am merely looking for a suspect."

"There is no one I can think of who would ... concoct such a plot. Steal a coat, maybe, but not use it in the manner that has been suggested."

Audley tried a different tack. "How does the marquis treat his servants? Again, this will be kept in confidence."

"He pays everyone on time," Durand said. "Beyond that, I can not be helpful. He has been very kind to me."

Clearly, this man would be of no help in this regard. "Are there any servants who have been dismissed still living in the area?"

"A few, I believe. Not many. You can ask at the *Verrat* – someone there will surely know."

The *Taverne Principale Du Verrat* was beneath the inn where Audley was temporarily installed. "Very good. One last question – Did you know Simon Roux?"

"I did not, Inspector. I know few people beyond these grounds."

"So he was never employed here?"

"Never, sir."

"Very good." He closed his book. "I will need to speak to every servant in this household – tonight."

"Some of them have retired, sir."

Audley turned back to him. "Then you had best get them up."

~~~

Because of the hour, he made the process as quick as possible. He only needed a few questions to narrow down the list of servants to those who were suspects or with whom he wanted a longer conversation, and those who needed to be watched over in case of escape. No one seemed to know much about Simon Roux beyond what he had already learned in town – that Roux was a womanizer and general troublemaker, but had never been employed by the marquis. It was the frazzled cook who solved the mystery of the staff changeover – "It was when term began at the seminary. Or, shortly before it."

"So when Lady Littlefield arrived?"

"Yes. I was hired because I used to work for the British officers during the occupation, and have knowledge of English cuisine."

"So he wanted to impress his betrothed."

"He made that clear, Inspector."

That did not quite explain why he would change the entire staff, down to the under gardener and the laundress, but he made no mention of that to the cook.

Audley hit a verbal wall with the subject of the marquis himself. The servants would not discuss his behavior – a sign that it was bad and they had been actively silenced. It was understandable that the marquis, seeking the approval of the Littlefields, would not want vile rumors circulating around about his behavior and would silence his staff, but it was no help to an inspector trying to root out a thief and possible murderer. The connection was not clear in his mind. If someone wanted to smear the reputation of the marquis, there were easier ways to do it than to steal his coat, dress up like a wolf, and kill what appeared now to be a random townsperson. *What is the connection between the marquis and Roux?* It remained most tenuous. Did Roux know something the marquis didn't want known? Then why would he incriminate himself? Had he over-thought the situation?

There was one interview that was particularly disconcerting. One of the upstairs maids, Sophie, responded quietly and numbly to all of his questions, her hands shaking as he watched. No matter how much he assured her – and he usually could be quite assuring if he wished to be – she would not say what she was so clearly thinking. *He probably beat her,* Audley noted. *At least once.* Another connection or another false lead?

The marquis had not killed Simon Roux. Of this he was sure. Not as a werewolf or dressed as one. Someone else had done it to some end, and it may have been unrelated. And maybe it was made relevant later – the spreading of rumors about a fancy coat, then the coat being stolen in the aftermath to confirm the rumors – he did not have enough information.

But he would get it.

CHAPTER 2

Inspector Robert Audley was an early riser. He supposed it was the militarism in his blood. His father was a kind man, but he was a soldier, and rose early, before breakfast was ready, for exercise, and his son followed in his habit. In fact, Robert Audley nearly terrified a passing maid by appearing fully-dressed so early in the morning as he descended the steps to the tavern below, where last night's drunks were still being tossed out.

"Oh, Inspector Audley! My apologies, your breakfast is not ready yet!"

"That is fine," he was quick to assure. "I only require some directions, if you would. And perhaps a biscuit for the road."

An hour later he was down the road some miles, his legs well-stretched as he passed through the village, filled with the sounds of people waking. On the other side of the road was the forest, its trees tall and foreboding, even on this beautiful sunny day.

He found the site of the crime easily enough, marked by a small wooden cross, barely more than two planks of wood nailed together and quickly shoved into the ground. No one left flowers for Simon Roux at the site of his death – or, at least, the dumping of his body – but someone had felt some Christian compulsion to mark it while he awaited burial.

As Audley suspected, there was no other evidence. Days had passed, and even the morning dew – especially from a forest – would have helped any blood stains to sink into the soil. There was only an indentation where his body had fallen – or where he had been dropped. The inspector knelt before it, and ran his hands across the mark in the dirt. Such a strong indentation meant Roux either fell or was tossed awkwardly on the ground, but he had been found, by the mortician's description, lying on his back quite neatly. *Thrown*, he decided, *then rearranged so the wound was visible.* He had been told the outlying area had been searched, but he stepped towards the woods anyway. There were human footprints everywhere, from the initial crowd of would-be investigators, but no obvious paths from any direction.

Had the body been carried to the woods or from it? Simon Roux had no business being in the woods unless he was hunting, and he would need permission from the marquis's huntsman for that.

Audley made another note in his book. But hunting at night? And some gear would have been found on him, or would still be at the murder site – or had it been cleaned up?

This was not the time to go wandering. He stopped by a large boulder in a particularly pretty area and ate some of the hard cheese and bread he'd taken from the inn. By now it was a more reasonable hour, and he had an appointment to keep.

~~~

The Robinson School for Women was no shanty operation nor a grand university. It seemed to be, at least from the exterior, a quiet place for the rich and titled of England to send their daughters for additional education, and its white paneling and multiple-winged single structure spoke of a subtle, tasteful British elegance, especially after all of the houses and shacks he had passed on the way. The seminary was like a nunnery without the religion, though he was sure there was a chapel. His own presence was obviously an intrusion, but he was accustomed to feeling that way about his presence in different places. He climbed the front steps and was received by a very strict-looking door-woman. "Inspector Audley," he said in English, handing her his card. "I am here to speak with two of the students concerning the death of Simon Roux."

She appeared offended. "There is no one here that would be involved in such a matter, Inspector."

"I have questions related to it that they may be able to answer. Now, I must speak with the Headmaster. Am I to be admitted?"

She hesitantly opened the door further, allowing him to enter. She offered to take his hat, realized he was not wearing one, and escorted him down a plain, undecorated hallway to the office.

There was nothing exceptional about the office of the Headmaster, who rose to greet him with irritated eyes. "I am Mr. Stafford, the Headmaster of this school." His accent was clipped, obviously aristocratic stock of the stuffiest kind.

"Inspector Robert Audley," he said with a bow. "Excuse my appearance. I've been walking for some time." For his coat and pants were still wet from the morning dew. "I will take no more of your time than is necessary. I am here to speak to Lady Littlefield and her companion, Miss Bingley, concerning the murder of Simon Roux."

"Yes, yes, that was why you were called here, no?" Reseated, the headmaster picked his pipe back up from its resting stand. "I can assure you, the ladies here would have nothing to do with someone of the likes of Monsieur Roux."

"So you knew him?"

The headmaster was startled.

He said something he shouldn't have said.

"...Well, of him. Sir, it is my business as protector of these girls to see that I know the name of every wandering ruffian who occupies these lands and comes within a day's travel of our grounds. For safety reasons, you understand." When Audley was silent, he was forced to go on. "The monsieur had a reputation of being ... flirtatious with the women in town. So you can see how that would be a concern to someone like me."

"Indeed, I can."

"I never met the man, no. But as I said, I knew of him. But you wish to speak to my students?"

"Yes."

"Why?"

Audley couldn't bring himself to be surprised by the question. The headmaster would of course be distrustful of someone who went about asking questions, some of which would no doubt be improper and speak of unladylike things. *Like murder.* "I met both of them last night, at the marquis's manor. I understand Lady Littlefield is engaged to the marquis."

"She is." Comprehension finally dawned on Headmaster Stafford. "You can't be taking this werewolf nonsense seriously?"

"Of course not," he said. "That said, I cannot rule out that the incident had something to do with the marquis, or was intended to look like it did, and they know the marquis on a level I do not. So I wish to question them both." He added, "I am an officer of the law and have full authority to question whomever I wish. If you have a problem with it, you may send a letter to the general inspector in Paris, but know that the sooner I find the person who killed Simon Roux, the sooner we will *all* be safer. Surely you cannot disagree with *that*."

"No," the Headmaster said with a swallow. "I cannot."

~~~

Inspector Audley was ushered into an empty classroom, and given a seat at the desk. He opened his notebook, inked his pen, and looked over his notes, waiting until Lady Littlefield entered, escorted by Mr. Stafford. "Inspector Audley."

"Lady Littlefield," he bowed. "You may leave us now," he said quite plainly to the headmaster.

"I cannot allow – "

"If you are concerned about propriety, you are welcome to look in through the window. However, I must be allowed to speak to her ladyship in privacy, for the sake of this investigation." He used his *voice of authority* again, and this seemed to scare Stafford off, so he closed the door to them. Audley immediately changed his attitude, smiling warmly at the woman – barely more than a girl – in front of him. "Please be seated, Lady Littlefield. I apologize for removing you from class."

"It is no trouble," she said, taking a seat in the chair placed opposite him, with only the desk separating them. But it was clear it was not 'no trouble'. She was nervous in her mannerisms, playing with the trim of lace in her gown, but he did not yet detect a level of nervousness beyond what he would expect of a young lady who had never been questioned about a murder before.

"I will try to compensate by taking up as little of your time as possible, so we will come right to the point – did you know Simon Roux?"

"No, I did not."

"Had you heard of him?"

"Yes."

"How had you heard of him?"

"Some of the other girls met him once on the road – I don't know the story – and he spoke to them. They were quite frightened by the experience. Apparently he made some rude suggestions."

Now he was getting somewhere, perhaps. "The names of these young women?"

"Miss Ashley and Miss Stevenson."

He wrote the names down. "Do you know anything else about it?"

"No. I did not take an interest in it."

"All right. Now we must turn to the marquis."

"Oh! He is not implicated, is he?" She seemed genuinely concerned. For what or whom, he could not determine.

"I do not think he killed Monsieur Roux," Audley said. It was an honest answer. "However, I do not think he is entirely unconnected to the incident, even if unintentionally. Someone may be trying to harm him by spreading false rumors. Do you know of anyone who would want to harm him?"

She put her hand over her mouth and shook her head violently: *No*.

That, of course, meant a very solid *Yes*.

"I will repeat myself," he said, more kindly than he was inclined to be, only because she did seem terrified. "Do you know of anyone who would want, even indirectly, to harm the marquis?"

"No," she whimpered.

"You are aware that lying to an inspector is in and of itself a punishable crime?" Not that he could do anything to an English lady of her stature – her family would buy her way out of it. But she didn't have to know that. Instead, he softened his tone. "My lady, I am only trying to help. Someone murdered Simon Roux and I think he did it to hurt the marquis. Surely you don't want any harm to come to your fiancé?"

"No, of course not."

There was more here. He had barely scratched the surface, but a very tender surface it was. His heart went out to her. "Very well. We will speak again, another time, perhaps. If I have other questions. Thank you for your time, Lady Littlefield." He rose to indicate she was free to go, and she curtseyed and scurried out of the room. He was glad to have done it before she burst into tears.

Answered no to all questions, implicating something is wrong with the marquis, he scribbled into his notebook. *Meant to say yes every time.*

~~~

He did not have very long to wait for his second interview. Miss Bingley, similarly attired, curtseyed and politely kept her eyes down. In her hands was some kind of charm on a chain, maybe a locket, and she played with it incessantly as he began his interview, "First of all, a small matter. How did you come to join Lady Littlefield on her visits to the marquis?"

"Oh," she said with a soft, pleasing tone. "It is quite simple. We share a room in the dormitory, and we have been friends since our first day here. When she was first invited, she did not know the marquis or much about him, and she wanted someone to come with her, so I offered. And I have been every time since."

"So she is still uncomfortable in her visits to the marquis?"

"Perhaps."

What kind of answer was that? "What do you know of the marquis?"

"Oh, surely you know more than I." She, at least, could speak to him in more than monosyllables, but then, she was not so personally connected to the marquis. "You've been investigating him."

"But you have known him longer. My acquaintance with him is not more than a day."

"But you have an acquaintance, where I have never spoken two words to him," she said. "So I cannot presume to know more of him than you."

What? "Then, from afar – what is your judgment of him?"

"The bible teaches us not to judge each other before we have sat in judgment ourselves," she said demurely.

So far, she had not answered a single question. She had quite an effective tactic of evading him. He switched topics. "Did you know Simon Roux?"

"I met him once."

He raised his pen. "Can you describe that occasion?"

"No."

He raised his eyes. "What?"

"I cannot. Or, rather, I have been forbidden by the good headmaster, who is only interested in the best interests of his students and their good standing in society, from speaking of Mr. Roux or any encounters I might have had with him." Her voice was still meek, but there was a more assertive undertone to it now. She continued boldly without giving him a chance to speak, "Your English accent is impeccable. Did you study in England?"

"My father was an English soldier. He came over after the Revolution for a minor engagement and stayed," he answered quickly, thrown off by the question. "Miss Bingley, I am far more interested in Monsieur Roux."

"He is dead and I believe he is going to stay so. Am I not allowed a simple question?"

He had dropped his pen. Ink dribbled over his previous notes. He rushed to pick it back up as discreetly as possible. She was not being shy – she was being coy. "Tell me about Simon Roux."

"The headmaster – "

"I don't care. Do you?"

She smiled. He had not yet seen her smile, except for the tiny polite one she produced in company – he realized that now, now that she was smiling for real, because something amused her. "No, I do not. You have caught me."

"Then answer the question. What transpired between you and Mr. Roux?"

He thought she rolled her eyes, though it was hard to see with her eyes lowered. She had stopped playing with the locket. "It is more what didn't happen, Inspector. To be plain, I was walking down the road when I saw that two of my schoolmates were being accosted by Monsieur Roux."

"Accosted?"

"He was on a horse, carrying a gun, and was making his intentions clear enough. He was not merely flirting. Must I supply the details?" she said. "So I shouted for him to leave them at once. He was, of course, more amused at the conquest of three women instead of two, and he was the *man* with the *gun* and the *horse*. What were we to do?"

"What *did* you do, Miss Bingley?"

She raised her eyes – green, almost like emeralds – and looked straight at him. "I told him to leave again and said if he didn't, I would make him. He refused, and so I made him."

"Made him?"

Nothing about her was coy now. "He charged. I hit his horse in the eye with a rock. It was spooked and ran." She continued, "You can see how the headmaster would be interested in this story not being in general circulation. It would imply that he was allowing his students to wander the dangerous roads unattended, and that two of them were nearly violated by a rogue on a horse. That would not speak well for his skills as a headmaster and for the school as a whole."

"Of course," he said, stupefied. "You threw a rock at the horse?"

"You can't hit a horse straight on. To really spook it, you have to hit it on the side. I was lucky and got the eye." Once again, she did not let him ask his next question. "Sadly, that ends my association with Mr. Roux, so I can't tell you any more than that, nor can anyone from this school. He stayed far away from the ladies of Mrs. Robinson's after that for some reason."

"Do you know who killed him?"

She did not break her gaze. "I heard it was a wolf."

"Surely a practical, intelligent girl like you doesn't believe that nonsense about werewolves?"

"I didn't say werewolf, Inspector. I said *wolf*. No, I do not believe a man turns into a wolf at a certain time of the month and kills whoever crosses his path. That is silly superstition. But if he was clawed to death, then logic would dictate it was an animal, and we have no bears or mountain lions in these woods."

He was still crafting his response when there was a knock on the door. "Enter." It was the woman who'd answered the door. "Is something wrong?"

"The constable has sent a messenger," she said. "There has been another murder."

CHAPTER 3

After quickly mentioning that their conversation would continue at another time, Inspector Audley left Miss Bingley and rushed out of the school, very nearly running. "It's a lady," said the messenger, a hired hand of the local constable, named Andre.

And then they did, literally, run. Fortunately the inspector was in good health, and they had not more than a few miles to go before reaching the cabin and the crowd surrounding it. "Inspector!" called the constable.

"Did anyone move the body?"

"No, the mortician is still on his way."

"Then I will look around before he gets here and disturbs the scene of the crime."

"You'd best cover your nose, then."

He did not need to be told twice. He poured some wine from his flask onto a rag he carried for this purpose and covered his mouth with it.

Despite his precautions, the stench was overwhelming as he entered the cabin. The dead woman, a portly lady in her mid-fifties, was on the floor near her bed, her throat slashed, blood staining the rug beneath it. The cabin had one room of assorted knick-knacks, furniture, and an iron stove. He touched it – cooling off. She had lit it for heat at night and never doused the flames. And from the stench, he presumed that she had been killed sometime after sunset the evening before. As the constable shrunk back to the door, coughing into his rag in disgust, Audley marched over and raised one of her arms. It was stiff, and there was blood and grime under her fingernails. No doubt he would find bruises on her body – there had been a fight of some kind. The few things she had had were strewn about. He looked back at the lamp he had stepped over and picked it up. The glass was smashed and he plucked the candle from the frame. From where the wax fell, it looked like it had been upright when it had last been burning, so either she snuffed it or the murderer snuffed it to prevent the house from burning down. *Not exactly the actions of a wild animal.* "Who was this woman?"

"Mrs. Christelle Bernard, Inspector."

"Who was she? What did she do?" He noticed a ring on her finger. "She was a widow."

"I believe so, yes."

"Did she have a living? Or savings of some sort?"

"I don't know. We can find out, but I believe – she used to work at the manor."

He dropped the arm and stood up. "For the marquis?"

"Yes, Inspector."

That was all he needed to hear.

~~~

Later that afternoon, Inspector Audley found himself again in Monsieur Lambert's workshop, this time with two bodies before him instead of one. He had sufficiently recovered from the original shock to his system of the stench of death, but had lost all appetite for lunch and spent the time instead in his room at the inn, going over his notes and writing more as furiously as he could.

He was lucky in one thing, which was that the body of Mrs. Bernard had not been found a day, even half a day later. He had given permission for Simon Roux to be buried, but now he wanted the body to compare. He only needed a minute before he turned to Lambert and said, "The wounds are different."

"Yes, they are," Lambert said, walking past him to put the last of the paint on Roux's face. He had not been pretty when he died, but he would leave this world at least with a decent face, however false it was. "She fought back."

"Unarmed. But the mouth wound is different. Like – knife wounds." He looked closer, tilting his head to the side and raising the lamp closer. "Yes. One slash to the throat to kill her. Then as she was bleeding out, two more slashes on either side to match up. And then, a claw of some animal was run across the wound to make it look like Mr. Roux's wounds." He pulled away. "A different killer. So now we have not one, but two."

"So it seems," said the mortician.

"And still, no solid motives. We know only that Roux had enemies, but most were female. And we do not know what Mrs. Bernard knew that got her killed last night." He looked sadly at her pale face. "We may never know for sure, but I have my suspicions."

~~~

The only people to attend Simon Roux's funeral were the people necessary for it to occur. Audley had to authorize it, Constable Simon had to organize it, the mortician and his assistant had to deliver the coffin, and the priest had to say the blessings. The ceremony was carried out with extreme brevity.

Audley wouldn't even be here, watching some wandering ruffian be covered with earth after a death that he probably had coming, if it hadn't been for the connection to the marquis, if there was one. There was still no distinct line between them. But the death of Mrs. Bernard insisted everything was tied up in a very intricate knot, or was getting more tangled as it went along.

If he couldn't solve these murders – at least, not immediately – he could at least try to stop more from happening. After the ceremony, he crossed himself and walked away from the graveyard with the constable. "I need a list of everyone living in walking or riding distance that used to work for the marquis."

"That will take some time."

"It's not a large town."

The constable shrugged. "It's not Paris, Inspector, but there are many people here, more than you see at the *Verrat* or the market. People on the farms, people in the forest. Gypsies."

"Gypsies?"

"A small band. They live deep in the woods, they say."

He shook his head. "Gypsies move around, Constable. Is this another local legend?"

"*Non*, Inspector. We can see their fires sometimes, on a clear night. Perhaps you should look tonight, when the moon is full. But if you go into the woods – I will have to answer to Paris if you disappear."

Oh yes, the full moon. We'll see what it brings. "Duly noted, Constable. Now get me that list. Those people are in danger."

"Danger, Inspector?"

"Yes, danger! The day after I question all of the marquis's servants, a dismissed servant is found dead before I can speak to her. You think that is a coincidence?"

"Simon Roux never worked for the marquis."

Audley frowned. "True." He did not want to say that he knew there to be two killers. Not only did he not fully trust the constable, but he also doubted the little man's abilities to comprehend it. "We shall see what turns up."

"Where are you going, Inspector?"

He was turning off the path, towards a certain manor. "I have an important question to ask the good marquis."

~~~

The sky was beginning to darken when he was ushered into the sitting room to wait for the marquis. He paced behind his chair, ignoring the tea set out for him until the Marquis de Maret appeared, looking a bit rushed. He had yet to dress for dinner. "Inspector Audley."

He bowed. " I am in need of a moment of your time."

"Of course." Despite his polite response, the marquis did not look pleased at the unannounced interruption. "Please, sit."

Audley did so, but did not relax. "Have you heard about the death of a Mrs. Bernard?"

"No," said the marquis, sitting down across from him. "When was this? Recently?"

"She was found this morning. I believe she used to work for you."

"Yes." He swallowed. "She worked in the kitchen. I confess that I did not know her very well. An older woman, yes?"

"So she was among those who were dismissed five months ago?" Audley said, which seemed to rattle the marquis, who was intelligent enough to sense he was being interrogated.

"Yes."

Audley opened his book. "Why was she dismissed?"

"I – I don't remember." The marquis sunk further into his chair. Either he was genuinely shocked or was trying to appear so. Audley admitted to himself that he couldn't tell.

"You dismissed the entire staff before the arrival of Lady Littlefield. Is this correct?"

"Not all at once, but yes."

"Why?"

The marquis blinked. "How is this relevant to Monsieur Roux? Was she involved with him?"

"It doesn't matter. What matters is that she was murdered, in the same way that he was, except she was in her home and was not a universally hated person in town. And I may ask whatever questions I like to try and solve this case." He continued, "You can refuse to answer any one of them, if you wish, or even have me tossed from your house, but you can understand that it won't look very good after you brought me here."

"Of course, of course." The marquis was recovering. "There were two reasons. First, when I arrived here in 1817, I had to scrape around for servants, many of whom I never found to be competent, but I kept them on for the sake of convenience and because the town was uncomfortable with the nobility returning. But I needed a competent staff to impress Lady Littlefield, whom I am eager to impress." He hesitated. "The second reason – you will keep in confidence?"

"Of course."

The marquis looked sad, even vulnerable. "My wife died – was killed – in our former home in the west. She was in the gardens – she did so love to work with the soil – when some passing soldiers of General Bonaparte attacked her. They violated her, abused her, and left her to die. When we found her, it was too late." He rested his head on his hand. "After that, I was in a mood of perpetual despair. I was not, I admit, the best gentleman. This was how I was when I arrived, and I was not entirely ... polite with the servants I did succeed in finding. But over time, I have healed – or so I hope. But I did not want old stories of my gloom to spread to my fiancée unnecessarily." He looked up desperately at Audley.

"Of course, my Lord. Thank you for the information, and it will be kept in confidence." Audley stood up. "I think perhaps the best way to express your regained senses is to keep an eye out for your former servants. I wouldn't want any more of them to end up like Mrs. Bernard."

The marquis nodded, "Of course, Inspector."

"Then I will be off and trouble you no more today. Thank you for your time, my Lord," he said, bowing. He left, satisfied that his threat had been perfectly understood.

~~~

His appetite finally returned – with a vengeance – and he consumed his meal at the *Verrat* enthusiastically. One of his first acts in town had been to befriend the barkeep, Anton, and the server, Camille. When Camille approached him to clear away his plate of well-picked-at chicken bones, he asked, "Do you know of the gypsies who supposedly live in the woods?"

"Yes, sir. But..." She paused. "I don't believe they're gypsies, Inspector."

"No?"

"Gypsies move around, don't they? And they put on their shows and do their little tricks. I've seen their wagons pass through here. But these people seem to live out there, never coming out of the woods."

"Never?"

"Not that I know of."

He did not open his notebook, but his hand instinctively fell on it. "How long have they been there?"

"A few years. Not much longer. I don't think they're gypsies, Inspector. I think they're ruffians. You know, ex-soldiers and refugees – the bad sort."

Like Simon Roux. "Where is their camp, exactly?"

"Way out, deep in the woods." She gave him a look of concern. "Inspector, if you're thinking of looking for them, you shouldn't. It's dangerous."

"So they're violent?"

"I've never heard anything, but why else would they be living out there, building fires so high we can see the smoke from here?"

"Why didn't anyone tell me of this?"

"Did you ask?"

It was the kind of answer that made him want to slap either the person asking or himself. In this case, it was the latter, for he would never truly consider hitting a woman. "I would prefer to know, for the record, if there are any violent people living in the woods when someone is found murdered just outside them."

"Oh, no one's seen them come out this far. You're safe for a mile or so in." She leaned over. "I am serious, Inspector. If you die because of some bandits, I doubt they'll send another inspector that's half as cute as you and we'll all suffer for it."

He smiled at her flattery. "I will take all the necessary precautions."

"Good to hear, Inspector."

Taking his satchel and book, he headed upstairs. Audley had no serious designs on Camille, but he was not going to discourage her to be friendly with him if it would lead to information not otherwise granted. It did not pass the professional line – he had forgotten her flirtatious comment (not the first she had made) by the time he removed his coat and vest and laid down to sleep for a short time. He would need to be rested for the evening's planned activity.

~~~

Among his things that stayed in a locked trunk beneath the bed in his room at the inn was a rifle. This particular evening, he took this along with his normal pistol. He had no intention to use it on anyone, but animals could not be discounted, and it would hardly look good if the young inspector from Paris was knocked off by a bear. *Or a wolf.*

Lantern lit, he donned a wide-brimmed hat and set out, taking only the precaution to leave a note on his bed stand, lest he not return. It was nearing midnight now, and the full moon lit most of his path on the road until he came to the spot where the cross for Simon Roux had been planted in the ground. It had fallen over, knocked over, by a passing animal or the wind, and no one was caring for it. He picked it up and was about to force it back into the soil when he noticed writing on the back. Not writing – more like scribbles. Holding the cross close to his lantern, he tried to make out the characters. He realized that while they were unidentifiable, they were not scribbles. This had been done with a careful hand.

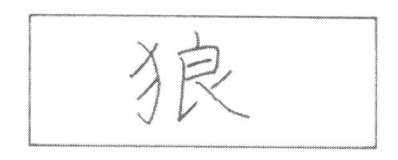

狼

It looked something like a lowercase "t" and an uppercase "R", but in the wrong order, and bizarrely done. Some kind of ancient script? None that he recognized. *I've paid my respects to Simon Roux*, he thought, and broke off the part of the cross that was marked and stuffed it into his satchel.

He could, as Camille had described, see the smoke of the fires, from somewhere deep in the woods. Using his compass, he determined the direction. *South*. With that, he blew out his lantern and entered the woods. The moon provided enough light, even through the trees, as his eyes adjusted. He treaded silently except for the occasional crunch of a branch or leaf pile. He passed several small streams running through various parts of the woods –there was a larger river somewhere, probably coming down from the mountains.

Audley did not realize how nervous he was until the silence was broken by a howl. He jumped, then tried to reason himself out of it. It was the deep woods. It was night. There were bound to be things that howled at night. Not necessarily werewolves. There was no good reason for his breathing to be so heavy, or for him to wait so long against a tree for it to steady again. And then, another howl. Damn it, he would get nowhere with this!

He focused on the compass, squinting to see its directional indicator. South. He focused on south, and continued for a while, until he could smell smoke and hear laughter in the distance. So, the rumors were true. He squinted in the distance, but saw no wagons or horses. He saw tents and shacks. The voices were almost entirely male. This was no gypsy camp, as Camille had warned him. It was, however, a camp of very likely suspects, especially if Simon Roux had crossed them somehow.

How to approach them? Should he do it at all, or just observe? The second option seemed safer, but he had not yet decided when a blunt force rammed against the back of his head and everything went dark.

CHAPTER 4

It was like waking from a deep sleep. Actually, it was precisely that, aside from a slight bruise on the back of his head that, reaching back, he quickly discovered. Sighing, he lowered his dizzy head again against the soft grass and took in the rest of his surroundings.

The sky above him signaled the beginnings of daylight. He had been unconscious – or first unconscious and then plain asleep - for hours. The spot was not the one where he had been struck, he was fairly sure. In fact, it looked familiar. He slowly sat up on his elbows, less dizzy this time, and found himself on the edge of the woods again – exactly the place that he had entered it. The place that Simon Roux died.

There had been something resting on his chest. He picked up the piece of wooden cross that had been in his bag. The strange symbol was still there, but when he flipped it over, there was a new, more recognizable print in French.

Be more careful next time.

Unintentionally, he found himself smiling.

Audley stood up and did a quick survey of his items. His satchel was still at his side, over one shoulder. His rifle was lying on the ground next to him. He checked it – still loaded. His pistol was still in his belt, safety on. *My notes!* He scrambled through his bag and retrieved the notebook. It was intact and unaltered, as far as he could tell. Whether someone had been through it, he knew not.

He looked back at the woods. He had not been dragged, but carried, because there were no marks in the dirt to indicate otherwise. Like Simon Roux's body had been carried. There were also no footprints aside from his old ones from last night. How had someone carried him and left no prints? Had they used the road?

He checked the woods one final time, this time kneeling by a trickle of a stream to wash his face. He had no intention of going back to town quite yet, not while he had business in the area. The girls' seminary, he realized, was not far. Nor was Mrs. Bernard's house. As the sun came up, he rested on a fallen tree and ate some brown bread he had brought along in his satchel and took a swig from his flask. With any luck, there were no search parties looking for him; perhaps they just thought him sleeping in, or had not even noticed his absence yet. Though he certainly looked a bit scruffy this morning, after spending a night sleeping in the woods, he doubted the Headmaster would think any less of him than he already did.

Walking along the road, he felt almost himself again by the time he came up to Mrs. Bernard's house. The door was hanging open, the house empty, the body at the mortician's. He stepped inside, only to find the same mess he had seen the day before. It had not yet been looted for what few valuable items she might have owned.

Why had she been killed? To silence her, or only to bring more attention to the mysterious 'wolf'? Or both? What did she know about the marquis that was so dangerous, or had he just overacted?

Still, the inspector was fairly sure it had not been the marquis himself or any of his immediate servants who had committed this gruesome crime or its predecessor. He would never lower himself to that, and his servants were too soft. A hired killer, then? The same one who had rescued him last night? Or one of the bandits in the woods?

He sat down on her stool and sighed. Maybe this had nothing at all to do with the marquis. Maybe one of the bandits had killed Roux for whatever reason, and someone who didn't like the marquis had spread the ridiculous rumor and stolen the coat to connect him to the crime. But that did not explain Mrs. Bernard's death, obviously done by another person trying to imitate the first. No, there was a connection. He had to discover it – and then, even worse, he had to prove it in a court of law.

Audley quickly searched the place, but found nothing to point him in any direction. Someone had entered, there had been a struggle, and then he'd slit her throat. That was the whole of the crime here as far as he could tell. There were some francs still in the drawer, so it was not a robbery. She'd still had her gold wedding ring on, too, he remembered, which would have been taken by someone looking to rob her. A man so cruel as to slash her throat would have no scruples about taking her ring if robbery was his intent.

Audley was getting nowhere. He already knew there were two killers – he just hadn't told anyone (other than the coroner), intending to draw at least one of them out. He had to move on.

It had reached a reasonable hour when he approached the school. A flash of red against the green of the foliage drew his instant attention, even if it was hidden beneath a white bonnet. "Miss Bingley?"

It was indeed. Miss Bingley was on the side of the grounds, picking wild flowers and putting them in a basket so very daintily, as if she were putting on a show. "Hello, Inspector Audley," she said without looking up.

"Forgive my intrusion – do you have lessons today?"

She finally stopped her activity and stood up to face him. "I have been excused for this morning."

"To pick flowers?"

"It is a proper womanly thing to do, is it not?" she said serenely. "Why, some day I might use this invaluable skill to collect enough for a table setting for my husband's grand table."

"It is a very ... um, *womanly* activity," he admitted, "but how were you excused from your lessons?"

"I passed."

"You passed?"

"Mrs. Halliburton said she had nothing else to teach me."

"What was she teaching?"

"For these few weeks, proper posture."

"What, as in balancing a book on your head?"

"Precisely," she said with a satisfied smirk.

"So I assume you are capable of balancing a book on your head?"

She put down her basket and approached him. "Hand me one."

Willing to go along with her, he opened his bag. He had his notebook, but he would not put that in someone else's hands. The only other option was what he was currently reading, a small book with a hard cover. "Here."

Miss Bingley took it with a curtsey, which reminded him to bow belatedly as she opened to the first page with curiosity. "*My Travels in the East* by Brian Maddox. I didn't know it had been exported."

"I hear it sold quite well in England. You are familiar with it?"

"I have a copy back at home, but I've not read it through yet."

"The same. I mean, I've not finished it yet either."

She closed the cover. "I promised you a display."

"I never said a *display* – " But she had already removed her bonnet. Her hair was unnaturally short, seemingly self-cut, as it was uneven in some places. She placed the book very carefully on her head, holding her arms out to steady herself. Slowly she stepped towards him, the book wavering only slightly on her head

"Very well, enough of this," she said, and stepped back a few steps in normal posture, the book staying where it was.

She then suddenly swung her body around, ducked so that the book had to drop to catch up with her, and then stood back up with enough force to toss the book forward. As it sailed through the air, she spun around several times, hopped over a stone, and landed just in time to catch the book back on her head as it landed – all on one foot.

Audley found himself clapping as she turned back around towards him, walked casually over, took the book off her head, and handed it to him. "So, as I said, she told me she had nothing more to teach me about posture. Manners and propriety are another thing, but until the curriculum advances, I am free for this hour."

He took the book back. "Are you perchance intending a career as a circus performer?"

"Only if no man in England will have me and my vast inheritance," she said. After a pause that was surprisingly comfortable, she continued, "But I am keeping you from your business with the headmaster."

"My business is not with the headmaster," he said. "It is with some of the students, yourself included."

"Then shall we take a turn about the grounds? That is an English custom for women and men who wish to speak.

Apparently we can only do it while walking."

He smiled as they began to walk. "You are very critical of your own culture."

"You are quite observant," she said. "Perhaps you should use these skills of perception in your work and you will get farther."

He stopped in his place, more serious now. "How do you know what skills I am using and what I am not?"

"I know you are not asking the right questions, or you would already have your answers. You hear a 'no' or a 'yes,' and just write in your book something like, 'She's lying – I wonder why?' instead of simply *asking.*"

How does she know that? "Interrogation is a very careful art."

"Are you so careful with all of your suspects back in Paris?"

He had to counter, "Are you considering yourself a suspect?"

"In what, I don't know, but I care not at all for the marquis, and neither does Heather Littlefield, but she's too scared to say anything. If there is a plot against the marquis, does not thinking ill of him make me a suspect?"

He felt blinded – but not by the sun, for his hat was protecting him from its rays, but not from the brightness of this young woman. She had replaced her bonnet as they were talking. "Miss Bingley, why don't you care for the marquis?"

"Again, wrong question. And you're the famous inspector?" she said, with a half-smile. That smirk! It was driving him mad. "Opinions are formed by events and knowledge. Try again."

Audley sighed. "What do you know about the marquis?"

Their casual stroll now stopped abruptly, and her body language changed. She stood straight and serious as she answered, "He beats his servants and rapes some of the maids. His previous wife, who was penniless, died under suspicious circumstances on her own grounds. Now he is engaged to a young woman from England whom he had not met before her arrival here, for the express purpose of meeting him with only the shallow excuse of being in seminary. This woman, aside from her natural attributes of being young and beautiful, is to come into a grand inheritance that will, by English law, become entirely his the moment they are married. Oh, and he changed all of his servants before we arrived, so anyone who might have known anything about his past – how he treated his wife, the circumstances of her death, how he treated his servants – is suddenly gone in time for the arrival of his new bride. The only one who did stick around ends up dead as soon as an authority figure starts asking questions. Now, Inspector Audley, tell me what part of that *isn't* suspicious?"

He stood there stunned into speechlessness, and she giggled a very girlish giggle. Was she serious or was she not? She seemed to flip back and forth at will. He could not comprehend it. "How do you know all this?"

"The very first time we visited the manor, it was for tea. In England of course we wouldn't be allowed to visit a gentleman's house without a wife or a sister inviting us, but here we are in France. We sat there, and the maid named Sophie served us. When she approached the marquis, I noticed her hands were shaking and one of them had several nails broken. When we were invited back for dinner the next week, I spoke to her while the marquis spoke privately with Heather for the first time, and after a bout of hysteria, she confessed everything to me – rumors and things that had actually happened to her."

"Why – why didn't you report this?"

"And to whom was I supposed to report this? The constable, who is paid by the marquis? The headmaster, who will not let one negative piece of news come from his school, even if it was unrelated to the school itself? Mrs. Robinson's has a reputation to maintain, after all. Just like no one knows about Simon Roux."

"Tell me about Simon Roux," he said, his voice more demanding than it had been since he arrived.

"I've already told you everything. He tried to rape two girls from my school, and I stopped him in time for them to escape. That didn't go reported because though it would have possibly gotten him hanged, it would have hanged the school as well. What father wants to send his daughter to a seminary meant to be an experiment in forced nunnery that instead lets its girls have their virtue stolen by common ruffians?"

She started walking again, and he realized he had to continue their pleasant stroll to keep up with her, even if they were circling the same land again and again. "Why didn't *you* report it?"

"To my father? Or any of my wealthy and powerful relatives? I would just be brought home, and Lady Littlefield would be left at the mercy of the marquis." She looked at him again. "She doesn't want to marry him."

"Does she know about Sophie?"

"Not the whole extent of it, no. But she has learned of his temper first hand. Literally."

He paused. "He yelled at her?"

"Worse."

"He ... hit his own betrothed?" Audley could not believe it. Was this the same man who had almost wept when discussing his dead wife the previous afternoon?

"He did give her makeup to cover the bruise so she could rejoin the dinner. You can ask Sophie; she applied it."

They walked in silence for a moment as he digested all of this information. Miss Bingley seemed to have returned to her proper girly self. Was she playing with him? She definitely was, but he could not tell which half was doing the playing. "Why are you doing this?"

"Doing what?"

"Why did you investigate the marquis? Why did you question his servant? Why do you seem to keep your own school open – a school you are obviously bored with – just so you can do all this? Why are you protecting her?"

"Because," she said casually, "she asked me to."

"That's it?"

"That's it." She added more seriously, "When someone asks me for help, especially someone without any allies and many people lined up against her, I give it." The sound of the bells interrupted them. "That would be my class in Italian. It seems our little walk has come to an end, Inspector Audley, because I would rather not miss this lecture. I have fallen a bit behind."

"We will continue," he said, a little more harshly than he intended, "another time."

"Of course, Inspector Audley." She gave a proper little curtsey and skipped off towards the building. He did not bow in return. Instead, he stood there numbly until she was gone, then turned around and headed back to the mansion.

~~~

"Monsieur Inspector! You cannot enter now, His Lordship is not – "

"I am not here to see His Lordship," Audley said as he invited himself into the entry hall of the Marquis de Maret. "I am here to see a maid named Sophie, or Sophia. Is she here?"

The butler looked a little flustered by the inspector's behavior. He had never been so forceful in his mannerisms when dealing with the marquis or his household so far, and he was still carrying his rifle from the night before. "Yes sir – she will be fetched immediately. May I take your hat and coat, Inspector?"

"No," he said. "I will wait here for her." As much as he would have liked to sit down and have a cup of tea, he wanted privacy, and he wouldn't get it within these walls.

Something about speaking with Miss Bingley had set him off. It had taken him a moment on the road, sorting through his mental notations, to realize the scope of what she had told him – all things she had done on her own. Granted, she had had more time than him and was acting under less scrutiny, but she also seemed to know everything about everyone. Her ability to toy with him – when he should have been toying with her – was maddening. While not particularly verbose, everyone else was at least giving him plain yes or no answers with plainly readable faces. He had noticed something amiss with Sophie in their initial interview, but he had not immediately pursued it.

He forced himself into a calmer state when the maid was brought to him. She was a young woman, blond and dressed in the reasonable French fashions expected of a maid. "Inspector Audley."

"Perhaps there's something you can assist me in," he said. "I would like to have a word with you. May we go outside?" He forced himself to add, as a likely excuse, "The weather is very lovely."

She curtseyed and followed him out, to the clear disapproval of the housekeeper, who looked on from the top of the stairs. Well, he could deal with that. The grounds were indeed quite lovely, even if he had decided he had had enough of nature in the past day. They walked out to a stone bench beneath the shade of a grand oak tree. Was this where younger de Marets had romanced their intendeds?

"Please, sit," he said as he set his rifle down and removed his hat. When she hesitated, he realized. "Oh, of course." He ruffled through his satchel and retrieved a dry cloth, which he set down on the stone for her to sit and not wet her dress.

"Thank you, Monsieur Inspector." She didn't seem to know quite what to make of this exchange.

"I apologize for my appearance. I've had ... quite a long night. And day." He sat down next to her and removed his notebook and charcoal pencil, good for moments like these. "I have, if you do not mind, a few more questions."

"I – I did not steal the coat, Inspector."

Of course. Servants are always accused of theft. "I did not think you did.

My questions are about the behavior of the marquis." The mention of this particular subject did startle her, he noted. "You realize, I am an impartial investigator to the law and do not answer to anyone here, not even the marquis. My investigations are private unless I choose to make them otherwise."

"Of course, Inspector."

"What I mean to say, to be perfectly clear, is that you can trust me. In fact, I am quite eager for your trust, for it will help me get to the bottom of this case. Do you understand?"

"Yes," she said, but she was quivering.

He gave her a reassuring smile. "Now, did you know Simon Roux?"

"No."

"Had you heard of him?"

"I had heard his name once or twice in passing conversation in town, but otherwise, no, Inspector."

"Are you often in town?"

"My parents live on the outskirts. My father is very ill."

He took down a note in his journal. "So you visit him. And I assume your work here is very helpful to your parents' finances?"

"Yes, Inspector."

So that explains it. "Now I must ask some delicate questions about the marquis."

She nodded slightly but said nothing, her body visibly tensing.

"Please be assured – I do not answer to the marquis, unlike everyone else in the area. And I know many of the answers to the questions already – but I would like to hear them from you." His voice was gentle, his blue eyes pleading. He had what his mother described as a 'puppy dog' face when he tried, though it would wither with age. For the moment, it was intolerably useful. "Has the marquis ever laid a hand on any of his servants?"

Her eyes met his, and he watched them painfully search him for dishonesty and corruption before she finally answered quietly, "Yes."

"Did he lay a hand on you?"

She turned away, burying her face in her hands. "Yes."

"Had he ingested a vast quantity of spirits when he did?"

Sophie was not quick to answer, "The first time."

He sighed sympathetically and lowered his voice. "And the other times?"

She shook her head. She was trying to hide it, but she was beginning to cry. He put a cautious hand on her shoulder. "I know, Miss Sophie, I know. You are not the first person this has happened to. I wish that you will be the last."

Sophie raised her watery eyes to his again, "Oh please, Monsieur Inspector, don't tell him."

"I will not speak a word of this conversation. I promise."

"He does know – he must know. There must be talk. But – I haven't told him and I don't know how to. Or even if I should."

He was not entirely sure where the conversation was turning. He only knew he had to pursue it. "You haven't told him what, Sophie?" But she couldn't answer. Now she was sobbing quietly into her hands. "Miss Sophie, are you with child?"

She nodded.

"And it is his?"

Again, the same gesture. Audley sat back, tightening his grip on her shoulder protectively and sympathetically, but that was all he could do. They were undoubtedly being watched from afar. "Have you told anyone?"

"No one. Not even my parents."

He stood up. He had too much tension in his body and he had to find an outlet for it. He paced in front of her – which would look much more inquisitional to anyone watching through a window –

with his hands behind his back. "Miss Sophie, as I am sure you are aware, the marquis is a dangerous man."

"I know," she whimpered.

"Has he – done anything – to anyone else? Even just threatened them?"

"No. Not that I know of, sir, please."

He frowned. "Do you have somewhere you can go, if I tell you to leave the manor for good?"

"I need this work, Inspector – "

"Your life is more important than money, Miss," he said. "And it may be in danger. Do you have somewhere you can go, if I asked you to go further than your parents' house?"

She looked puzzled for a moment before answering, "I have – a cousin in Mon Richard, and his wife and children. They would take me in."

"Their family name?"

"Murrell. The same as mine."

He nodded, writing this down. "Miss Murrell, my duty is to the law, and I am sure the marquis has violated it in at least two ways, but I need time to gather evidence. If I tell you to, can you be ready to leave for Mon Richard at a moment's notice?"

Hesitantly, she nodded.

"Good. That will be all, Miss Murrell." He offered a hand to help her to her feet, and implored her to use the clean side of his cloth to wipe her face before they headed back to the manor house. "Nothing will be said to endanger you, I promise. In fact, it will be very much the opposite, God willing." She gave him a weak smile of thanks as they stepped up to the front door, where she scurried back into the house and to work.

Audley left her at the door, ready to return to town – and finally, a warm bed and a change of clothes – when Monsieur Durand stopped him. "Inspector Audley."

He sighed. His awkward night of sleep and exhausting day was catching up with him. "Yes?"

"His Lordship wishes to see you." He added for emphasis, "*Now*."

CHAPTER 5

Never one to question an order, especially when he was interested to know why someone had the audacity to give it without the necessary authority, Inspector Audley followed the butler in. This time he let the man take his coat and hat, and shelve his rifle, and he was invited into the sitting room where the marquis was apparently taking tea. "Inspector. Are you always in the habit of questioning servants without the master's permission?"

Audley sat down opposite him as a servant poured tea into a second cup. "I was not aware that I required it when I have been called in particularly to investigate a crime. Apparently I must read up on the new appendixes to French law." He dropped a cube of sugar into his cup and held it, letting the heat warm his hands while he waited for the sugar to dissolve.

"What did you question Sophie about? I was under the impression you already spoke with her."

"I did." He took a sip, sure that his love of tea made him truly was a Brit at heart. "I will trade you the answer to your question for an answer to one of mine – what happened to your forehead, my Lord?"

It had not escaped his notice that the marquis had a bruise and a nick on his right temple, not swollen but purple and blue, and that he was also wearing heavy gloves, odd for indoors. "I fell while gardening."

"Gardening?"

"Yes. It seems I am not as talented as my wife, may she rest in peace. I slid on the wet stone and banged my head smartly on the ground before the gardener could catch me."

"Well, it must have been hard for him to see you in the middle of the night."

"Excuse me?"

"It is now - ," Audley made an orchestrated performance of checking his pocket watch – "half-past two, and yet your bruise has healed enough that the swelling has already gone down. It is on its way to yellowing already, so I would say – and this is just an estimate – that you acquired it very early in the morning, while it was still quite dark." He looked down. "Did you hurt your hands as well, during the fall in your garden?"

Finally, the marquis looked decidedly put-off. Audley decided to revel in the moment of truly having the upper hand.

"Inspector, you're not buying into this werewolf nonsense, are you?"

"I said nothing of the kind," he answered. "It had not even occurred to me until you brought it up just now."

"Enough, Inspector," the marquis said firmly, deciding to change the course of conversation as he pleased. "Now answer my question. What were you asking Sophie?"

"I was inquiring about my investigation. You will recall the matter of that missing coat that caused all this trouble to begin with. That and a dead man with his throat slashed."

"Ah, yes. Did she steal it?"

"No," Audley said, pleased with himself for having avoided the real answer but still managing not to lie. "I am quite certain she did not."

"Hopefully your skills as a detector of thieves are better than yours skills as a medical examiner," the marquis said as he rose. Very aware that he was being dismissed, Audley quickly gulped the last of his tea and rose with him.

"My Lord."

"Inspector Audley."

Despite the earlier conversation with Sophie, Robert Audley walked out of the manor with a satisfied smirk on his face. The marquis, in attempting to intimidate him, had shown his hand. He might not be a werewolf, but he had some nocturnal adventure on the night of the full moon that was mysterious enough.

~~~

Audley returned to the *Verrat* as quickly as possible. He needed to recoup and record and begin to sort the mess of information in his head, which was still throbbing from the knock last night. He was frustrated when, as he entered, Camille approached him with some urgency. "Monsieur Lambert is waiting for you."

The old mortician was not a tavern regular, so Audley was not wont to dismiss it, but he was also very tired. He found the ghastly pale man in the corner, and set down his rifle and satchel across from him, determined to do this quickly. "Hello, Monsieur Lambert."

"Inspector Audley. I found something that might be of use to you in my little collection," he said, and brought something up from underneath the table. Audley was relieved to find the collection he was referring to was one of books, as an old tome was passed to him, its bound pages frayed with age.

Audley opened it to a picture of what appeared to be some sort of wolf with chicken feet and the tail of a mule. *The Beast of Gévaudan*, it read.

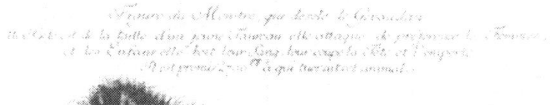

"You do not take this seriously, do you?" Audley said.

"Despite my profession, I am not obsessed with the underworld or any creatures that may come from it," Lambert said. "It is merely a book that I own. Have you read it?"

"No," he said, "but I recognize the picture. And I've heard of the Beast of Gévaudan. The legend of the mysterious beast that ate children in our woods – it must have been circulating for almost a century, now." He flipped through the book despite his best inclinations. "I always thought it to be a metaphor for the nobility. Or a metaphor created by the nobles for the revolutionaries."

"There was a beast that they killed. A wolf. They brought it to Versailles."

"Then it must have been missed when the place was seized decades later," Audley said. "We are dealing with a human killer, Monsieur Lambert. Perhaps one dressed in costume, but human all the same."

"I thought there were two killers."

"There are," he said, lowering his voice, "but it is best not to say it, so soon in the investigation, or the second one will not be so easily drawn out."

Monsieur Lambert put his boney hands up. "I will say nothing, Inspector Audley."

"That would be best, I think, for your own safety. Clearly one of our killers has a problem with people knowing too much."

~~~

Taking his food with him, Audley retired to his room while it was light, and called for some water to be warmed. They managed to get a bucket for him, which he dumped over himself, and after some scrubbing, began to feel human again. Refreshed, he ate his dinner and removed the contents of his satchel onto the table that served as a writing desk. He flipped through the book Lambert had given him, and promised himself that he would read it later.

This is not about a beast, he thought as he opened his notebook, inked his pen, and began to flip through the pages of notes – names, places, recordings of conversations. *There is too much at work here. Someone planned this.* Either someone wanted to keep him from finding the men in the woods, or someone wanted to protect him from them – that much he had learned well last night. *It could also be both.*

The wolf – protector. *Protector of women?* Audley wrote under *wolf*. It – he – had killed Simon Roux, a known villain and at least *attempted* rapist. *Protector of him?* Was it the same person who had "attacked" him last night? He was thoroughly convinced he had not been attacked by one of the bandits, otherwise he would be dead or at the very least, not carried and left in such a significant spot. But if the wolf had carried him, then the wolf was not one of the bandits. And the wolf was not the marquis, he was fairly sure. There was nothing to connect the marquis to Simon Roux.

In fact, the marquis had everything to lose by me coming here. Or perhaps the marquis had assumed Audley would do what a regular constable did, which was ignore the wealthy and find someone to hang for the crime and then leave, job well done. Certainly, Audley had no *real* business investigating the marquis's affairs with his servants and his fiancée – unless they were connected to the wolf. But he could not make the connection.

The only thing he was fairly certain of – with no way to prove it – was that the marquis had hired someone to kill Mrs. Bernard and make it seem like it was the wolf, as he had now officially dubbed Roux's killer. He had decided *that* as soon as Miss Bingley had told him about Sophie. Miss Bingley – he needed her as his assistant. She would be much more helpful than an ancient mortician who believed in fairy tales and a constable he doubted he could trust. Unless she had an angle, too.

Yes, she did – she had stated it. She was out to protect Lady Littlefield from the marquis. She had gone above and beyond the call to point Audley in the direction of Sophie, whom she clearly associated with Lady Littlefield. What were their names? He had to look them up. Heather Littlefield and Georgiana Bingley. Maybe his mind was still rattled from the previous night and the drink he was mindlessly ingesting now to deal with his headache.

It was all connected – he just didn't know how. He put all of the names on a blank sheet and tried to connect them, but could not draw enough lines. There were too many degrees between Roux and the marquis, the two principle characters.

Maybe Miss Bingley knew – Miss *Georgiana* Bingley. Looking back on their conversation, she was so clearly holding back more information, as she had done in every previous encounter with him. Other people did it because they were scared (*Lady Littlefield*) or because they did not wish to implicate themselves (*the marquis*). She had no motive that he could see. If he'd been sharper that morning, maybe he could have gotten it from her. He tried to recall everything she had said, down to the last detail. ("I have a copy back at home, but I've not read it through yet.")

What book? Oh yes. He scrambled for the last item from his bag, the book he had been intending to read while in transit but had not been able to find the time. He opened *My Travels in the East* by Brian Maddox. It seemed to him from the first few pages a standard travelogue, but it was a bestseller in England and was all the rage in Paris, to the point where even his mother in Normandy had sent him a copy.

The man had apparently been an Austrian prince, then run off with his bride, traveling through Russia and then somewhere in the Japans or Cathay before returning to England. It was a wild story, but the press had substantiated it. Audley flipped to the biography. *Mr. Maddox lives outside London with his wife, Princess Nadezhda Maddox.* There was an address to write to him, a box in London.

As he read, the sky darkened, his eyelids grew heavy, and the fluttering of the candlelight became hypnotic. He could barely concentrate on the words as Mr. Maddox described his first contact with his future father-in-law, Count Vladimir, over a game of cards. Audley instead started mindlessly pushing through the pages, almost ready to close the book. And then almost at the end, he stopped.

He'd stopped on a page of a script he had never seen before. The letters – described by Maddox to be basic Japanese script – were more like whole drawings to themselves in their complexity. *It must take the Japanese a long time to write even the shortest note.*

He realized that he needed to correct his own thought. He had seen these letters before. He sorted through the rest of the contents of his satchel in a flurry. There was a leftover roll of bread, an extra case of bullets for his pistol, his flask, and most importantly, the broken cross from Simon Roux's death site.

Be more careful next time, it said to him. He flipped it over, looking at the letters on the other side that had been so unfamiliar to him, and compared them to the ones in the book. Either it was a strange coincidence, or someone had written a message on the back of the cross – in Japanese.

Audley abandoned thoughts of sleep and drew a new sheet of paper from his tablet. *Dear Mr. Brian Maddox*, he began.

Robert Audley did not end up settling down for the night until some time later, when he had written and sealed the long letter, and had woken a courier to have it posted to England immediately. Only after that task was completed could he find any rest.

~~~

"Did you see the paper this morning, Inspector?"

Those were never words an inspector wanted to hear, especially first thing in the morning, before he had any wine or a chance to hear anything himself. "No, I've not."

Anton, the barkeep and owner, passed him the town's paper, which was barely more than a pamphlet on paper so flimsy it would hold up maybe a week. Only the very official-looking lettering at the top gave it any authority. It had only one story.

THE MARQUIS DE MARET BELIEVED TO BE WEREWOLF!

Audley cursed under his breath. This would cause more trouble for him than anything else. If anything, it would further obscure the actual wolf-man, who Audley believed thoroughly to have no lycanthropic tendencies. The article, short and poorly-spelled, explained that howls had been heard on the night of the full moon (true) and that the marquis had been spotted the next morning with mysterious injuries (also true). Well, he could not attack them for the veracity of their comments. It went on to speculate all kinds of nefarious deeds he could have committed, omitting any direct reference to the two murders (neither of which had occurred on the full moon) but certainly implying something in that direction. "Who publishes this?"

"A man named Gerard. He has a press in his house. He does it for the town's amusement. Makes quite a few francs doing it, too."

"I take it he is not known for his journalistic integrity?"

Anton, who had probably never been outside the town in his life, did not understand the concept.

"I mean, does he always print wild rumors?"

"What else would he have to print?"

Audley sighed, finished his breakfast, and headed out. He intended to speak with Gerard, who might well be getting in over his head. He did not get very far in this quest, as he was approached by one of the marquis's men immediately upon leaving the tavern. He resignedly gave the man a tip of his hat. "I assume His Lordship would like to speak with me?"

Ten minutes and one coach ride later, he was sitting in the study of the Marquis de Maret, having the very same one-page paper with its one story waved in his face. "*Do you know about this?*" Audley noticed that the marquis's now ungloved hands had several broken nails.

"It was the first thing I heard of today," Audley said. "I have also heard it is printed by a man with a press and nothing better to do than print town gossip."

The marquis seemed to calm, walking back around his desk. "This is true. This is not the first article he has written about me."

"And the others?"

"I know the difference between mindlessly jabbing at the returned nobility and actual protest," the marquis said, crumpling up the paper and tossing it in a bin. "I am not concerned about Monsieur Gerard. I am concerned about his sources."

"Surely you do not think I am one of them?"

"No. Despite our disagreements, I know you to be above this," the marquis said, and Audley bowed in thanks. After a pause, the marquis continued, on a seemingly unrelated note. "I have dismissed Sophie."

"What?" Audley answered as calmly as he could.

"I did not leave my own apartments yesterday, except to speak with you, so this information must have been leaked by one of the servants."

"And you assume it was her? So you think she has special reason to hold something against you?"

The marquis frowned but did not fall into such an obvious trap. He instead played with the pen on his desk. "I had to make an example. You will take comfort in the fact that she was happy enough to leave."

Audley gave a noncommittal murmur. He would make no confession, either.

"Putting this business aside," the marquis said, "I wonder if I could ask you a favor?"

Audley looked at him curiously. "My Lord?"

"My fiancée is joining me for a brunch and she is bringing her companion. I would like to speak with Lady Littlefield privately, but propriety does not allow it except under special circumstances. Would you join us and make conversation with Miss Bingley?"

Audley surprised himself by the speed and ease of his own answer, "I would be honored, my Lord." He added, "But, I would recommend, if your purpose is a quiet moment with your intended bride, that we take a walk around your gardens, as is the English custom. That is considered very proper."

The marquis smiled. It was an unnerving experience. "I will cede to your authority on the matter and agree, Inspector."

~~~

The ladies arrived soon after that. Inspector Audley had been offered considerable resources to clean up beforehand, all of which he took advantage of, short of borrowing the marquis's clothing. It was nice to be perfectly-shaven and combed by an attendant, something he usually only enjoyed while at home in Valognes. He emerged a cleaner, fresher Robert Audley, and it put him in a rather good mood for the appearance of Lady Littlefield and Miss Bingley.

"Welcome, welcome! My darling," the marquis said, kissing the hand of his betrothed. "Miss Bingley. It has been recommended to me that we first go for a walk in my gardens, if you ladies are not too hungry." He spoke to them in his relatively fluent but strongly accented English.

Both ladies agreed with perfect smiles. They certainly knew how to act. *They are in a school for manners and have probably been taught from birth how to be polite*, Audley reminded himself. As they stepped outside on the beautiful spring morning, the marquis took his betrothed's arm and went ahead. Audley and Miss Bingley did not touch, but hung back and walked side-by-side, keeping both pace and distance.

"So how did you get dragged into this, Inspector Audley?"

He kept his smile as he said, "If he is going to talk to her, he will do it within my sight. This seemed the best arrangement." He noted her quiet smile of approval. He had actually done something right in her eyes. "Have you read the papers this morning?"

"Our school does not provide the local paper for us."

"It was only one article. Apparently, the marquis is a werewolf. Did you know that?"

Miss Bingley did not look overly surprised, but this news about the paper did seem new information to her. "A werewolf, if you believe in such nonsense, is only a wolf one night a month, correct?"

"That is the legend, I believe."

"That would imply the marquis, as a werewolf, is but a humble man the rest of the month. That I cannot agree on, so I do not find myself in agreement with the local papers."

"Very well." He decided to turn to news she would surely want to know – if she didn't already. "Miss Sophie has been dismissed for starting the werewolf rumor."

Miss Bingley stopped in her tracks. "*What?*"

"Just what I said. The marquis told me but half an hour ago."

"What did he do with her?"

"He said he dismissed her. Where she goes is her own volition."

He had not before seen such conviction in Miss Bingley's eyes as she grabbed his hand – which startled him, "*Find her.*"

"I don't have any – "

"Find her. Promise me you will find her and make sure she is safe." She tightened her grip. "*Promise me.*"

"I promise."

"Thank you." She released him, and in a moment regained her calm and coy demeanor. "Now, come," Miss Bingley said, continuing on their path and giving him a small smile. "We have strayed away too long from meaningless conversation."

"Yes," he said, his heart racing for some reason. "I have, I fear, addled your feminine mind."

She swatted him, barely brushing against the fabric of his coat. "So, Inspector Audley ... I realize I do not even know your Christian name."

"Robert."

"And where are you from, Inspector Robert Audley?"

"Valognes, in Normandy. I grew up there. It's quite lovely."

"Is it on the sea?"

They were both keeping an eye on the marquis and Lady Littlefield, who were ahead of them some distance but appeared to be simply walking and talking. "No, but we have a manor – more of a castle, really."

"Oh," she said. "Your mother's family?"

"No. It was a noble estate before the revolution, and the family never reappeared, so the place was put up for a very reasonable auction, and my father purchased it. As far as we know, they followed the rest of their family, who moved centuries ago, to England. But the manor often feels like it's still theirs; many of their things are still around."

"So now they are a good English family?"

"Yes," he said. "I forget the name ... ah, yes. D'Arcy."

"No!"

He paused in his step, turning to her, surprised by the surprise on her face. "It is true."

"You are serious – the Darcys?"

"You know of them?"

She recovered and began to walk again. "Mr. Fitzwilliam Darcy is my uncle."

"Really?" He himself could not believe the connection. "Do you know him well?"

"He lives but three miles from me, in Derbyshire. His wife is my mother's sister."

"What a coincidence," he said, and meant it. "I vaguely recall a visit from Mr. and Mrs. Darcy – but I was very young. Maybe five or six."

"I know they made a journey at some point – but I was also very young. It was after my brother and sister were born, but before he went to Austria – Oh, I must have been only two or three."

"When were you born?"

"1805."

He raised his eyebrows. "1801." He had no idea they were so close in age. She was a tiny, fragile-looking woman and he was a hardened inspector for the Parisian authorities. She was nearly a head shorter than him.

"You look older. You have a certain wisdom about you. I suppose that's why you're the famed inspector."

"I'm a famed inspector, if that is true, because I solve cases."

"Then solve this one," she said, her voice oddly pleading. "For Heather."

"You are not concerned with the dead, Miss Bingley?"

She answered without hesitation, "I am more concerned about the living."

~~~

The brunch was a more casual meal than supper, especially because it was only the four of them, and with not nearly the same number of courses. The marquis seemed to be in an uncommonly good mood, or at least was attempting to look like he was in front of Lady Littlefield – if so, he was doing it very well. He ignored Miss Bingley almost completely, as seemed to be his habit, and she drew no attention to herself. When he discovered the marquis was willing enough to let the inspector ask Lady Littlefield casual questions about her studies, Audley seized his chance to get to know her better. "So, what are you studying at Mrs. Robinson's?"

"Languages, painting, drawing, all of that," she said, perfectly pleasantly. "Some manners, but it is just a formality. And, of course, religion."

These girls were not girls. They were in their late teens, and had been sent to France for further education for whatever the reason. For Lady Littlefield, it was to marry the marquis. For Miss Bingley? He considered discipline. She was certainly good at making herself a handful. He wondered what she could be like to her parents when she wanted to be. But the point stood – they were English ladies raised in the right circles and had nothing to learn in the way of being pleasing company and proper women. He smiled amiably. "Your French is extremely proficient. What other languages do they teach?"

"Italian. And for those who master that, Latin. Georgiana is in the top of the Latin class," Lady Littlefield said, to which Miss Bingley just gave an appreciative nod, but said nothing.

"Do you find France favorable? At least, what you have seen of it, Lady Littlefield?"

"Very much so," Lady Littlefield said, unconsciously shooting a nervous glance to the marquis and then quickly turning it back. The marquis did not notice; Audley did. Miss Bingley had taken on, as usual, the appearance of a wall of silence and obliviousness, as she quietly ate her luncheon meats. "This is my first time outside of England though, so I've little to compare it to."

Their little chatter continued for the whole of the meal, and while it was convenient that the marquis was so willing to let Audley question his fiancée, if very informally, Audley found it frustrating that Miss Bingley offered almost nothing to the conversation and gave monosyllabic answers when addressed directly. The marquis didn't seem bothered, and maybe that was for the best.

The meal finished and they saw the ladies off into their carriage to return to the school grounds. Once the carriage disappeared down the road, the marquis immediately turned to Audley with a more serious expression, "I want to sponsor a wolf hunt."

Audley shrugged, as if to say, 'And?', not knowing where the marquis was heading with the sudden introduction of this topic.

"I would like you to head it, Inspector Audley. As part of your investigation."

"I did not come here to engage in sport," Audley countered. "Nor do I think it would do anything to forward my investigations."

"I think it would."

"How so? We both know the killer is perfectly human."

"Oh yes. I know," the marquis said with odd determination. Audley frowned; the man was hiding something. Well, more than he was usually hiding. "But I wish to draw him out."

"So the purpose of the hunt would be...perhaps a man who kills people will be sympathetic to the creature he is associated with by rumor and the press?"

"I am referring to a man who dresses as a wolf, in case you'd forgotten."

Audley glanced at the marquis intensely. "Those are nothing more than rumors – unless you tell me otherwise." When the marquis didn't contradict, he went on, "You've seen him, haven't you?" Still, no response, but no dismissal. He hazarded another speculation. "You fought him?"

The marquis looked uncomfortable, shifting his weight around where he stood, not making eye contact. "On the full moon, obviously."

"Obviously. And would you care to give me a description of the killer I've been searching for, if you are so interested in forwarding my investigation?"

The marquis motioned for them to go back inside, where Audley quickly retrieved his notebook and inked his pen as the marquis paced around him. "He attacked me."

"Unprovoked?"

"Yes, unprovoked."

"When was this?"

"About two in the morning."

"What were you doing up at two in the morning?"

The marquis said calmly, "I've not slept well since this all began."

"So you went on a walk?"

"Precisely. As I've said before, I don't believe in werewolves, so I had no problems with wandering my own grounds, which are well patrolled, no more on a full moon than any other night. I was attacked in my garden."

Audley skipped the obvious question and merely asked, "What did he look like?"

"It was hard to see, but he was wearing a wolf skin – over his head, shoulders, arms, legs – and had a white shirt and breeches on, otherwise."

"How tall was he?"

The marquis estimated, "I would say, about your height."

"How was he armed?"

"Claws. Presumably taken from the wolf he skinned."

"What color was this wolf?"

"Grey – the typical color of wolves in this area."

"Did he speak?"

"No."

"Did he growl?"

"Yes. And howled. But not totally inhuman – he seemed simply to be very good at what he was doing."

Obviously. "So – you could not identify this man if you met him?"

"I could not say in all honesty that it was not you, Inspector Audley," the marquis said without hesitation, "between the disguise and the poor light. Though I highly doubt it was."

Audley gave him a false smile. "Thank you for your trust, my Lord."

"Of course."

"And he attacked you totally unprovoked?"

"Yes."

That the marquis was withholding at least something, Audley did not doubt. In fact, he could not be sure if he could hold the story in any veracity whatsoever. It would be a convenient cover story for many other things, and the marquis was clever enough to first attempt to conceal it, and let Audley think he discovered it. "Is there anything else you'd like to mention?"

"No. Now, what about my proposal?"

Audley put aside his pen and closed the ink jar. "If you do arrange a hunt, I will join you on the hunt for observational purposes. But this is not an official action of my office, and I will not aid you in hunting down some innocent wolves for the purpose of public relations."

"So you side with the wolves?"

"You know very well that the situation is far more complex than that, my Lord."

"Very well."

The marquis seemed to miss that Audley hadn't said, "No."

CHAPTER 6

Robert Audley removed his hat and held it respectfully over his breast as the priest recited the benediction over the grave of Mrs. Bernard. A few people from town had come forth for this event on the warm Saturday afternoon, far more than for Simon Roux. Mrs. Bernard had been a lonely widow, but had supported herself with a vegetable garden and was considered a kindly neighbor, always visited by the local children. *She did not deserve this*, he thought. Of course, no one deserved such a death, especially not a kindly old widow, but added to that was the additional frustration that he knew who'd killed her, or at least the person who had given the order, and could prove nothing.

Yet.

He left quickly afterwards on a mission of mercy. Returning to town, he quickly discovered from Camille that Sophie's parents lived on a farm just outside of town. As much as he preferred walking, he saddled the horse he had been loaned by the department in Paris and rode until he found the fields of the Murrell family. They had been laid to waste by the passing of soldiers and bad years of harvest, and stood unsown, as had been described to him. The house itself was in good enough repair, with smoke rising from the chimney indicating life inside. He cautiously knocked on the door, and then bowed to the old woman who was cleaning her hands on her apron when she opened the door. "Monsieur?"

"I am Inspector Robert Audley," he said, removing his hat. "I am here to speak with Miss Murrell, on behalf of a friend, if she is here."

"What sort of friend?" she asked cautiously.

"Miss Bingley." Clearly, saying 'the marquis' would not get him in the door. And besides, this *was* a favor to Miss Bingley.

She disappeared back inside, closing the door behind her. This woman was no good at deception, if she was even trying to make the flimsiest attempts to disguise her daughter's whereabouts. She reappeared quickly. "Come in, Inspector."

He entered the small house, and was ushered into the living room, which was no grand place but was respectable enough, all things considered. She offered him a tiny glass of afternoon wine, which he accepted. Sophie Murrell emerged from wherever she had been in the back of the house, and he rose to greet her. "Miss Murrell."

"Inspector. I was not expecting – "

"I am here on Miss Bingley's behalf," he said. "She wanted to know that you were well despite your dismissal."

"Yes." She sat down, wringing her hands nervously, and he retook his seat. "I have no income now, but I suppose I will find something ... Anything is better than staying in that house."

"How did it come about, precisely?"

She would not look him in the eyes. "He accused me of stealing his red coat and then spreading rumors about his activities on the night of the full moon. Please, Inspector, I did neither of those things."

He raised his hand to her protests. "Of course you did not. But if you would spare me a moment, I would like to know more – for your safety and for my investigation." He did not take out his notebook for this interview. She was too nervous. "What did happen to the marquis on the night of the full moon?"

"I do not know, sir. I was already asleep. All I know is that when I saw him in the morning, Monsieur Durand was caring for his wounds."

"What was he wearing? The marquis, I mean."

"Sir?" she asked. "He was wearing – I suppose they were the clothes from that evening, although without the coat. They were very soiled."

"And this was – how early in the morning?"

"A little after the rooster crowed. Maybe an hour."

He continued his mental notation. "So one would assume he was up the course of the night."

"Yes. But I said nothing!"

"Of course. I do not believe he dismissed you because of that. Miss Murrell, he is removing all of his liabilities – and you are one of them for reasons we both understand, whether he knows the whole of it or not." He added softly, "Sophie, I believe you are in some danger, and it would be best for you to perhaps leave town. Can you be ready to leave at a moment's notice?"

Very hesitantly she answered, "You asked me before, and my answer is the same. I can, if my life depends on it."

"It may. I would not ask otherwise." He rose. "If you will excuse me, I must deliver this news to Miss Bingley. She will be greatly relieved."

"Thank you, Inspector," she said. "I do not know why she has bestowed this kindness on a servant, but please thank her for me."

He smiled. "I will."

~~~

There were definitely advantages to a horse. He traveled easily back into town, and past it, down the road to the seminary, stopping only to compose a letter before realizing he could not deliver it to their post box. They were proper ladies in a seminary where, no doubt, any mail not from their families would be opened and inspected by their headmaster. He would have to deliver it in person. He thought the plan admirable, and rushed to complete it before dark. It was Saturday, so the ladies of Mrs. Robinson's were tending their gardens and walking along the paths nearby. He nodded politely to many of the girls, who curtseyed and then ran away giggling as his horse snorted. He did not see Miss Bingley, but came upon someone else he recognized.

As he addressed her, Lady Heather Littlefield looked up from her picking of flowers, holding up her bonnet as she did so. "Inspector Audley." She curtseyed properly as he de-saddled and dropped to the ground.

"I was looking for Miss Bingley," he said as he approached, holding the folded letter.

"She is out walking. I do not know when she will return." Her demeanor was different than he had encountered before, but then, he had only seen her when she was beside the marquis, or during an interrogation. Casually met, she was a pleasant girl, more at ease in safer surroundings.

"Then can you deliver a message to her?" he said, holding the letter out for her to take. She did not do so.

"Inspector Audley," she said politely, "I cannot. A gentleman cannot correspond with a lady in such a manner."

"It is of utmost importance."

"Propriety is of the utmost importance. It is what protects a lady's virtue."

When she didn't seem to waver from her position, he sighed. "Then can I trust you to deliver the message in words? Do I have your confidence?"

"Since you have so freely given yours in the past, I will offer mine," she replied.

"Miss Bingley wanted to know if Sophie is safe. I have just spoken with the lady in question and she is, despite being dismissed. That is the entirety of the message."

"Oh," Lady Littlefield said. "Then, of course, I will gladly deliver it."

"Did you know Sophie?"

"Only of her. I have had no time to wander about the manor as she has had, as the marquis pays me every attention and none to Georgiana."

So he does, he thought. "Miss Bingley has done quite a lot on your behalf. Did you know her before coming here?"

"No, I did not. She grew up in Derbyshire and I in Sussex, but I became her companion when she arrived – "

"You? *Her* companion?"

She blushed, clearly having said something she should have not. "Within the school, I mean. It is not of relevance to your investigation."

"You would be surprised as to what has relevance to my investigation. Please, do go on. You befriended Miss Bingley, not the other way around? Or was it mutual?"

"We share a room, so it was mutual, but I am her only friend here. Not to speak ill of Georgiana, but the other classmates – they do not understand her."

"And you do?"

"I do not attempt to. I accept her for who she is."

He was even more curious now. "And who is she?"

"You can hardly expect me to answer so personal a question, nor even know the answer in such a short acquaintance. All I can say to you is that she is an outstanding scholar in everything but lessons in etiquette and the like, which she has no patience for, and she prefers solitude to conversation with the other girls."

"Did her parents send her, or did she want to come here?"

Again, it was not a question she was eager to answer, but under his gaze, she did so. "She said quite clearly to me that she chose this place specifically and decided to come here as opposed to spending a year in London. She did not say why."

But all things considered, it was understandable. If she grew up with green trees and fields, she might not have wanted the city life that would be required of her while she searched for a husband. Or maybe, she was not ready for a husband at all and wished to put it off. That was what many girls did – the obvious exception being Lady Littlefield, who came to France *to* marry. "And so she agreed to accompany you to visit the marquis, and does so each time on the premise that you need a companion. And she has done much more beyond that, as we both know."

She averted her eyes. "Yes."

He didn't have to ask why. Lady Littlefield did not want the marriage; Georgiana did not want to be completely lonely. They were united against the immediate world around them. "Thank you, Lady Littlefield. I am in your debt if you would deliver this message." He bowed, and turned to his horse.

After a pregnant pause, she ran up to him and blurted, "Inspector Audley! Please, I must say something."

He immediately stopped all pretenses of getting on the horse and leaving. "Of course. What is it, Lady Littlefield?"

"You must stop this."

"Must stop what?" Because honestly, he could think of a dozen things she could be referring to.

"Despite her appearances, Georgiana is a woman of wealth and stature from a great family. Between her father and her uncle, most of Derbyshire is owned by her family. On the other side of the family, her uncle is a knight of the realm. You can have no intentions for her that will bear fruit."

"Intentions?" he said, legitimately puzzled.

"You know exactly of what I speak."

"You are mistaken, my lady. I have no idea of what you speak."

Her face hardened. "I refuse to believe that, Inspector Audley. But you cannot be after her inheritance, as you do not know of it, to my knowledge. But her father would never consent."

"Her father would never – " He stumbled. "You think – No!" he laughed a little. "Goodness, no! Did I give that impression?"

"You gave every impression, Inspector. I am not blind."

"Oh." He laughed. "Oh, no, no, please do not be mistaken. And make sure Miss Bingley is not mistaken – I am an inspector and I am investigating two murders, and I will question anyone concerned with them, and she has proven to be a very knowledgeable source, perhaps the most knowledgeable. And she has been willing to speak honestly with me. Nothing more."

She crossed her arms. "Do not be ridiculous. You walked with her, you laughed with her, and you had your eyes on her for the entirety of our meal together."

"It was only – "

"You may continue insisting, Inspector," she said, smiling herself now, but very slyly. She was a woman, and she was in her element. "But I will still not believe you. Your face betrays you. Even now you are blushing."

He was surprised to notice he was. This of course only made it worse, and he had to look away. "You are assuming too much. I *assure you*, this is a professional matter only."

"Good," she said, though not convinced, "because her heart belongs to another."

She turned away and seemed to be literally skipping down the path as he shouted, "*Who?*"

"Oh, no one relating to your investigation, so there's no reason for it to concern you," she replied. "Good-bye, Inspector Audley."

He realized that was a dismissal, and bowed quickly before climbing on his horse and storming out of there at top speed.

~~~

The case. He had to think about the case. The best way to do it, logically, was to sit at the bar and order a stiff drink before beginning to look over his notes and record his conversation with Lady Littlefield, at least the parts that were *relevant* to the *case*. He began to read over his notes, looking at the underlined words, the charts, the names, the dates, and places. Around the fourth drink, he was willing to admit he wasn't reading so much as *looking* at them.

He ordered his last drink, downed it in record time, and headed up the stairs before it would become too difficult to do so. If he was going to be furious at himself and his case, he would do it in privacy. After all, he was a *professional.* He had that aura about him and he liked to maintain it. It gave him authority where he might not have it otherwise, being so young and un-grizzled for a famous inspector.

He had made his reputation with the priest case and his keen intuition – but really, it had been a large case that fell in his lap mainly by happenstance. He really owed his career to that murderous priest. Otherwise, he could have easily spent decades in the lower ranks, filing case reports and following the senior inspectors around in the hopes that he might "learn something." He didn't find his business particularly hard. It simply required a lot of thought – preferably done when not drunk. Wolves, dead people dumped in the forest, bandits, the marquis, Miss Bingley – it all made his head spin. He couldn't attack it. He couldn't take the pieces apart and then reassemble them. At least if he had them together, he could see what was missing.

The most frustrating thing, what every detective truly hated, was knowing the ending without the beginning or middle. He knew the marquis was a murderer (probably not directly, but he had certainly ordered at least one death) and a rapist, possibly a sadist. He knew there was a second person out there who was messing with the marquis – messing with *both* of them. The Wolf wanted the marquis dead, but couldn't seem to do it, so he had other pieces in play.

The thought haunted Audley. Was he one of those pieces?

The marquis had called him in, he was sure. There was money behind it. The marquis had welcomed him into his home and assisted (somewhat) in his investigation. The marquis wanted the original murder – the one he *wasn't* responsible for – solved. With the murderer found, an enemy of the marquis would be eliminated. Now it was more complicated than that. The wolf hunt would either do nothing or make it worse. Sophie was yet another complication. Lady Littlefield was no mere puppet, either. Today even she had played with him. How dare she suggest such a thing! How dare she insult his professionalism as a detective!

He hurled his notebook across the room. It hit the wall and landed on the ground with a thud. That soft sound was sobering enough, and he slumped into his chair with a groan.

It wasn't Heather Littlefield's fault. She was a daughter of a peer – she had been raised to be married, and would obsess about the notion until she did so. Then she would bear children and obsess about their marriages. It was the way of life – how could she bring herself to think of anything else? How would she believe that his interest in Georgiana might be for strategic reasons? Because Georgiana seemed to have all of the answers?

A knock on the door. To say it startled him was putting it mildly. He jumped to his feet – a mistake, but he managed – and opened the door a crack. "Yes?"

It was Camille. Pretty Camille, with her black hair and her reasonably ... ample ... corset. Camille, who was always so nice to him, and looked pretty and fresh, without finery. He should really appreciate her more. "We are retiring," she said. "Is there anything else you will require, Inspector Audley?"

There were different ways to interpret that question. He was imagining some of them because he was drunk. But he just leaned into the doorframe. "No, thank you. I will be fine."

"You are sure?"

No. "Yes, thank you."

She curtseyed. He was too dizzy to even acknowledge it. He watched her leave, shut his door, and collapsed on his bed to what he hoped would be a dreamless sleep. He would be quickly disappointed.

~~~

Sunday meant church. It meant the town gathered to socialize, to observe each other in their piety, and possibly nod off during the sermon. It was the one day of the week when the marquis lowered himself to sit among his neighbors, as he sat in the front row beside Sir DuBois and the Rousseaus. Inspector Audley at his best would scope the church and take a seat where he had the best vantage point to observe the parishioners, watching them interact. Robert Audley, slightly hung-over and feeling slightly repentant about the contents of his dreams, was not at his best. He rose for the annunciation of the host, which managed to catch the colored light streaming in from the little stain-glass window above. Some traditions even the revolution had not destroyed – the quiet moments of the beauty of God, or at least the notion that a higher spirit was watching over them, deserving of praise. He was not a religious man, but he had his ideals. Justice was one of them. Morality, another. It was the axis his life revolved around, perhaps more than others because of his profession.

The ladies of Mrs. Robinson's School for Women were not present. They were good English Protestants, after all, with their Book of Common Prayer. His father had given him a copy when he turned sixteen out of some primal *Englishness* but did not expect him to use it. He did read it a few times. The girls would be bent over theirs in their own private chapel, listening to the sermon in English, all hellfire and –

No, he was distracted again. No good. Especially in the house of God.

He stepped outside after the main ceremony as quickly as possible for a breath of fresh air. The adults hadn't left yet, but children were running around unsupervised in the field beside the church.

"Boo!"

He did jump a little, not at the child approaching him but at the strange sight of a child in a crude wolf mask made of cloth. The boy held his fingers up like claws and howled at him. Some of the other children joined him.

Audley smiled at them and turned away. The townsfolk were coming out the front doors of the church, spilling into the square as the marquis shook some hands before climbing into his carriage. Audley hung back, exchanging pleasantries but making no earnest attempt at conversation. He was watching the crowd. One topic dominated all: the hunt.

The marquis, it seemed, had put a prize up for the largest wolf caught on Tuesday's hunt. The number of francs, while no dent in the marquis's wallet, was stunning to anyone Audley saw before him. And what good would it do? There were probably a few wolves in the woods to hunt and kill, but Audley was positive that that would have little effect on his murder investigation – unless this brought *the* Wolf out, which it might do.

"Joining us, Inspector Audley?"

Sir DuBois slapped him on the back, breaking Audley from his reverie.

"Oh, yes," he answered quietly. "But not as a hunter; merely as an observer."

"Well, you'd best bring a rifle nonetheless, something could happen to you if we *do* find that wolf nest up the hill."

"Is there one?"

"We've thought so for years. There are always a few wolves around, so there must be a lair somewhere, and the marquis sent his huntsman out to try to locate it."

Audley merely said, "I'm sure he's said so."

"Between you and me, Inspector, he could be letting wolves loose out there tomorrow for all we know, just to make sure someone comes back with something and ends this town myth about the Wolf."

"I wish it were that easy."

DuBois punched him in the arm. "Don't be so glum, Inspector. Not when there's a hunt on the week's schedule! Oh – are you a city man? Never been on a hunt?"

"Hardly. I grew up shooting geese with my father in Normandy as they came over the channel. But hunting wolves to stop a rumor – that is another matter entirely."

"I suppose, but I'll be out there with the rest of them. These sorts of things don't come along every month."

Neither did murders. But Audley said nothing, merely nodding politely before finding a reason to excuse himself.

"Hunt on Tuesday!" someone shouted. Audley recognized one of the marquis's servants. "Open to all! The person to kill the largest wolf gets the reward!"

If that was true, the marquis would hardly be willing to pay out for yet another murder. But Audley's concerns were not for the unsuspecting wild wolves in the woods who were about to be decimated – they were dangerous predators anyway – but lay instead with the Wolf. How would *he* react? Would he ignore it entirely or try to turn it against the marquis?

Was he among the crowd, planning it right now?

CHAPTER 7

Inspector Audley set out with the hunting party in a foul mood. He had accomplished nothing with the previous day's inquiries. People were coming into town from afar to take part in the hunt (and perhaps win the prize), and though none of them were particularly savory characters, they had little to say about Simon Roux or Mrs. Bernard. Most of them knew the marquis only by reputation. As for the Wolf, they chalked it up to myth and superstition.

"Do we still get the prize money if the biggest wolf turns out to be the marquis?" said a hunter from the next town. Everyone around him laughed; Audley did not.

The group set out early, after a small gathering of pre-hunt celebration (sponsored by the marquis), as the sun rose. It was full in the sky when they entered the woods, totally disorganized and moving in all directions. Audley watched the hunters more than he watched the wildlife, but all that they seemed to be doing was scaring off what deer there were. Audley watched another one go by.

And that was when he heard the first scream.

The man ahead of him, a bearded leatherworker named Henry, had fallen into a hole with a crash. He was easily helped out by the other hunters as they gathered around the pit. Audley knelt to examine it. "A trap." It had been hastily-dug and then covered with leaves and branches. Henry had sprained his ankle in the fall and cursed his rotten luck as he limped back to town. "And it's been set recently. Those leaves wouldn't hold up more than a few days."

"Someone doesn't want us to win!"

Audley rolled his eyes and sighed, and the hunt continued in earnest.

The first shot was at something grey. It ended up being a large rock with cloth shaped like wolf ears attached to it. The bullet ricocheted off the rock and nearly hit DuBois. "Christ!"

"Are you all right?"

"It missed – I think. I'm not bleeding anywhere, am I?"

Audley checked him over, and found only a tear in the cloth of his jacket where the bullet had grazed him. "You were lucky." He turned to the others gathered around. "No more shooting at rocks!"

There was some laughter at this despite the earnestness with which he said it, but it was a nervous laughter as they headed deeper into the woods. The ground sloped down briefly before heading back up, towards where the huntsman from the manor said there was thought to be a wolf's den.

Next, a man experienced the wonder of almost being hit with an arrow, which whizzed about a foot over his head and embedded itself in the tree behind him. "Shit!"

The others raised their weapons and furiously searched for the bowman, but found none. Following an instinct, Audley knelt on the ground, sorting through the dead leaves and brush to find the rope trap that the hunter had triggered. "Hold on." He picked up the rope and pulled at it, seeing where it would take him. He gave it a strong tug and it led him into bushes. The others stayed back hesitantly with their guns raised until he re-emerged with the crossbow in hand. "Another trap. Someone does not want us to hunt these wolves."

Audley took note of the height of the arrow shot. It was far above the tallest man's head. It was clearly not meant to hurt anyone, just frighten them off. However, he could not guarantee that all of the traps would be so harmless. "I am calling off this hunt."

The hunter who had almost been killed by the arrow approached him, his gun raised at his side. "You may be an inspector of the law, but unless you can prove that it's illegal to hunt in these woods, we have every right to do so. And if you do want to do that, you'd best take it up with the town committee."

By "town committee," the man obviously meant the gang of heavily-armed woodsmen that surrounded him. He knew how to pick his battles. "Then continue as you will, gentlemen. But I do not advise it."

They did not listen to his advice. As they walked up the hill, they heard the first howl, and Audley fingered the safety of his own rifle.

"Shoot it in the head," said the hunter. "That's the best way to do it, city boy."

He smiled politely. "Thank you for your advice."

DuBois was proceeding more cautiously. He had an eyeglass, and was able to finally spot a wolf some distance away, up the next hill. "Don't shoot it. We need to find the lair."

The crowd seemed to be more or less interested in following *his* advice. They closed in a bit and proceeded more slowly as he tried to track the wolf, which would disappear behind trees and shrubbery. He lost it a few times, only to re-find it within a minute, until they were close enough to start noticing tracks.

The hunter Maurice, a burly man who did field work for the marquis in the spring, knelt down and tasted the dirt in the paw imprint. "Fresh."

They began to move more quickly now, so much so that Audley was almost running to keep up with some of them. Everyone wanted the prize but no one was sure how many wolves there were or which one would be the largest. Audley was fairly sure it would descend into chaos quite quickly after the wolves were dead. His heart was beating faster, the thrill of the hunt affecting even his own even temperament.

The next howl broke all order they might have had. They ran forward, and a blast from a rifle somewhere to Audley's left signaled that someone had taken aim at a wolf. A wolfish scream was heard, and then more howling in other directions.

"Inspector! Help!"

He turned toward the familiar sound of DuBois' voice. In his peripheral vision, the wolves were emerging from the woods. The den could not be far away. But his attention was on the human, and he followed the pleading voice until he found

DuBois, fallen into a pit – another trap laid by what he suspected was *the* Wolf.

The difference this time—there was a wolf sniffing around it. If DuBois tried to shoot it, as he undoubtedly would, it would probably jump and kill the trapped man.

Damnit! "Sir DuBois! Don't shoot it!" He approached the edge of the pit cautiously, standing across from the wolf, and raised his rifle. The others had gone on ahead for the bigger kills inside the den, and this wolf seemed to have been missed. It did not appear agitated. *Perhaps it is just curious.*

The wolf looked up at him, sniffing in his general direction. Audley aimed but didn't fire. The wolf had two different eyes, one blue and one brown; odd, but not unknown. It yawned, but still kept its eyes on Audley, apparently having forgotten about DuBois stuck in the pit.

"Now!" Dubois whispered from his pitiable position. "Shoot it!"

It was almost like a dog, at least one of the dogs that still looked like its wolfish descendents. Those hunting breeds with their unnaturally smooth skin – not enough fur to keep them warm in the winter – and those small dogs for women's pets seemed now unnatural to him, a freak of nature. Or, more accurately, a freak of mankind. They'd taken a perfectly beautiful, natural creature and bent it out of shape to their will through centuries of breeding. He wondered if this wolf, so raw and wild, would even know what to do with one of those little dachshunds the women of Paris carried around with them. Would he feel something in common, or would he just eat it? He could probably scarf one up in a few bites.

Audley lowered his gun. Instead, he stamped on the ground around him, shaking up the leaves and branches. "Go!" he said to the wolf, waving his arms to emphasize his size, as if he were a bear. "Go! Get!"

The wolf got the message, and, seemingly startled by the strange movements of this strange but tall creature, it hesitated a moment before scampering off. Not with its tail between its legs – even it had a sense of dignity to maintain.

"Inspector?"

He knelt beside the pit and offered DuBois a hand. "Sir DuBois." He helped the man out. The pit wasn't especially deep, so it wasn't hard.

"What got into you? I suppose I should be thanking you – and trust me, I *am* – but this *is* a wolf hunt."

Inspector Audley replied calmly, "I am not here to hunt. Not that creature, at least." *I'm more interested in finding the creature that set that trap. Can't you see that?* "Go on, if you haven't learned your lesson yet."

"I'm not so easily startled, Inspector Audley," DuBois said, raising his gun again. "Not while there's game afoot."

And I think we're the game, Audley thought as he saw DuBois run off in the direction of the shouts from the other hunters. Within half the hour, the small den was cleaned out, and though many of the wolves had scattered, there were four significant kills. One was too small, but the other three would have to be determined by weight for the purposes of the contest.

"At least none of them are wearing a red coat," DuBois said as they walked back.

Audley smiled at him to be polite but said nothing.

~~~

Food and drink were ready when they returned to the town square, again sponsored by the marquis, who was awaiting their return. ("So we didn't kill 'im after all!") The day ended as it had begun, in drunken revelry, as wolves were lined up to be weighed. Audley looked them over as they lay on the ground, and noticed none of them had two differently colored eyes. A part of him that he was not aware of before sighed in relief that 'his' wolf wasn't among the dead.

Audley sat down on the bench near the tavern door. He was not interested in jovial conversation, taking only enough wine to quench his thirst. The weighing came in – the one with brownish fur was the heaviest by less than a pound. The winner was Maurice. He held up his bag of gold as the rest drunkenly cheered him on and the marquis shook his hand. Then the wolves were hung up instead of being immediately skinned by their necks, for all to see. It sickened Audley, they were so much like hanged convicts to him.

"A successful day, no?" the marquis said, sauntering over to where Audley was staring at the dead wolves instead of drinking with the crowd.

"Only at making the deer so populous that they'll ruin some of the crops," Audley said.

"Come now – you don't think me that simple a man, do you?"

Audley did not have the energy to toy out what he already knew. "So you have the Wolf's attention, as if you did not before. There will be repercussions for this, and perhaps it will make him show too much of his hand, and perhaps not. But if men end up dead because of this – I'll hold you on charges, my Lord."

The marquis was still in a good mood, so he did not respond unkindly. "Is that a threat, Inspector Audley? And how would you even connect the two enough to charge me?"

"I would find a way," Audley said, perfectly serious as he put down his mug and went into the tavern, not even bothering to bow to the marquis as he left.

~~~

Robert Audley retired that night frustrated and angry, but also thoughtful. Yes, the marquis was needlessly taunting the Wolf to try to draw him out – if Audley could see that, so could the Wolf, who may well have been in the hunting party today. He would have been able to avoid his own traps, knowing where he'd set them – or he could have set a few off as he went to make sure they were acknowledged. From what Audley could tell, aside from Simon Roux, he had not killed anyone. Even today the traps had been mainly harmless, except when they got the wolves riled up, and that was the hunters' own fault. He could not stop the nagging feeling that the Wolf had saved *him* that night that he tried to approach the bandit camp.

Audley briefly wondered if the Wolf *had* even killed Simon Roux. It was the most likely scenario, but not something Audley could say he was positive about. He had taken it for granted from day one. In fact, very little had changed since day one. Simon Roux had been killed by a man, not a beast, the marquis acted suspiciously, but to the obvious aim of pleasing his fiancée, who had her best friend looking out for her by gathering information against him. To what purpose? Would she write Lady Littlefield's family? Apparently, Heather Littlefield herself had no power to call the wedding off.

Or would she tell the detective who was investigating a murder case? The idea was unnerving.

Opening his notebook, he looked at his notes again and drew a line between Georgiana and the Wolf, halted only in the middle by a question mark. *Does she know who the Wolf is?* She knew a lot, more than she was willing to tell Audley or Heather Littlefield. Maybe she didn't know who he was but knew something about him somehow. Or maybe she did know but was just another one of his playthings, as Audley knew himself to be.

He paced. *The Wolf wants me to chase the marquis. My job is officially to chase the Wolf. But I can't do either with just the information I have.* So he was back to the basics. *Information gathering. Forget Simon Roux for a moment,* he thought. *This is all between the marquis and another man. Everyone else is a distraction.*

That meant Georgiana was a distraction. Was she intended to be? That did restore some of his fortitude – he was being played like everyone else, by her and including her. She was charming him by being confounding. It was a trap and he had fallen into it when he should have been looking for the Wolf.

Start at the beginning. That was what he had been taught; that was what always worked. The first night, he went to a party, and met a crowd of people. Many were fat or spineless nobles; who stayed to play murder? He wrote the names down so he could see them. *The marquis. Lady Littlefield. Georgiana.* He crossed that out. *Miss Bingley,* he wrote in its place. *Lord and Lady Rousseau. Sir DuBois.* Georgiana, who agreed to be the murderer; DuBois, who agreed to be murdered.

DuBois, who he'd forgotten all about, by focusing on the obvious: the marquis, Miss Bingley, Simon Roux, Sophie. Mrs. Bernard. He was convinced that, sadly, she was just a victim of a larger scheme. In fact, he hadn't investigated *any* of the local notables.

What was *wrong* with him?

Simon Roux had been a suitable distraction at the same time being a murder victim. How much else had been plotted? Was Sophie really pregnant? Was that wolf today trained?

I'm getting paranoid.

He needed a good night's rest, after a couple of drinks. It didn't matter, he could hold his liquor. He was French! Half, anyway. He fell asleep to the sound of a wolf howling, which he consciously decided to ignore.

~~~

The next morning, Inspector Audley did something that he had never been called upon to do before in the course of any investigation. He inspected livestock. Dead livestock.

"Four."

"What?" the constable said, annoyed by the inspector's lack of concern. "What did you say?"

"There are four of them."

"So? Who cares how many it killed?"

"He."

"What? What is this nonsense?"

He straightened his hat to protect himself from the morning sunlight. "No animal did this." He knelt beside the body of the first cow. "First, no animal would take the time to perfectly line up four dead cows in a neat row. Second, no animal killing for food would just leave it after one slash, uneaten. Third, these wounds – " and he probed the neck slash, already knowing what he would find, " – are identical to those on the neck of Simon Roux."

"And Mrs. Bernard."

Audley decided not to contradict him. "Four is also the number of wolves that were killed yesterday."

"You think – "

He stood up, not wanting to blather on with this man. "Where is the man who owns these cattle?"

"He is inside – I told him to fix us something."

"The man has just lost a fortune and you asked him to serve us?"

The constable shrugged.

The farmer's name was Monsieur Javier. While his wife cooked in the kitchen, the farmer sat at his table, counting a stack of francs in amazement. Beside them was a small leather pouch.

"What is this?"

"I – have been paid," Javier said. "The amount four cattle would bring from the market. I found the pouch tied around the big one's neck."

"He paid you?"

Javier shrugged in his own confusion. "And if you think it is not poisoned, I can sell the meat – make more. I am tempted to say that the Wolf should have killed more."

"I think you may sell them – but leave the areas where they were slashed," Audley said, sitting down opposite him and putting his hat on the table. "When did you discover them?"

"This morning, when I went out to feed them, they were not in the barn."

"You keep them there each night?"

"*Oui*, Inspector."

"Is there a lock on your barn door?"

"*Non*, Inspector. Just a latch. It was opened this morning."

"Damage?"

"None."

So the Wolf let four cows out, slaughtered them quickly enough to not have the others make a sound to alert someone, and positioned them so it would be obvious something was amiss. And he paid the poor farmer for his loss – making it a harmless crime. The meaning, however, could not be clearer. "Did you tell anyone?"

"There were some field workers passing by earlier – I imagine it has spread to the town by now. Or it will soon enough."

Exactly the intention. "I do not think any more cattle will be harmed, unless we hunt wolves again. You are probably safe."

"Safe? I'd rather be rich," said the farmer, overwhelmed by the amount of money in front of him. He had probably never seen that amount in his life, not all at once. "Hunt all you can."

Audley smiled. "I am afraid it does not work like that."

"Too bad."

He doffed his hat and took his leave.

~~~

Audley had plans for the day, but it seemed they were not in the cards. In the morning it was sunny, but by the time he returned to town it was dark, and when he was finished with his quick lunch, the downpour had begun. Normally he was not terribly averse to a spring shower when he had business to take care of, but this was no spring shower. He wiped the dust off the window and stared out it. He couldn't see past the courtyard.

"Sorry, Inspector Audley," Camille said from behind him. "You will have to wait with the rest of us."

He sighed and wandered over to the bar, where Anton was cleaning glasses with a dirty rag. "What do you know about Sir DuBois?"

"Am I under interrogation?"

He smiled, his sudden exhaustion sapping his desire to be serious. "You would know if you were. What do you know of him?"

"I don't think I know much more than everybody else, Inspector – can't be of much help there," Anton said. "He has some land and a house – nothing like the Maret Manor, but respectable enough.

"Is he nobility? Descended from?"

"Nobody knows. Folks like us don't see much of him. All we really know is he was knighted by Napoleon."

"For what?"

"Sharp-shooting, I think. I heard that he survived Russia."

Anyone who survived Napoleon's disastrous campaign probably deserved a medal. "So he's not from here?"

"No. He could have been anybody before he was in the army."

"And he's not married." That was odd – Sir DuBois was in his forties, easily. "How long has he lived here?"

"Since about 1816 – and he's a widower."

"Widower?"

"Wife died last year. Clarisse, I think her name was."

Now Audley's attention was more focused. "He doesn't seem as if he's in mourning."

"You never met his wife. Married for a long time – since before the war. I think he enlisted to get away from her. When she died last summer, nobody was wailing at that funeral."

"What was she like?"

"Hard to talk to. Very insistent, very mean. Died by swallowing a chicken bone. Somebody once said to me that she choked on her own bile."

Audley nodded. "I know the type. So Sir DuBois is on the marriage market?"

Anton shrugged. "Might be why he's cozying up to the marquis. Having rich young ladies around, even if they're English?"

"Lady Littlefield is engaged to the marquis. Surely he can have no serious intentions there." He said it mainly because he knew Lady Littlefield had no intentions on DuBois – otherwise, he would have come into the picture much earlier. She did not seem smitten by *anybody*.

"But there's the other one, isn't there? The red-haired one? She must be worth a fortune."

Audley pounced on it. "How do you know Miss Bingley?" His heart was racing again. "I thought the students weren't allowed in town."

Anton stopped his cleaning motion, a little embarrassed. "You're not going to tell the headmaster, are you?"

"No! Now tell me how you know Miss Bingley!" he said a little too insistently for his own liking.

"All right. But – 's just between us, Inspector."

"Of course." *Get to the point, man.*

Anton leaned in, lowering his voice. The only other patrons were far off from the bar, but he whispered nonetheless. "Some nights the ladies sneak out. Must be awfully stuffy there. And sometimes they come here. Nothing serious – I don't give them the heavy stuff. They just like the atmosphere. The thrill of doing something wrong, you know."

Of course. British ladies of their class were like caged birds. "I know. Go on."

"Well, Miss Bingley comes with them sometimes, whoever's going."

"Lady Littlefield?"

"Nah, other girls. Doesn't matter – the point is, Miss Bingley goes with them but she doesn't sit and chat. She sits at her own table and just watches them."

"Does she drink?"

"Almost nothing."

Audley was now in full interrogation mode, and he didn't care who noticed it. "I assume she talks to you."

"She has ... on occasion."

"About what?"

"I ... don't think I should tell you, Inspector. Private conversations and all that."

"May I remind you that I am an – "

Anton put his hand up. "Fine. You don't have to get out your papers – I know who you are. So she talks to me, but like you – she just asks questions. About the town, the marquis – everybody. She asks about the men sitting at the bar. Wants to know who they are." He paused, biting his lip. He was weighing whether or not to give out this information. "She got in a fight once."

"Over what?"

"A man – name of Peter – was getting a little too forward with one of her schoolmates. Miss Bingley stepped in, and he tried to slap her."

"Tried?"

"She caught his hand and broke his arm."

Audley said nothing.

"Anyway," Anton said nervously, "that was it. The girls left and she paid me ten francs not to say anything to anyone. I think she meant her Headmaster, but I still don't feel great about telling you."

"I'm sorry to inconvenience you," Audley said, even though he wasn't. They sat in silence for a moment, until he continued, "There isn't any hot water about, is there?"

"Plenty of water, none of it hot. We can get something ready for you, if you want."

"I would be most appreciative," he said, wondering what kind of bill he was running up with this case. "Thank you, Monsieur Anton." He let Anton make his escape. Audley made his own, retreating to his room as they readied water for a bath. He needed to think.

~~~

He woke the next morning to howling. Or, as he was later able to assess when his mind was clear, he woke from a *dream* about wolves howling to the pounding of rain on the roof. It was not the most pleasant way to wake, but it signaled that he had no need to hurry about his business, as there was nowhere to conduct it, unless his suspects showed up at the tavern and had a roundtable discussion of his case for him.

Robert Audley was tired, and he didn't know why. It was a complicated case, each scratched layer revealing another one like an onion, but that should not be so draining. He'd been working almost without sleep on the dock strangler case when he had been pulled off it to come here into the misty woodlands for some dead body found in the woods. This was practically a vacation. So why did he go to bed every night exhausted, only to wake up more agitated and lonely than he had been before?

Well, he needed a vacation from this vacation, something the rain afforded him. He put away his notebook and opened the Maddox book, starting again from the beginning. He was soon lost in the narrative – either Brian Maddox had had a most exciting life or he was quite a weaver of tales.

An Englishman with huge gambling debts and a wound that crippled his leg from a fight with a creditor, Brian Maddox left his native land to marry an Austrian princess after *losing* a bet with her father, a count of Transylvania. His wife was a beauty beyond pearls, but her father was overbearing and eager for her to marry. Political alliances against him prevented any local stock to come forward.

'*And here, my readers, I will close the curtain,*' Maddox wrote, after spending some time describing Romanian custom. '*Suffice it to say, I remain besotted with her as much today as I was on the day I married my princess.*' Mr. Maddox often left out names, dates, and personal information. He mentioned that he had a younger brother in England who was a physician and had married into a wealthy family. Most of the book, he explained in the introduction, had originally been written in the form of letters composed to his brother, Danny, never sent because he was on the run. He kept them instead and delivered them two years later.

When they produced no heir (he left out why, but it was obvious enough – she was barren), the count became restless and threatened '*to put my head on a spike, in so many words. I'd seen him do it often enough with criminals, so I had no doubt of his delight in the demented spectacle.*' But he could not leave without his wife, whom he loved beyond measure, and they fled – not north or west to England as the count would suspect, but east to Russia.

'And there we lived the life of fugitives – though it was an unexpected pleasure to be free of spying servants and my father-in-law, may God rest his soul.' Eventually the count's men did catch up with them, so the couple fled even further, boarding a ship with no known destination. Everyone on the ship became ill with some kind of plague, and he decided it was best to take his wife on a boat and row to the nearest landmass. They washed up in Northern Japan, though they had no idea where they were at the time. *'I could not find myself on a map. Even today I must estimate where we might have landed.'* The book had a map on the next page, with a dotted line from the port town in Russia to the top island of the islands of Japan. Again, Maddox did not name the village, but went on to describe the culture of the 'Ainu.' They realized they had to get to Nagasaki, the only port in Japan where foreigners were permitted to live, much less come and go, and so they began their epic journey down the length of the country, in heavy disguise under the protection of a hired warrior with a name Audley found unpronounceable.

His tales were too wild to be believed at first. Men who were allowed to kill anyone as freely as they pleased, and with no reason, if they were born into the right class; high-class whores who commanded great respect and people who paid just to eat with them; and a thorough bureaucracy surrounding the warlord who ruled Japan (the 'shogun') that they were constantly avoiding. *'As gaijin, our lives were always forfeit if we were discovered.'*

Maddox's tone was at times mystified, at times sympathetic, and at times removed with a sense of humor. (*'They crucify Christians here. How ironic!'*) He had drawings of hairstyles, dress, armor, swords – but no guns. They did not believe in them. Having written the book later, the author could look back on his adventures with perspective and decide what tone he would take, but it was clear that he and his wife came, over their year-long journey, to respect this blood-thirsty and un-Christian way of life. *'A Japanese would rather die than lose his honor. Often they will commit suicide if they have been shamed, or to avoid a shameful situation. This is considered an act of great honor and courage.'* This paired well with the ending and the muddled description of their protector's suicide. The author was too emotional about it to discuss it in detail, or else he had some part in it. His last section, written on the ship back to England with the Dutch East India Company, was a long treatise on *bushido*, the way of the warrior. It was more all-encompassing than any knights' tales that Audley had read as a child, even the Arthurian ones.

Sadly, there did not seem to be any other secrets. Brian Maddox never discussed wolves or anything wolf-related. He did not translate all of the Japanese script in his book, admitting that he was no expert. The postscript by the editor of the edition noted that Mr. Maddox now was partial owner of an import company that brought Japanese and Chinese silk to England. The other partner was his sister-in-law's brother, the wealthy man from the north. Once again, no names or places. Audley knew there was a sequel, just released, but not available in France yet.

What was he supposed to learn? Or was it just another distraction? *Forget this case.* He had spent a useless day enjoying a good book and he had no regrets. He turned on his side and went to sleep.

~~~

"Inspector! Inspector!"

Audley did not dream of Japanese warriors or Austrian princesses. He dreamt of the same thing he'd dreamt of every night for three nights now. It was almost painful to be pulled from that, and he ignored the banging on his door as long as he could. "*What?*"

"Inspector Audley! You must come!"

Groaning, he pulled off the covers, put his vest on over his shirt, and opened the door. "What is it?"

It was the constable. "Another body, Monsieur Inspector. By the Murrell farm."

Audley, still half-caught in a wonderful dream now slipping away from him, was instantly awake. "Animal or human?"

The constable swallowed. "Man."

CHAPTER 8

"How is this possible, Inspector?"

Audley sighed. He knew how. "There are two killers, Constable. We seem to have found one by way of the other."

Indeed they had, without any effort on their part. A bearded man who had not yet been identified had been found in the fields next to the Murrell house, his throat slashed and his body bloated from the rain. He had been there for at least a day, but not having left their home, the Murrells said they had not noticed it, or so the constable told him. The most interesting thing was his hands, which had swollen around two metal weapons that looked like claws. He had to tug at the flesh to pull one off and stepped away with it. The claws were metal and hastily-assembled, little more than hooks molded to a set of metal knuckles. Still, they were sharp – drawing blood when he held one point to his finger – and could kill.

"What do you mean by that?" the constable, who was not particularly speedy in his thoughts, finally replied.

"I mean there are – and always were – two killers, Constable. The Wolf and a copycat trying to blame Mrs. Bernard's murder on the Wolf. Perhaps this man, perhaps one of his associates. He met up with the real thing sometime before or during the storm and lost." Claw still in hand, he turned to the constable. "Can we get anyone who can identify this man?"

"If Lambert cleans him up, I suppose we could get some people to look at him. Doesn't look familiar to me, though."

"How about the bandits? I mean, 'gypsies'," he corrected himself sarcastically. "In the woods?"

The constable rubbed his chin. "Could be one of them, I suppose. In fact, from his clothes, most likely."

The man was in worn and stained clothing, part of it from bits of various uniforms. He did have a striking enough appearance that, Audley guessed, if he was from around here, he would be easily recognized by the constable, but he was not. "Get Monsieur Lambert."

"Where are you going?"

"To talk to the people with a body on their lawn."

~~~

His entrance frightened the Murrells – wife and ailing husband, both in the kitchen. They relaxed a bit when they saw it was him and not someone else. "Where's Sophie?" he said, making no pretensions of why he was there.

"Gone," said Mrs. Murrell.

"To her relatives in Mon Richard?"

"Yes, Inspector," said Mr. Murrell, a pale man made even paler by the events surrounding him.

"When did this happen?"

"The first night of the rain. We didn't even hear it – we were both asleep until she came back in the house, soaking wet. She said she had to leave – that the Wolf told her to leave, that her life was in danger if she didn't. It all happened so quickly – she was gone within the hour."

"And the man in your fields?"

"She made no mention of it. Please, Inspector, she might not have known. It was so wet and dark and hard to see! We didn't know of it until this very morning." Mrs. Murrell rose, and grabbed Audley by his sleeves. "Please, Inspector, leave him alone!"

"Who?"

"The Wolf. He has done so much for Sophie. He protected her the other night, he gave her money for the road – "

"Money for the road?" he said. "How much?"

"Twenty francs."

A considerable sum for them, probably. Audley just nodded. "So she spoke to the Wolf."

"She said she did."

"Did she describe him?"

They both shook their heads. Audley did not believe them to be lying. "You know, he has now killed two men."

"And saved our Sophie! Oh, please be kind to him! We know he's a murderer, but – you know there are people in this town who are so much worse!"

He could name one, just off the top of his head. "I will do what the law requires, Mrs. Murrell." He added, "But I will not put your daughter in harm's way. However, I must find her immediately to learn what really happened here. I fear she held much back from you. You are sure of where she went? To her relatives in Mon Richard? The tailors?" They nodded. "Thank you." He doffed his cap before putting it back on. "I must be off – to make sure your daughter is safe. If anyone asks where I have gone, I have gone to find the Wolf – you understand?"

"Of course we do," Mrs. Murrell said. "Godspeed, Inspector Audley."

"I hope He grants me speed," he said, and excused himself.

~~~

"What? You cannot go."

"I am doing a terrible job of discovering the Wolf here. Perhaps I will have better luck elsewhere," Audley said as he stuffed his satchel with supplies. "I will be gone for a few days – a week at the most. When I return, I expect that someone will have identified the body if anyone knows him. Can you see to that?" *Are you competent at all at your job, Constable?*

"Y-Yes, I suppose."

"Good." He debated on bringing the travelogue book. It didn't weigh much – it was rather small. Eventually he stuffed it in his bag, shouldering it. "I will be back as soon as I can."

He left before the constable could say anything. Downstairs, they had packaged food for him as he requested. Camille blew him a good-bye kiss, but he was unaffected. He saddled his horse and rode on.

~~~

Sunday services in the little cathedral in Mon Richard ended relatively early. One woman stayed in the pews, her hands clasped together in prayer, staring up at the wooden Christ statue. She was startled out of her reverie by the noise of shuffling in the seat beside her. "Inspector Audley!"

"Miss Murrell," Audley said, giving her a half-bow while still sitting. He was too tired to get up. He knew he must have been a sight – traveling for over two days by horseback, sleeping by the side of the road. He had whiskers on his cheeks, and his blond hair resembled a bird's nest. His clothes were durable, but they needed a good wash. "Don't worry – I only have a few questions for you."

"You've come a long way then, for a few questions."

"They are very important questions."

They sat in silence for a moment, as both of them privately gathered their thoughts.

"So – you can probably guess why I am here," he said. "The story you told your parents – either what they told me was incomplete, or what you told *them* was incomplete."

Sophie didn't speak immediately, but then she quietly told him, "I was inside, sleeping, when a noise on the roof woke me up. My parents don't hear very well. I went out to the porch and a man dropped down in front of me – I recognized him."

"You did?"

"He's one of the gypsies that live in the woods. Or, he was. I don't know his name," she said in a whisper. They were, after all, in a church.

"How did you recognize him?"

She looked at him in confusion. "The bandits come by the manor house occasionally. The marquis must have some kind of deal with them."

"Somehow, that does not surprise me in the least," he said. "Though, I wonder why no one thought to mention this to me." He lowered his head. "It is my belief that one of the bandits murdered Mrs. Bernard but tried to make it look like it was the Wolf."

"I don't know about that, but I don't think it's impossible, now that I think of it," she said, playing with her long braid of hair nervously. "The man who attacked me – he had these sort of metal claws. He had a pistol as well – but I do think he intended to kill me with those claws."

"Did he say anything?"

"No, Inspector."

"But he did not kill you. The Wolf saved you."

"Yes. I do not know why the Wolf seems to protect me, precisely. Surely the Wolf has better things to do with its time," she said. "But it came out of nowhere – it leapt off the roof of the porch and landed between us. They fought briefly and then it – killed the bandit."

"And you spoke to it."

"Yes." She bowed her head shamefully. "It told me to run to safety, as fast as I could, and tell as little of this as I could to my parents. The rain would give me time to escape."

"Because the body would not be found," Audley noted. "Go on."

"There is not much more to say. I packed my few things, said good-bye to my parents, and left."

"Did the Wolf say when it would be safe to return?"

"When the marquis is dead."

That hung in the air for a considerable silence.

"What did he look like?"

The question seemed to take Sophie by surprise. "It had a wolf's skin over its head. I could not tell you a thing about its upper half – except it – he – had a brown shirt on of some kind, and breeches. Oh – and sandals."

He stopped writing in his book. "*Sandals?*"

"Yes. Wooden ones, too. I have no idea how he managed to fight in them."

"Wooden? You mean, clog shoes? Like the Danes wear?"

"No, Inspector. I mean sandals – but they were wood. I can't describe them well. The Wolf was covered in mud and I didn't get a good look at him."

He sighed. "But you know who he is."

Sophie looked away. "No."

"Did you know it is illegal to lie to an inspector of the law?"

She turned to him, her braid whipping around, her eyes cold. "Why do you persist?"

"Because I was told to find Simon Roux's murderer."

"You were told to do so because the marquis probably paid off your officer. He wanted you to dispel these rumors about him being a werewolf by finding some man to hang. Only you refuse to do it – why is that? You could find a likely suspect easily. Many people disliked Monsieur Roux. He was a gambler and a womanizer. He tried to seduce wives and girls from the school. But you are obsessed with this wolf business."

"And I will continue to be obsessed – until this stops, Miss Murrell. It is my duty to see that it does. Are you more loyal to a murderer than to me?"

"The Wolf saved my life twice, while you have done nothing but alert the marquis that I might be engaged in suspicious activity. So yes, my loyalty does lie elsewhere, Inspector. Can you blame me?"

He blinked numbly and said, "No, I cannot. But I must have my answer."

"Then figure it out for yourself. The Wolf has given you enough clues. He said that himself."

"He spoke of me?"

"He did. He said you were quite intelligent, but easily blindsided, or you would have solved this case long ago. Or maybe you have no real desire to solve it."

He was officially taken aback. "Did the Wolf explain what he meant by that?"

"No," she said simply. She wasn't lying, but she was holding something back. She knew something else, and it gave her power. Here, far away from the marquis, she had some strength in her. "We are both under the Wolf's spell. It is not human, even though it is."

"Oh?" he said. "Then if the Wolf is so magical, does he know if I will solve the case?"

"He said you will regret it when you do."

"Miss Murrell – "

She stood, wrapping her shawl around her. "Inspector, since you have been so good to come out here to find me. I will ask my aunt and uncle to open their house to you. But you will get no more from me. I promised. The Wolf promised to protect me and it did. Now I must keep mine to protect it. I'm sorry, Inspector Audley, but you have come for nothing."

"No," he said softly, "I am here on Miss Bingley's behalf. Like you, I prefer to keep my promises."

She smiled.

~~~

After washing up and shaving, Robert Audley took dinner with Mr. and Mrs. Murrell and their niece Sophie. It was a modest meal in a modest house, a step up from the Murrell family back in town. The conversation was light; Audley did not know how much Sophie had told them and did not want to violate her trust. She was lucky not to be showing yet, but he had no doubt that she would be soon enough. Audley talked a bit about Paris and his childhood in Normandy. After dinner, Mr. Murrell, who spoke no English, insisted on inviting him to the study for the "English way of doing things" – a cigar and port, or in this case, just a sweeter wine.

Relieved to be back in civilization, Audley allowed himself to relax as he sipped his 'port' and slowly perused the small collection of books on the shelf. One title immediately struck him. "You have read Brian Maddox's book?"

"That? Oh, yes. When they translated it a few years ago, a bookseller came in a wagon selling copies. I'm awaiting the translation of his second book."

"So it is popular in this area?"

"Very popular, Inspector Audley. Or it was when it came out. Though, I do assume he made up most of his tales. Some are simply beyond belief."

This was important information, but only useful in that it widened his list of suspects if *everyone* who could read had this book. "My copy is the English edition. May I see yours?"

"Of course."

He plucked it off the shelf and rifled through it, putting his port on the shelf. He instantly turned to the pages of kanji – and the translations beside them. "I did not know he translated the Japanese."

"You say you have the English version? Perhaps he added them in a later edition."

Audley found the symbol he was looking for – and the French beside it. *Wolf.*

The suspect list grew even longer.

~~~

"You will be careful?" Sophie, despite her coldness to him during the previous day's questioning, was genuinely concerned for him.

Inspector Audley climbed on his horse the next morning, suitably refreshed for a long journey home. "Of course."

"The marquis is not pleased with your presence. You should be careful."

"As should you," he said. "Miss Murrell, promise me you will stay here in safety until this is all settled."

"I promise," she said, smiling at him. "And I always keep my promises."

He had intended to be off at first light, but was delayed by oversleeping and then Mrs. Murrell insisting on packing food for his journey. Whatever Sophie had told them about him, it was very good, and he didn't question the offerings, thanking them profusely before saying his good-byes. Sophie watched him go, waving as he disappeared into the distance.

Audley did have to return, but this time the trip was a bit more leisurely, mainly because he needed to concentrate a bit less on the road and more on the case. His questioning of Sophie had revealed just how little he knew and not much else. Was the Wolf really right in front of his face, as she implied? That only narrowed it to most of the town and the marquis's associates.

Ah, yes. He had ruled out Lord Rousseau, unless he had a man doing the tasks for him. Rousseau was old, fat, and not particularly clever, or so he struck Audley in their brief acquaintance. DuBois was another matter – a battle-hardened warrior, perhaps looking for a new wife and using the marquis for access to one. It was obvious that Georgiana (when had she become that and not Miss Bingley, as she should have been?) worked for the Wolf to some extent. If DuBois was the Wolf, that made sense. Perhaps she sought to marry him.

No, he struck that from his pool of ideas. *Her heart belongs to someone else*, Lady Littlefield warned him, yes, but he could not imagine it to be DuBois. If that was true, then her playing with Audley's emotions was just cruel. *Who said she was playing with my emotions?*

Stupid Robert, another voice inside his brain chided him. *Of course you don't see what's in front of your eyes. Admit it.*

I won't, he answered. *I can't. Besides, she is promised to someone else –* But whom? Someone in England, surely. Then what was she doing in France? Was she fleeing her own demonic marquis? Was her obsessive protection of her classmates – to the point of putting herself in danger – merely the manifestation of her own aggression against her position? What awaited her when her term was up?

Why am I thinking about this?

He stopped midday to water his horse and take a breather himself. He leaned headfirst into the tree, banging his head against the trunk to knock the images and ideas out of his brain.

Give it up, Audley. You'll never have her.

But he just couldn't.

~~~

He made one stop on the way back to town, beyond what was necessary for sleep. Back in Mon Richard, he had requested directions to the estate of Sir Louis DuBois and was given that information. Uninvited, he rode up to the front door and was greeted by a polite but inquisitive doorman.

"Inspector Robert Audley," he introduced himself. "I wish to speak to Sir DuBois, if he is at home?"

"He is," said the doorman. "Is this an official police matter?"

"I have a few questions," Audley said neutrally. The servant bowed and called for someone to take care of his horse as he was ushered in. The DuBois house wasn't as fancy as the De Maret manor, but it had its charm. When DuBois had said he liked to hunt, he wasn't kidding. The walls were decorated by his kills – mainly deer, but a few bears, and a wolf. "I'd like to meet him in the library, if that's not an inconvenience."

"Not at all, Inspector. He should be here in a few minutes – he is in the gardens. Would you like refreshment while you wait?"

"I would be grateful," he said, not hiding his exhaustion from the road. But that was not why he requested the library. As soon as he was left alone in it, he began a systematic search. Fortunately, it was alphabetized, and he found the Maddox travelogue easily enough, in the French edition. To his surprise, the second volume – in English – was by its side. He must have paid a small fortune to get it ahead of local printing.

"I see you are admiring my poor collection." Sir DuBois had returned from some outdoor work, from the look of his dress.

Audley stood up. "Yes – I admit to being a fan of this Mr. Maddox, but I've not acquired the second volume."

"It's not been translated into French or imported in English. I had to have it specially ordered from London, for I was too eager to read it. The translation process is very slow – the first volume came out nearly ten years ago. He is working on a third, I heard."

"What is the second one about?"

"He goes to the Indias with his business partner before visiting Cathay, and then Japan, to buy silk. He's made quite a fortune with these trips, I understand. But his documentation is priceless."

"Do you believe it's all true?" Audley asked as he quickly flipped open the French version and found, once again, the kanji for wolf and the translation beside it. "He's been questioned on his veracity numerous times by the press, but nothing serious."

"I believe it's too bizarre *not* to be true. There's a scene in the second volume where his partner decides to fight a man who is a master of martial activities in China, who is accepting all comers. Just as a joke, of course. Mr. Maddox immediately bribes the champion not to break his partner in half. Instead he's knocked around a bit and given a nickname – Chinamen language for 'red-furred monkey man.'" His smile faded. "But I assume you are not here to discuss travel literature."

"Not entirely, no," Audley said, replacing the book. "I have some questions for you."

"Oh dear. Am I under investigation?"

"Everyone is under investigation until this case is solved, Sir DuBois. Please don't take it personally." He gave him a reassuring smile as they sat down and tea was served. Audley did not take out his notebook. "Tell me – what do you know of the marquis?"

"Am I on the record?"

"A very confidential record, I assure you."

DuBois was not a man to back down easily. "The marquis is a hasty man. I know little of his life before he returned to the old family estate after the Restoration, but I understand his first wife died under suspicious circumstances, and that this new match with Lady Littlefield will benefit him financially – to the tune of fifty thousand pounds." He sipped his tea. "He's impulsive, and at times brutal, but for the most part, he puts on quite a kind face for his guests – especially in front of his fiancée."

"And her companion?"

"I forget her name. She says very little at the dinners I have been present for, and I have been present for a number of them. The marquis has very few friends, so he cultivates them."

"If you don't mind the intrusive question," Audley said, stirring his own tea, "I have been given to understand that you are a recent widower."

"Yes, but it doesn't seem like it, no? My wife of fifteen years died last summer by choking on a chicken bone – she did love her chicken. And while I had respect for her and honored her passing, I cannot say I was particularly bereaved. Our marriage was arranged for financial reasons – much like Lady Littlefield's – and we were never particularly close, but after I returned from the war, it only went downhill. We were two different people. The war shaped my character, and she had not changed. We were not a match. Beyond that, I will not spoil her memory. You understand?"

"Yes," Audley said, and he meant it. He sipped the tea – very good stuff. "Are you putting yourself on the market after your year is up?"

"I suppose. I do not approach it eagerly, though nor am I particularly uneager. I came out here to rest after Russia – the services which I performed there earned me my knighthood, which so far, the new government has respected. I would have to go to Paris or at least some minor city to find a bride – and at my age! Who wants an old soldier?"

"You are hardly old," Audley observed. "And there is Mrs. Robinson's seminary."

"Oh, those ladies are beyond me. They're all from wealthy families in England and half of them are probably already betrothed – or here to have some discipline so they will be more amiable to being betrothed when they return. I know how it works. What English gentleman would say yes to his daughter being married to one of Napoleon's soldiers, eh? Out in the middle of nowhere in a foreign country?"

"France is not so foreign."

"Still, you see my point, no?"

Audley nodded. "I do." He did not detect that DuBois was lying about his disinterest. He had clearly considered it carefully at one time and then dismissed his chances. His logic was sound. He did not really have a chance with any of these women, unless he deflowered one of them and *had* to marry her – and unless Audley was mistaken, he did not seem the type. "If you don't mind – this is purely procedural, but did you know Simon Roux?"

"Yes," DuBois said, to Audley's great surprise. This was one of the first positive responses he'd gotten. "I hired him last spring to cut down some trees that were hanging over my garden and preventing the flowers from getting sunlight. He was good with an axe, but that's really all I can say about him."

"Were there any problems?"

"None. He showed up, worked for a few weeks on various projects on the grounds, and left. I paid him when he was finished. Sometimes he arrived late or hung-over, but you have to expect a certain amount of that, and as long as he got the work done, I didn't care. We spoke very little."

"And he was happy with his payment?"

"He expressed no discontent."

Audley sipped his tea. "Did he speak to your servants?"

"Not the house servants, no. The groundskeeper supervised him, but he passed away of old age a few months later, so I cannot help you there.

This was probably a dead end, but at least he could connect *someone* to Simon Roux. "Thank you for your time, Sir DuBois, but I must return to town."

He rose, and they exchanged bows. "Of course, Inspector Audley. Perhaps we shall see each other again soon."

Perhaps we shall.

~~~

"Inspector! Inspector Audley!"

He had not even made it to the tavern. He was instead assaulted (not literally) by Monsieur Durand, the marquis's man. "Inspector, His Lordship wishes to speak with you immediately."

"What about?"

Durand seemed insulted that he was being asked. "Monsieur Inspector, you've been gone a week now, and this case is still unsolved."

"I was out trying to solve it. Has anything occurred involving the marquis that I should know about?"

"No, but he still wishes – "

"I will speak to him when I am settled in," Audley said. "I have been on the back of a horse for nearly three days now. If the matter is not pressing, then it will wait."

Eventually Durand left. The truth of the matter was that Audley knew the marquis was likely to deride him, and he wasn't in the mood. His head was too full of other things. He needed to speak to the constable. He needed to speak to Anton. He needed to gather himself. He stopped a man on the street, a farmer he did not know. "Is there news? I've just returned. Any strange happenings?"

"*Non*, Inspector. It's been quiet, as far as I know."

Odd, but still a relief. He tied up his horse and stepped into the tavern. The door had not closed behind him before Anton, usually behind the bar, was in front of him. "Inspector Audley."

"Monsieur Anton. What is it?"

"I did not know when to expect you back, but there is a man here to see you. He said he has come a long way." He gestured over his shoulder.

Audley peeked over Anton and noticed a man sitting at one of the tables, dressed like a proper English gentleman, his walking staff at his side, leaning on his shoulder. He was quietly sipping tea, looking rather at ease. "Who is he?"

"I don't know, but he has rented the room next to yours."

"Has he been waiting long?"

"*Non.* He arrived earlier today."

"English?"

"Yes, but he speaks French almost perfectly."

"Thank you. And could you ready a meal for me?"

"Of course."

Audley tapped him on the shoulder. "Good man. Thank you."

"Of course, Inspector."

Anton scurried away, and Audley walked across the mainly empty tavern – it was early yet – to the Englishman. His black, frizzy hair was nearly out of control, but everything else about him was neat and proper. "Sir?" he said in plain English.

"You are Inspector Audley?" said the Englishman, his face pleasant and calm.

"I am."

The man rose from his seat, not relinquishing a hold on his walking stick as he offered the other hand in greeting. "Pleasure to meet you. My name is Brian Maddox."

CHAPTER 9

Audley gladly shook the man's hand, so stunned that he had not yet decided whether he was in a state of belief or disbelief, either one reasonable. "You – you are?"

"Yes," Maddox said, reaching into his waistcoat and producing the very letter Audley had written him, now almost two weeks ago. "I came immediately upon reading it. Couldn't help myself – very interesting stuff. And I'm obviously a bit of a nomad. But you look exhausted – would you care to sit with me?"

"Of course," Audley said, scrambling into his seat. "You have no idea – well, I'm a bit surprised to see you, to say the least. I only requested a translation – "

"– of the kanji. It's 'wolf', of course. I had to look it up myself." Brian Maddox, a man with graying black hair and probably in his forties or fifties, had a very pleasant manner of speaking. "But the story you told was very interesting. Not the sort of thing we see everyday. I had to be in this area on some business anyway, so I thought, why not stop by? I hope I'm not intruding on your investigation."

"No! Not at all," Audley stammered. "Not at *all*. Though you did translate the kanji in the French edition, which I only discovered yesterday in someone else's home. It seems your book is quite popular."

"Good for me, I suppose, but bad for your case, no? It doesn't narrow down the list of suspects, assuming we're looking at your murderer."

"No," Audley said, still flustered that Brian Maddox was sitting across from him so casually. He gratefully took the wine Camille brought for him. "But that is assuming it was written by the murderer. And that there is only one." He continued, "Mr. Maddox, since I wrote you, there have been two more murders."

This seemed to disturb Maddox. "*Two?*"

"Yes."

"Goodness. I didn't know my work was going to be inspirational in such a fashion!" he said. It was meant to be lighthearted, but it didn't come out that way. Maddox was suddenly rattled, possibly by the severity of what he was facing – but what else was he expecting to find? "Well, I suppose you can hardly tell me everything. I'm no French detective."

"Just as you left things out of your book."

This did bring a smile to Maddox's face. "So, you figured that out? I suppose so, as you're an inspector. I'm more regularly accused of making things up to put them in than purposely leaving things out. Except for names and places, of course. I don't want to force the publicity on my family."

"I read your book recently," Audley said, "and I admit that parts of it were a bit – hard to believe – but there were definitely things you left vague. Like what happened to your bodyguard in the Japans."

A shadow crossed over Maddox's face. "Yes. Miyoshi. That was very personal, and Nadezhda – my wife – and I decided to leave out the details."

Audley nodded. So it had all been true – Maddox was too invested in it for it to be otherwise. That or he was a terrific actor. "There were things that amused me and fascinated me, but at the moment, I seem to be called to a thousand places at once. Perhaps we will trade details later tonight?"

"I would be honored, Inspector Audley."

Audley raised his eyebrows. "*I* would be honored, Mr. Maddox."

~~~

Now that the infamous Brian Maddox was in town, and at his disposal for some unknown reason, the last person Audley wanted to speak to was the marquis. He recognized, however, that it was a necessary part of the job, and so when he had eaten and washed his face, he went quickly to the de Maret Manor. He was ushered into the marquis's study. The marquis himself did not acknowledge him at first, seemingly rifling through some book instead. Audley knew the tactic – making a man wait, trying to humiliate him.

The marquis finally closed the book. "It is good to see you back on the case, Inspector Audley."

"I was never off it," Audley said. "I had investigations elsewhere."

"And they were?"

"Once again, I am forced to remind you – I am not obligated to report to you, My Lord. I keep my own counsel and will until this matter is settled."

The marquis turned to him angrily. "And when will it *be* settled, Inspector? We have three dead people and four dead livestock. Your only lead – these so called 'bandits' in the woods – disappeared while you were gone."

Audley swallowed, but controlled his expression admirably, and certainly did not verbally reveal that this was new information to him.

"Yes, that's right. A group of men from town got together, put the pieces together themselves while the famous inspector was off gallivanting to God-knows-where, and went into the woods. It would have been a blood-bath, but it seemed the bandits had already moved on, and quite hastily. Their camp was still set up, the fire still lit – or so I am told. But now the killer – or *killers* – are gone."

Audley was not cowed. "It seems as though someone must have tipped them off for them to leave so conveniently quick. I wonder who could have done that. Someone with something to gain for the killers not to be found?"

"What are you implying, Inspector? Or attempting to imply?"

Robert Audley made the decision to have no more patience with this man. He was still standing, not invited to sit or offered refreshment like a normal guest. He was still tired from his journey, and he was eager to get back to the tavern and speak with Mr. Maddox. "If you are attempting to cover up your previous records by dismissing your servants, then it does seem convenient that the last remaining former servant, an old woman with no connection to Simon Roux or the bandit found outside the Murrell house, would be killed as soon as people start asking questions. You would certainly benefit from that, would you not?" He stepped forward. "And what of Miss Murrell, or Sophie, as you know her? Surely your intended would not take well to the idea that you took liberties with your female servants, willing or unwilling. Unfortunately for that man, still unnamed, he met with the real Wolf, saving Sophie's life. Had she been killed, it would have been *another* victory for you – if not for the Wolf."

"Very clever, Inspector Audley," the marquis snarled, not backing down either. "And Simon Roux? The very reason you are here? The very reason I hired you?"

"That you bribed my superiors to get me here is of no concern to me. I answer only to the law. And no, I have not made that connection yet – but I intend to, if it is to be found."

"So you will forget his killer, then?"

"I will find his killer and however many more killers there may be here. I sense I will not be terribly surprised with the outcome." He bowed, excusing himself. "Good day, My Lord." Then he turned, and walked out.

"Audley!" the marquis howled. "Don't get foolish ideas in your head from town rumors! It is dangerous to accuse a noble."

"It is dangerous to kill a noble," he replied, "but it was only a quarter century ago that they were so readily doing it. Remember your place, Maret."

"And you remember yours! Audley! Get back here!"

But Audley ignored him, and turned his thoughts to other things as he breezed past the footman and back out into the afternoon sun.

~~~

"Is it true?" Audley asked Anton upon returning to the tavern. "Did a mob really descend upon the woods to look for the bandits?"

"Yes, Inspector," Anton said. "But they found nothing – only the camp."

"Which they ransacked, of course."

"I imagine. I was not there."

Audley rubbed his chin. "I don't suppose any of it is left – or maybe something is." Already, a plan was forming. "Well, we shall see. Tell me, where is your other guest?"

"Mr. Maddox? I believe he has gone out on some business. He said he will be back before dark, hopefully."

Yes, Mr. Maddox said he had some business in the area. But what could he possibly have? Maybe he was just interested in the case. From the way he wrote, and the way he spoke, the Englishman was obviously an obsessive fellow, curious about all kinds of oddities, and rumors of a werewolf and a murder mystery would entertain anyone. Maybe Audley had revealed too much in the letter when he briefly summarized the case to explain why he needed a quick response – but he hadn't expected the response in *person*.

Or maybe Maddox would be an asset. If his stories were true, he was an incredibly resourceful person, and he owed allegiance to no one. He seemed to favor Audley and might be willing to help. Audley did not dismiss him yet. He decided to proceed cautiously. These new developments would take thought. "I will take my meal upstairs. And will you have Camille prepare an overnight package of food?"

"Going on another journey, Inspector?"

"We shall see," was all he said as he nodded to the barkeep and headed up the steps to his room. He would need his energy for tonight, and not just to talk to Brian Maddox.

~~~

Audley took dinner early. Not finding Mr. Maddox in the tavern, he knocked on the door next to his room in the upstairs inn. "Hello? Sir Maddox?"

There was some shuffling before Maddox opened the door. "The *Sir* Maddox in the family is my brother. Unless there's a tall, blind doctor staying here, you're out of luck." He was dressed in a multi-colored blue bathrobe and sandals.

"I'm sorry – I hadn't realized you'd retired," Audley said, bowing.

"What? No, I haven't. I simply – have been rather distracted." He stepped aside to open the door more.

Audley noticed Maddox's sidearm, in the form of a small blade tucked into his cloth belt. "Are you always armed?" he asked.

"Yes," Maddox said. "A samurai is always armed."

"You weren't when I met you before."

"Of course I was."

"You were not."

"Think hard, Inspector."

Audley focused on their first meeting at the bar. "Your walking stick?"

"Very clever. Come in, Inspector Audley."

Maddox's room was identical to Audley's except that Brian Maddox had a few more personal items with him. Audley noticed a curved sword on a stand that certainly didn't come with the room. There was a rack for another blade, and Audley noticed the matching, smaller version was the one in Maddox's belt. He said nothing about that as Brian picked up his walking stick and held it up vertically. It looked like an ordinary English walking stick from afar; complete with the copper top, but the wood was a lighter shade than normal. Now that he saw it up close, Audley noticed a small line in the wood.

"Observe," Maddox said, and pulled open the stick, revealing the hidden blade. It was straight but still seemed bizarre to Audley, and he watched as Maddox handled it with great skill, holding it up for inspection.

"What is that?" Audley said, not daring to touch the wavering line in the steel.

"The *hame* line – where the steel was folded to create the blade." He closed it back up in a quick but elaborate ritual of drawing it to the side against the case and inserting it. "Not a great blade, but good enough to take a man's head off."

Audley huffed. "That's still an excellent blade." He tapped the cane on the wood. "Is this – "

"- the walking stick I was given in Japan, yes. I added the English top to make it look the part when I returned."

"And you say it can take a man's head off?"

Brian smiled coldly. "As we discussed, I left things out of the book." He put the cane back in its place, resting against the wall. "Now, I apologize, Inspector, but I find myself quite exhausted from all my traveling and will be retiring early. I must be getting old. Can we perhaps delay our discussion until tomorrow? Unless you have a question relevant to the case, of course?"

"No, nothing I can think of. It can wait, certainly." Audley bowed again. Brian returned it, and Audley exited the room. "Good night."

"Have a good night, Inspector."

Audley doubted it, but he smiled anyway.

~~~

Audley set off early in the evening, not waiting for the witching hour this time. By now he knew the woods well enough to find his general direction without much trouble or a light. He moved in relative silence, heading in a straight direction to the old bandit camp. The trip took him well over an hour.

It was, in fact, abandoned – and hastily so. It was recognizable not only because of the remains of the fire, but also because some of the tents were still partly standing. There were crates around, and he rifled through them, finding them empty of anything interesting. These people had left in a hurry – but not *too much* of a hurry. They'd taken the time to collect all of their important things, leaving behind only enough scattered remains to make it look like they scurried away at the sounds of the approaching horde of townsfolk. In other words, they had been warned in advance.

Sighing, he wandered away from the camp, having exhausted his leads there. He did not dare head towards the wolf den, knowing full well they had not killed *all* the wolves. *I am just lucky this forest is now untrapped.*

He wandered through the woods, heading slowly in the direction of town, lost in thought, but not ready to return to the road. *I'm near the marquis's manor, am I not?*

That was when he heard it – the distinct shuffling of leaves not made by his own feet. He had stopped moving to ponder his location, so it was someone else. He spun around, drawing his pistol.

It was knocked out of his hands with a long metal bar. Where it went, he did not know, but he had the instincts to reach for his other pistol, hidden in his coat. He fired at the man approaching him, but missed, and the bar swung again, this time hitting him square on the head, near his left temple.

The howling, the terrible howling. Not from the man. He recognized that much as he helplessly dropped to his knees, struggling to remain upright. His attacker didn't strike again when *it* came out of the trees in a flash of light grey fur, landing between Audley and his assailant.

The last thing he saw before his vision faded was the furry back of the Wolf, and as he collapsed, he could have sworn he saw human legs on wooden sandals.

~~~

"Inspector? Inspector Audley?"

The sweet voice was not as much insistent as it was gently prodding, to draw him out of his state while a soft compress was applied to his head. "... Georgiana?"

The figure, blurry as he painfully opened his eyes to daylight, stepped back. "Since when have I been *'Georgiana'*?"

He swallowed. His senses were not coming back quickly, especially with the pounding in his skull, worse than any hangover. At least he had the good fortune to be lying down with his head on a pillow. Somewhere, he heard the rushing of water. Everything smelled of nature – were they still in the woods? "I'm sorry," he mumbled, as his vision focused on the red-haired figure that was, indeed, Georgiana Bingley. She was dressed up properly too, nothing askew in her appearance as she wiped a wet towel across his forehead. "Miss Bingley."

"Inspector Audley," she said. In her position, kneeling beside him as she tended to his wound, it was impossible for her to curtsey, but he sensed that she would have hidden behind that . His scope of vision limited by his position, he immediately tried to sit up – and the wave of dizziness brought him back into that blackness that had engulfed him earlier.

"Don't try that again," her voice came again, and when he reopened his eyes, she was in a different position, on his other side. Some time must have passed. "You're concussed. You shouldn't sit up yet. Here – drink."

"I – "

"I *said*, 'drink.' I won't say it again," she barked, forcing the cup to his mouth, and holding it there until he swallowed all of the water inside it. It tasted a bit odd, like she had added something to it – something slightly sweet, perhaps honey. "There. Now for goodness sake, stay still."

He settled into his pillow and the blanket he was laying on – not uncomfortable at all, but not matching his surroundings. They seemed to be in a cave of some sort, with light coming in from behind him – that much he could tell – and down at the end, a blur. A wall of water. "Where am I?"

"My little grotto. No one else has used it in a long time because now a waterfall runs over the entrance – you have to get soaked to get in. I discovered it a few months ago," she said, putting the cup away, and seating herself on the rock formation that served as a sort of bench. "In case your investigative mind is not working at full speed, which I wouldn't blame you for, the Wolf brought you here."

"How – how long was I out?"

"Since midnight, at least. It's nearly nine now." She appeared to be tired, as if she had been tending to him for a long time.

"You – don't you have school?"

She rolled her pretty green eyes. "The headmaster and I have an understanding."

Audley raised his eyebrows. It was quite painful, but it had its effect.

"I haven't reported the lax security in the seminary, for example, allowing girls to walk along the roads at night. I haven't reported the attempted violation of two of them by Mr. Roux. And other incidents I won't go into." She stood up, moving in and out of his range of vision as she tended to whatever things she had behind him. "My uncle owns half of Derbyshire. My father nearly owns the other half, and has a monopoly on the silk trade to England. My other uncle is a knight of the realm for his loyal service to His Majesty. In other words, despite my lack of a title, I am in a position of extreme influence, should I care to use it."

"You could have Robinson's shut down," he concluded.

"Precisely. And in return for not doing that, I come and go as I please. Within reason, of course. I still have to attend the lessons I haven't already completed the final exams for – most of the time. Besides that, my time is my own."

"Very clever," he said with a smile. "Blackmail."

"If money were exchanged I would call it that, yes." She had this self-bemused look on her face that distracted him from his pain.

"And you're working for the Wolf?"

"No, Inspector, I am not." She said it and he believed it – he was fairly sure he could tell when she was being outright dishonest. She lied by changing the subject or answering with a question.

"But you just said – "

"Whatever relationship you perceive me to have with the Wolf is irrelevant to me. The point is, you are here, and I am going to see to your well-being until you are well enough to return to town."

"Did you alert the authorities?"

"The authorities want you dead, Inspector Audley."

To this, he had no immediate reply.

"Not officially, of course. But there is an unofficial price on your head – 500 francs."

"Quite a sum."

"Yes," Georgiana said. "It does narrow down the candidates who could be offering it up in exchange for your head." She leaned in – something he did not mind at all. She did have such bewitching eyes. "You are upsetting his bandits, Inspector. That is a very bad idea."

"*His* bandits?"

She sighed. "Why do I have to do all of your detective work? The marquis controls those bandits. He supplies them with food and supplies in exchange for their loyalty – and their willingness to do certain deeds."

"Like killing Mrs. Bernard."

"Precisely. And attacking Miss Murrell's house."

"I did find her – Miss Murrell," Audley said. He did not give a thought as to why he was seeking her approval so eagerly. "She's safe in Mon Richard."

Georgiana's face genuinely brightened. "Thank you, Inspector. I am in your debt."

"It was my duty to see to her safety – to everyone's safety. Including yours."

"Mine?"

"You don't think you're making an enemy of the marquis by aiding me?"

"How does the marquis know I'm aiding you? He barely knows my name. Besides, the Wolf is aiding you, no?" She passed him a small bread roll. "Eat. And don't be fussy about it."

It was fresh bread, not the stuff he had in his bag. It was delicious. "Thank you."

She let him digest his breakfast and disappeared out of his line of sight for a while, messing with something behind him, probably supplies. His headache was feeling slightly better, but he didn't dare sit up. If she was right and he had a concussion, that would put him out for a few days, at least. "Will I be safe at the *Verrat* if I return there until I am recovered?"

"Yes. I've asked your new neighbor to guard you."

"Mr. Maddox?" How had she arranged this? It mystified him. "How do you know him?"

"You mean *Uncle Brian*?" she said. "Did you even *read* the book?"

"I did," he said defensively. "He doesn't name his relatives, except his brother Danny – who he said is now a knight – "

"Right. Daniel Maddox, who married Caroline Bingley, my father's sister. In the second book he mentions his business partner Charles – they work in the silk trade, I told you. Charles Bingley is my father." She offered him another roll, which he declined, but he took a sip of wine from a flask. "I confess I haven't read the book properly. I know the stories by heart because he used to tell us when we were children – it was terribly exciting stuff. A little gruesome, but exciting."

"Then you probably know the real versions."

She smiled. "When my father and uncle returned from India – which is the subject of the second book – they came home with two differing accounts of what they did while there. Papa's was much more sedate. He wouldn't admit to entering a martial contest with a *wushu* master just for the fun of it in Cathay. Uncle Brian paid the man off not to kill Papa. He just knocked him over three times before my father had the good sense to give up."

Audley laughed. It was more than a bit uncomfortable, but, he felt, well worth it. "You come from a very cultured family."

"Not very, I only have a father obsessed with the East, and an uncle who ended up there while fleeing his father-in-law. It's all happenstance."

"Do you speak any of the languages?"

"Japanese. Some Hindi, but it's too strange, and no one knows it but Papa. Unfortunately, the 'language of the Orients' is not considered an acceptable language to my teachers at the school, and I still must study Latin, a language that has not been spoken in over a thousand years."

"Clearly, they are not as enlightened as you."

She smiled brightly at him. He was lost in it for a moment, saying nothing. She must have noticed, because she suddenly broke the silent moment in a slightly louder and more insistent voice, "Are you tired, Inspector?"

"Yes." He had to admit his strength was fading. He was just enjoying the conversation too much to let it overcome him. "A bit."

"Then you should sleep a little. I have to return for drawing lessons anyway, so if you wake up and I've not returned, *promise me* you will not try to leave on your own."

"I promise."

"Good." She replaced the bandage on his head, which she had removed to clean. "Sleep well, Inspector."

He was sure he would.

~~~

When Robert Audley woke, he was indeed alone. Having no idea what time Miss Bingley had left him, even checking his pocket watch would not help tell him how long he had slept. If Georgiana had been telling the truth – and he could find little reason to doubt that she was – he was safer here than he would be returning to town alone, wherever 'here' was. She had left him some food and his satchel. A quick inspection revealed that nothing inside it had been disturbed, or did not appear to be. The only other thing in the cave besides the mat and pillow was a locked trunk in the corner. Normally he would make some cursory attempt to pick the lock, but he could barely sit up, much less navigate with his pick. Holding his head up on its own made the room spin, so he settled for leaning against the cave wall. He opened his notebook, but the words were too hard to focus on.

He'd fouled this mission, he was sure of it. His health was already in serious danger, and without aid he would not solve the case – when he was so close. He knew the marquis was guilty of murder. He knew the Wolf was guilty of murder. At least one of them was guilty of assaulting an officer of the law. But did he have evidence? Did he have witnesses? Did he have the whole story?

He cursed and fought another wave of pain as the world went blurry.

The next thing he knew, Georgiana was saying, "I told you not to," as she straightened him out, putting a pillow behind his head. "Now look at you. Do you even know what a concussion *is*?"

"You've touched me," he said. "On somewhere other than my hand; ungloved. I think we must be married now by English law."

"How unfortunate that we're not in England, then," she said, without skipping a beat as she guided him back down. He lay on his side this time.

"Lady Littlefield said you were promised to someone – back home," he mumbled. "Is it true?"

She looked away quickly. "Is that what she said?"

"In not so many words."

"... I'm not betrothed," she said, her voice wavering before she regained it. "No. I don't know why she said that."

He blushed. He had overstepped himself and it was agonizing. "She only told me – it was for your own good. I can't explain it." *Without making it worse.* "It was part of a larger conversation."

"Of course," she said coldly. "Because you ask so many questions." She stood up, walking out of his line of vision. "Even ones that are none of your business, Inspector."

"Miss Bingley, I'm sorry."

She said nothing. Audley heard some movement behind him – she was doing something or another and he couldn't see it. He swallowed and sat through the awkward silence before saying, "How was your lesson?"

"Fine."

And then, silence again. He sighed, and closed his eyes. It was too tempting to lie there, pretending to be asleep. He only realized he hadn't been pretending when he awoke with the metallic taste of sleep in his mouth.

"You're sleeping too much," Georgiana said, slipping into his view and kneeling beside him. There was nothing dismissive or playful in her voice – it was more like genuine concern. "Have some tea. It should keep you up a bit longer this time."

"I assume you don't know an apothecary that can be trusted? Perhaps Monsieur Lambert?"

"He's a mortician and you're not dead yet," she said, some of that playfulness returning to her voice. "Can you sit up on your own?"

He tried – he really did. Eventually he was sitting up, and each time he wavered, she caught him and got him upright again – something that, while frustrating, he could not help but enjoy quite a bit. When he could hold his own, she forced him to drink two cups of tea, which did something to straighten his senses. "Can I stand?"

"I don't know. *Can* you?"

He smiled. "*May* I, Dr. Bingley?"

"The sooner you are returned to civilization, the better, I think," she said. "Try. Here." She offered her hands and with a surprising amount of strength, helped him to his feet. "How do you feel?"

"All right," he lied. "Just – give me a moment, please."

"I'll carry your things."

"Thank you."

"And you, if I must."

"Thank you," he muttered, half out of his wits for a host of reasons. In the end, she put his arm around her shoulder and guided him along the walkway. The waterfall did cover most of the entrance. They had to walk on a path along the stone ridge, and at one point, through a wall of water before emerging into the sunlight, soaked. "Ow." The water hitting his head had been enough to rattle him. She helped him sit down, resting his head against a tree. The sound of the water was soothing, and the sunlight dried his hair and his clothing. *She must be wet too*, he imagined, because his eyes could not focus to see Georgiana in her muslin dress, clinging to her body –

God help me.

"You will keep my secret?"

Which one? "Of what?"

"This is my haven. Not even my uncle knows of it, and I have no intention of telling him."

Audley smiled weakly. "I won't say a word." He had only the vaguest idea of their current location, but imagined he could re-find it easily enough by simply following the stream.

"Why are you helping me?"

Georgiana returned to him, holding a stick. "Because you need it. Here. We can't be seen with your arm around me, leaning on me, or I *will* have to marry you."

"I would laugh, but I think it would hurt," he said as he got to his feet, leaning heavily on the makeshift staff. Her red hair against the green trees was easy to focus on, and their slow walk continued until he saw a figure in blue in front of him.

"Jorji-chan, (*are you sure this is the right thing to do*?)" Brian asked in Japanese.

"(*I need him*)," Georgiana said. "Please. He can barely stand."

Audley wasn't going to deny it. Brian Maddox – as the figure apparently was – took the sword he had been holding and slid it into his belt to free his arm to take hold of Audley's swaying body. "Audley-*Keibu*," he said, his voice deadly serious, "I've been hired to protect you. That includes guarding your health. We must return to the tavern." Brian, Audley now noticed as his eyes refocused again, was wearing a patterned blue robe and navy pants as wide and pleated as a skirt. "Georgiana, are you coming with us?"

"I have some time before I should be back."

Audley was honestly struggling too hard to stay upright to notice Maddox's expression as the three of them walked back to town. In fact, he remembered very little of the journey, at the end of which he was practically carried up the stairs and allowed to pass out on his bed in the inn.

It was night when he woke again. *Definitely sleeping too much.* His head still hurt.

He had been injured. The case was out of control. The most logical thing to do would be to request help from Paris – but he would be dismissed by the arriving investigator, who would not do half the job, and it would go on his record. Audley had other reasons not to follow this course of action. Once he got himself inside a case, he couldn't drop it. It was why he was so successful so early in his career. He wondered if all the great inspectors were so obsessive.

He was improving, in that he could sit up and see clearly, but not for terribly long. He made no serious movements. He needed time to think but was distracted by the noise of conversation nearby

"What do you think?"

"I don't know."

If he closed his eyes and focused, straining his ears, Audley could hear them. It was Georgiana and Brian Maddox, he realized, talking on their porch next to his. Why was she still here? He slid into the chair beside the window as quietly as possible, leaning his head against the wall for support.

"How could you not know?"

"I know how this has to end. I don't know how to get there."

He heard Brian Maddox sigh in response.

"You don't have to say it!" Georgiana said rather sharply, hard on Audley's ears. "I know I'm in over my head."

"At least you admit it." Maddox's voice was half-passive, sort of depressed and anxious. "But you don't know everything, Jorgi-chan. Even if you think you do."

"I know you didn't tell Papa you were coming here."

"Hmph. So you could have logically concluded by the fact that he didn't run here himself like a madman. Your parents sent you to seminary because they were concerned for you."

"They sent me because I asked to go."

Whether this was new information to Maddox, Audley could not tell. He was only listening to voices, still a distance away, and his own perceptive skills were not at their peak.

"How is everyone?" Georgiana asked more softly, perhaps seeking to change the subject.

"Fine. Except for Geoffrey, of course. You succeeded in your plan to put him in a foul mood. We had to put up with it at Christmas."

"*What?* Does *everyone* think that?"

"No. Only me. And, perhaps, Charles."

"Papa wrote me a Christmas letter."

"And he said the same thing?"

"Basically."

Again, silence.

"What about my patient?"

"*Your* patient? A young lady has no business nursing a man. Unless she is actually a nurse with medical training. Which, of course, you are not." His tone was a bit harsher than before. "Unless the customs are different in France."

"I saved his life!"

"Yes, congratulations."

There was a noise. Audley was not sure what it was – perhaps Georgiana storming off. Realizing he might soon have visitors, Audley returned as quickly as possible to his bed. He was not wrong in this assumption – Brian appeared moments later with a candlestick and a tray of food. "Good evening, Audley-*Keibu*." He was dressed in a similar fashion as before, two swords tucked into his belt. *This is what a Japaner person must look like*, Audley thought. He was also wearing sandals with white socks. They were not made of wood.

"Why do you call me that?" Audley said with curiosity, not accusation, as he slowly sat up.

"*Keibu* means Inspector. It is a very honored position."

"Is there a lot of crime in Japan?"

"Very little. He is more of a hero to the peasants, who have no one else to protect them. They cannot afford samurai and samurai don't care for them." Maddox sat down next to him and offered up a plate of food. "Eat."

"Is that an order?"

"It's a good idea."

He slowly consumed his food under Maddox's watchful eye. Maybe it was the swords on his side that made the Englishman that much more intimidating, but his concern seemed genuine enough – certainly enough for him to enforce it.

"Are you dizzy?"

Despite the fact that he had been upright for some time now, Audley replied, "No."

"Does your head hurt?"

"Like I was trampled, yes."

"I hear you practically were." Maddox took the empty plate from him, setting it on the tray. "As far as we know, you can trust the innkeeper – Anton?"

"Yes."

"And the girl; Camille. But I'll be on guard, anyway." He turned back to Audley. "Do you need to write to anyone?"

"If I report this, they'll take me off the case."

"So?"

"So? Someone will just come in and do whatever the marquis says, hang some innocent rogue for being the Wolf, and leave. Like it would have happened, if all went according to the marquis's plan. But they got me instead, and I have this rather silly idea that the law is not upheld to the whims of nobility."

"How unfortunate for this marquis that I've heard so much about."

"All good things, I'm sure."

"He seems to be a rather infamous character."

Clearly, Georgiana had told her uncle her version of everything. Audley had no doubt that she would have. This newcomer probably knew more about the Wolf than he did. Could he trick the information out of him? It depended how good his bodyguard was with his swords. "Indeed."

"Inspector, you look tired. The color's gone out of you. Here," Maddox said, passing him a cup. "Drink this before you pass out."

Audley did as he was told. It turned out to be a very sweet wine, and it was the last thing he remembered as he slid back into bed.

CHAPTER 10

Audley was not allowed to sleep through the night. He was roused twice, made to sit up, and drink some juice or tea. Finally he woke himself, and it was light. Only the curtains kept the sun from really hurting his eyes. "What time is it?"

"Nearly ten," came the answer from the floor. It was Brian Maddox, sitting cross-legged, his long sword in one hand and a metal ball with oil on it in the other. Audley watched with sluggish interest as he carefully polished his sword.

"There's – there's a mark on it."

"Yes," Brian said. "The name of the owner. Shiroho-no-Fuma. Miyoshi, as you may remember him from the book. That was an alias."

"So – these were the swords he gave you?"

"Yes."

Audley still hadn't moved much from his sleeping position, on his side, and he liked it that way. "How did he die?"

"It says it in the book."

"How did he actually die?"

"He committed suicide. I did try to talk him out of it."

"He hanged himself?"

Maddox stopped his polishing. "You are a rather gruesome man, like my brother, but you don't have the excuse of being a surgeon."

"But I am a man who examines dead bodies for a living."

"True," Maddox said with a sort of sad smile. He replaced his blade, and drew the shorter one, holding it against his chest. "In the ritual of seppuku, the person stabs themselves in the stomach with this sort of knife, a tanto."

Audley cringed. "What a painful way to die."

"If he has truly earned an honorable death, a second person vows to end his suffering by cutting off his head after a few seconds. So, a samurai carries around all of the equipment for suicide."

Audley said nothing, slowly chewing on this information like food before drawing his conclusion. "You were the other man."

"Yes," Maddox said sadly. "I didn't want to, I assure you. I hadn't truly 'gone native' as they say. But he asked me – begged me – and I would have insulted a dying man not to honor his wish." He replaced the smaller blade. "That is not in the book."

"People here would call you a murderer."

"Many times over. A *lot* of things are not in the book."

"It must be a very brutal society."

"Yes and no. They are not so taken with the notion that death is bad. It is, after all, an inevitable part of life. They are better at accepting that than we are." Brian looked up at him. "Have you ever succeeded in bringing a man back to life by bringing his killer to justice?"

"No, but I hope I've prevented other murders."

"So you investigate the past to affect the future."

It was too early in the morning for this – even though it was late. "Essentially, yes. But I usually concentrate on other things – facts, connections." He cocked his head, beginning to sit up. "What does a samurai concentrate on?"

"His mission." Maddox left Audley to ponder this, continuing his work in silence.

Audley did eventually sit up. He bathed, which was a wonderful luxury, and shaved himself – very carefully – after breakfast. Mr. Maddox insisted on him drinking some kind of tea with bark smashed up into it for his headache, and when it did seem to lessen, Audley put up no more fuss.

He passed his enforced convalescence quietly, flipping through his notes. It seemed as though the first ones had been written ages ago, perhaps by another hand. The names floated around on the page, and not just as a trick of the eye from a man with a rattled brain. The marquis. Lady Littlefield. Simon Roux. Sir DuBois. Sophie Murrell. Georgiana Bingley. All connected by only one thing – the Wolf.

Were his designs from the start only concerning the marquis? If so, the marquis only fit into the puzzle with that rumor about his wolfish habits in a red coat – that had never been found. He circled 'red coat' again. None of the servants claimed to have stolen it, and the marquis had no reason to have it destroyed – it would only serve to fuel the rumor. Who did that leave? People with regular access to the manor. Regular guests. The same people on his list – Sir DuBois. The Rousseaus. Heather Littlefield. Georgiana.

Georgiana!

Why hadn't he seen it? She worked for the Wolf. She was a regular visitor who was virtually ignored every time – the marquis, upon their first interview, barely recalled her name despite the fact that he saw her with great regularity. He knew she was occasionally separated from her friend Lady Littlefield – after all, the marquis must have taken his fiancée aside to hit her (if he indeed had, as Georgiana claimed). It would not have been in front of guests or during a dinner party. Maybe it was a quiet dinner – leaving Georgiana alone. Maybe she had agreed to it – after all, she had done enough snooping to interview Sophie. She was small and apparently could make herself unnoticeable. It was within a definite realm of possibility.

While he did not consider that mystery unsolved, he set it aside. This had more to do with murders than a coat. Mrs. Bernard, he was fairly sure, was a victim of his own investigations into the marquis's servants. She had needed to be silenced. Another name off the list. The third, the cattle, had been killed as a relatively harmless act of revenge by the Wolf for the killing of its so-called brethren. (But how had it gotten a wolf skin without killing a wolf?) Next, the unnamed bandit, who had been attempting to kill yet another servant of the marquis who held information against him. This time, the Wolf had been ready and gotten in the way, saving Sophie's life. And finally, the last murder – only attempted – his. For 500 francs, a man had attacked him, and the Wolf had saved him. Not an insignificant part of the case.

Go back to the beginning. Simon Roux. Was he an example? Was he meant to start the cycle? There was still no positive connection to the marquis. The only connections he could draw were to Georgiana and Sir DuBois, both tenuous.

What am I doing wrong? Why is this case so hard to solve? Why is everyone holding back information from me?

Thinking was making his head hurt worse. He closed his notes and managed to walk around a bit. He was somewhat recovered from the day before, a promising sign. Maddox attended him throughout the day, occasionally changing the bandage on the small nick on his head. "Can't be too careful," the Englishman said. "Some of my brother's medical neuroticism seems to have rubbed off on me."

"You talk about your brother in your book," Audley said during one of the washings. "But you never talk *about* him."

"Of course not. The book was born of letters I wrote to him but could never send, and he encouraged me to publish them, but he's a very private man."

"He's younger than you, I think. You mention that."

"When our father died, I was eighteen and he was ten. I raised him, even though I wasn't ready. He had medical problems – with his eyes. He'll be blind in a few years. He retired from the royal service because of it."

"The royal service?"

"I couldn't mention it for legal reasons, but at the time that I wrote, my brother was the royal physician to King George, while he was still Prince Regent. He retired because of his declining vision, and His Majesty knighted him for his loyal service."

"And his wife is – "

" – Bingley's sister, yes. Charles is younger than her. They have the same red hair – that's where Georgiana gets it. Her mother is blond. Hold still."

"It's cold," Audley said, referring to the compress.

"So?" Maddox said. "Be a man."

"So you came to see if Miss Bingley was in trouble, didn't you?"

"Clever man," Maddox said, pressing down the new bandage. "There. Done. Yes, I was a bit alarmed that she lived so near to a murder investigation. And I am a bit of a wanderlust, so I came." He stood up, putting the medical items away. "If you're feeling up to it, the marquis has extended an invitation to both of us to dinner tomorrow night."

"Really?"

"It seems he has heard of my celebrity, and once again I am to be the object of spectacle. A hardship a famous writer who went on all sorts of wild adventures must endure."

"But the invitation was also to me?"

Maddox shrugged. "Who knows? Perhaps he wishes to make amends."

But it was clear they both doubted it.

~~~

Inspector Audley was much recovered by the following evening. He spent the morning walking in the fields near the tavern with Maddox, and rested in the afternoon before swallowing copious amounts of Maddox's willow-bark brew and dressing himself for dinner.

Brian Maddox was dressed in his Japanese robes, this time with a black top and a matching black jacket over it – perhaps this was Oriental formal dress. His long sword he carried, the other securely on his waist. Some of it for show, Audley was sure.

Three days had passed since Audley had sparred with the marquis, and he still wore a bandage on his injured head, but he felt he was prepared. He needed a break in this case, and it would only come through the marquis, the man more central to the story than the Wolf himself.

It was an odd assembly that greeted them at the door. Lady Littlefield was by the marquis's side, with Georgiana of course a step behind them, blending into the background as usual. The other guest was none other than Sir DuBois, who greeted Brian most delightfully.

So the cast is assembled, Audley thought, feeling clearheaded and glad to have his mental faculties back. The marquis expressed his contentment at being able to host the "literary master of the travelogue", and on Audley's recovery. Audley shot a queer look to Georgiana, who rolled her eyes at the comment.

Dinner was a sumptuous affair, certainly in comparison to the soft and simple foods Audley had been forced to consume over the last few days, when pain distracted him from his appetite. If the marquis wanted to make peace, so be it. Audley wouldn't necessarily stop his investigations, but he would eat the man's food.

"Will you be staying in the area long, Monsieur Maddox?"

"Not very," Maddox said very politely. He was all smiles and congeniality. His long sword rested on his lap, out of sight for most of the table. Some of them probably thought it was a prop sword. "My plans are not set, but I must return for business purposes – and to finish my third novel."

"Please, sir!" the marquis begged, "You must give us a preview!"

"Hmm," Maddox said, leaning back in his chair as the fourth course, soup, was served. "First I must decide which part is most definitely a part I will be allowed to tell."

"Have you been holding back on your readers, Mr. Maddox?" DuBois said.

"Of course I have. One can hardly include personal information in a published work. But in this case, I was on a diplomatic mission to see the Emperor of Japan, so I must protect myself *legally*. I will say that we – my cousin and I – utterly failed to convince him to open the country of Japan to foreigners, obviously."

"You met the Emperor of Japan?" asked a nervous Lady Littlefield. She rarely spoke at these dinners, but this time, she could not withhold her curiosity.

"Not precisely. I was, briefly, in the same room with him and the shogun, a warlord who actually controls the country. The Emperor is divine, but politically, he is just a figurehead. However, we were not permitted to see him. He sat on a throne behind a red silk screen. His name is Emperor Ninkō, and I believe he is the 120th emperor, or so they claim."

"Well, what did he sound like?" DuBois said, obviously fascinated.

Brian Maddox was playing to his audience. "He had a very quiet voice and was extremely polite to us, the barbarian foreigners, because we had just accidentally fought on his side during the quelling of a rebellion." Of course, he could not leave this unexplained. "It was a matter of happenstance. The other ambassador and I had to get across a particular field where there happened to be a major battle against the shogun and the emperor. We were caught between two sides, and our party – which included some native friends of mine – decided that the best way to escape would be to cross the field dressed as soldiers. So we stole four sets of armor and set across, having no idea which side we stood for. It turned out to be the right side, and when it was discovered how we had so valiantly put our lives on the line for the government, we were rewarded with all kinds of honorific titles. No treaty with England, though. His Majesty King George was most displeased." He said it with a smile, ending his story with a punch line that made everyone laugh.

Audley watched them all, though it was hard not to be lost in the story. As far as he knew, the marquis had never expressed an interest in Maddox's work before (though, to be honest, it had never been brought up), but he did smile for his guests. As usual, he made an effort to be perceived as a good host.

"Well, I do hope you will stay a few weeks longer, so that you may dine here until I vacate the manor."

Audley couldn't help himself. He beat everyone else to the obvious question, "You are leaving your estate?"

"Yes, my fiancée has requested a ceremony in the north so that more of her relatives may attend. Unfortunately, she will have to leave school, but it will ease this period of abominable waiting."

Audley did not even have to look at Georgiana's stare of horror to know she was surprised. She would have said something to her uncle – somehow – as soon as she knew. He looked instead to Lady Littlefield, who smiled meekly. "And when is this joyous event to take place?"

"Always the interrogator, Inspector Audley, eh? In less than a month, if the arrangements can be made."

So he was speeding things up and escaping the area as fast he could without losing his bride. The gravity of it quieted everyone until DuBois bravely said, "If I learn you are doing this to escape from inviting me, I will have your head, Maret!"

He raised his glass. "A toast, to the happy couple!"

They raised their glasses, three of them very mechanically, and toasted the couple. Audley did it with his eyes open, Georgiana with her eyes closed, as if to block the entire scene out.

~~~

Audley and Maddox did not stay long after dinner. Inspector Audley felt drained, this being his first serious outing since his injury, and Brian Maddox saw it in his complexion and requested permission to excuse themselves, which the marquis granted. After the appropriate good-byes, they retreated to the inn, but despite his exhaustion, Audley could not put himself to bed just yet.

"I need a favor, Mr. Maddox."

Maddox bowed.

"The marquis invited you to come to the estate and tell some of your tales more privately, did he not? Before we left, in a low voice, in the hallway?" He said it most insistently, even though his strength was quickly going out of him.

"He did."

"Take him up on it. Go to the manor tomorrow and talk to the marquis for as long as you can."

Maddox frowned. "Absolutely not, unless you plan to come with me."

"Precisely the opposite. I need to speak to Lady Littlefield at the school – and Miss Bingley. And I need the marquis to be distracted, for once."

"I cannot protect you – "

He put his hand on Maddox's shoulder, "You cannot keep me from solving this case, either. I am only going to the school and back. I will walk on the main road. Hell, I will take a horse, my rifle, pistol, and a sword, if you wish. But I must go there and you must go to the marquis. Do this for me, please."

"I have my mission – "

"- And your mission is to protect me from the marquis. Going to him will help solve the problem."

Brian swallowed, resting his hands in the folds of his robe. "Very well, Audley-*Keibu*. But I don't think it's wise."

"Sometimes we must take risks. Death is inevitable, no? Part of life?"

To this, Maddox managed a wan smile.

~~~

Audley had lied to Brian Maddox.

His reasoning was not entirely sound, but somehow, the Englishman had accepted it. Perhaps for his own reasons. In truth, Audley wanted to interview Lady Littlefield and Georgiana without Maddox hovering over him. Specifically, Georgiana. She acted different within her uncle's presence – she was calmer, but more secretive than ever. They had a secret understanding, and Audley was sure she would reveal more if her uncle was not there. After all, she was an English woman on the marriage market, and he had to protect her honor so she didn't end up married to some poor French detective, no?

Despite that, the next morning, Mr. Maddox did separate from him as promised, after Audley woke from sleeping late yet again. He knew he was not fully recovered, but he was well enough to ride a horse to the school and conduct two interviews. They said their good-byes, and he was off.

He arrived early enough for morning lessons. This time, the headmaster did not even try to fight this heavily-armed inspector who demanded to see Miss Bingley. He was brought to an empty room and told to wait.

Before long, it was Lady Littlefield who appeared, curtseying politely as she entered. "Excuse me, Inspector Audley, but Miss Bingley is not feeling well today and cannot speak to you now. I hope I can answer all of your questions in her place."

He was stunned. "Where is she?"

"I said, she is not well – "

"So I could find her in the infirmary?"

"You are not permitted in the infirmary, Inspector."

He dropped all pretensions. "She's not there, is she?" The horrified look on poor Heather Littlefield's face confirmed it. And to think that this was all for *her*. "Where did she go?"

She looked cautiously behind her, but no one was outside. Despite her precautions, she whispered her response. "She left last night. She has not returned."

"And the school has not notified anyone?"

"They never do. This is not abnormal. She has a place that she sleeps, out in the woods. Beyond that, I don't know."

But he did. Georgiana had told him that she had an understanding with the school. He wondered how often she was 'under the weather.' And he knew where she would go, as well. "I do." Again, he faced another look of horror. "Please, rest assured. You have not betrayed your friend. She told me of her expeditions. I know she is working for the Wolf. I know she is doing it to protect you. I only came to question the two of you about the marquis's announcement last night. I will ask you only – Did you know of this plan before the announcement?"

"I did," she said. "But only earlier that afternoon."

"Has your family agreed to it?"

"Apparently they have. He showed me a letter from my parents."

"But you were not informed by them."

"No." She looked ready to cry.

Audley sighed and softened his voice. "Please be assured, Lady Littlefield. Miss Bingley is not the only one who means to protect you."

"And what harm will it all do? Just because he is not the best man in the world? No one should die because of one unhappy marriage prospect – and yet, three people have," she said. Her questioning of it also quite reasonable. "Promise me you will stop Georgiana."

"Stop her?"

"She said she would protect me. She promised me at the beginning, the first night he hit me, when I was crying in the carriage on the way back. And look where it has taken us all. But I know she will take it to the end." She whispered. "I know she'll kill him if she has to."

The fact that it was Lady Littlefield, the very picture of English demureness, who said it made it so much worse. "She will?"

"Don't doubt it, Inspector."

He swallowed. "Why is she so angry, Lady Littlefield?"

"I – I can't say."

"Who hurt her?"

She gaped at his question. He would have done the same. It was too great for both of them. It was not a planned question, not something an inspector of the law should ask. It was not theoretically relevant to the case. It just came from his instincts, the instincts that had made his career and carried him through previous cases. "Tell me who hurt her." His fingers hardened around his notebook.

"It doesn't matter. He's in England. And he didn't hurt her – physically. He's not the marquis. It was just a misunderstanding." When she raised her eyes to him, they were watery. "She won't speak of the details, but I know. Georgiana is a lonely woman. She has been all her life. He was the only one who understood her, and when they drifted apart, it crushed her."

"So she ran to France?"

Lady Littlefield could not bring herself to say it. She covered her mouth with her hand and nodded.

"I have to find her."

To his surprise, all she said was, "I know."

CHAPTER 11

Robert Audley abandoned all pretenses of caring about his own safety. He left the horse tied up at the school and ran into the woods. He had only the vaguest recollections of the location of Georgiana's hideaway, but he found a stream soon enough, and followed it as far as it took him. He soon found its source, the pool of water being filled by a waterfall, the cold water pouring down from the melting winter snow in the mountains above. And for the life of him, he could not remember how to enter the cave he knew was beyond it. Something about getting wet?

"Do you require assistance, Inspector?"

He spun around – a little too fast, making his head spin – to see the form of Georgiana approaching, her white gown a contrast to the greens and browns of nature surrounding them. "Georgiana," he said before he could stop himself.

"Inspector Audley." She curtseyed. If he did not know otherwise, she merely appeared to be on a pleasant walk in the forest. "I presume you were looking for me."

"I was," he swallowed. "How – how are you?"

"Fine. Better than yourself. And isn't Uncle Brian supposed to be your shadow?"

"I sent him to distract the marquis," he explained, closing the gap between them. "I needed to speak with you."

"The marquis does not keep a watch on me."

"I needed to speak with you – without your uncle around," he said, "to be perfectly honest about it."

She huffed. "At least you're being perfectly honest." She stalked off in the direction of the waterfall, and turned back only when he stood there, dazed. "Are you coming or not?"

He followed her in silent agreement as she stepped up to a small ledge and, with her back to the rock, inched her way through the waterfall, taking his hand as he followed. They both stepped through and emerged into her small cavern completely soaked. Georgiana removed her bonnet and ran her hands through her very short hair. "So – are you here to talk about the marquis's escape attempt?"

"I went to your school to discuss it with you. That's when Lady Littlefield told me you were missing."

"I wasn't *missing*. No one was missing me."

"How could you think that?" he said, surprised at how much his voice was raised. "You don't think there are people who care about your safety? That you might be putting yourself in serious danger by working for a killer, and for being a spy against a man who has people murdered? Lady Littlefield was practically in tears."

"Heather is a gentle English flower," she said. "She's my friend, but even she would admit that. And you know how women are so emotionally fragile, don't you, Inspector?"

"Did you tell her you would kill the marquis?"

Even the unshakable Georgiana Bingley was taken aback by that question. "Not precisely."

"But you would."

"If everyone's so inept that it comes to that," she snarled. "If you can't make an arrest despite the mounds of evidence I've piled at your door. Evidence I risked my life to collect. You have two women who've been beaten by him, one who was raped and is carrying his child. You know he's responsible for at least one murder and of hiring people to do his dirty work. If it hadn't been for the Wolf, there would be another woman murdered while you were staring at your precious notebook."

"I don't have enough. I only have speculation."

"Arrest him. You know that even that would ruin his reputation, even if he is acquitted, and the Littlefields would call the wedding off. That's all I want."

"Is that all you really want? Lady Littlefield safe? Or do you just want to hurt the marquis?" he said, not backing down this time.

"Why would I want to hurt the marquis? He's done nothing to me but ignore me, which is most convenient for my purposes anyway."

"I freely admit that he's a despicable man. He's a rapist, a murderer, and if I thought I could pin enough on him to hold up in court past all the bribery he would offer to get the charges removed, I would have him in irons tomorrow. So convenient, you say. Is it also because it gives you a target? Do you need someone to hit?" She turned away from him in anger, but he grabbed her arm. "Who hurt you, Georgiana?"

Apparently she did need someone to hit. Unfortunately, he was extremely available. Her slap was much harder than he expected, knocking him back against the wall. When his vision cleared again, she was holding her hand over her mouth, for once in horror at her own actions.

Finally, something that she had not planned. "I'm so sorry. I shouldn't have done that."

He straightened himself. His head was pounding, now from a combination of the slap and his injury. "I have had worse. Recently." He did not back away. In fact, he wanted to be closer to her. He saw the pain in her eyes, usually so well-hidden. "Georgiana - "

"You're not supposed to call me that."

"Miss Bingley. There, does that feel better?" he said. "If you want to help me, help me. Where is the Wolf?"

She swallowed, attempting to recover her composure. "You stopped looking for the Wolf a long time ago, Inspector."

Despite his instincts, he could not bring himself to deny it.

"You would have found him. It's so obvious, and despite my insults, I consider you a very intelligent person, Inspector Audley."

"Robert."

"What?"

He stammered, "My name is Robert, remember?"

"Do you want to be Inspector Audley or do you want to be Robert?"

He responded by kissing her. He would have judged that a suitable response, if any part of his brain was really working. He was too close, and she was too vulnerable, too human, and too beautiful. He couldn't stand it anymore. It was wrong, and he broke it as soon as he could manage, not because she rejected him, but because he knew he had to, as they staggered away from each other. "I'm sorry," he mumbled, hiding his face with his hat. "I – shouldn't have done that."

"*Obviously.*"

Despite it, he smiled. "I mean it, Georgiana." He lowered his hat. She did not look terrified, or angry, but then, her emotions were very hard to read. "I should go."

Her response was to kiss him. This time, neither of them backed away.

She put her arms around him and ran her hands through his blond hair. It felt divine, indescribable, really. When they finally separated, she buried her face in his shoulder, being just the right height for it. "I love your hair," Audley said. "I always have." He'd seen redheads before, but never had he seen a woman with such short hair, or a combination of the two. It was just lovely, like a perfect rose, silky to his touch. He was so taken in by it, by her, so close to him, it took him a moment to notice she was sobbing – very quietly, and muffled by his vest. "Georgiana?"

She raised her tear-stricken face. "It's not your fault."

"You weren't crying when I showed up."

"No, but I wanted to," she said, sniffling. "I've wanted to for so long."

He could have made a joke about the delicate composure of the female species, but it didn't feel appropriate. It didn't feel right. "You're lonely?"

"You guessed?"

He smirked. "I needed a hint from Lady Littlefield. Actually, I needed her to say it outright."

"Some detective."

"Yes."

Georgiana leaned into him again, this time not openly sobbing, but he couldn't see if she was still crying. He waited, and kissed the top of her head, listening to the sound of the water flowing behind them.

"I don't know what happened," she said, her voice wavering as she separated from him at least some distance. Her eyes were still red. "We were so close – we grew up together. We were born two weeks apart. We played together as children." She swallowed. "He was the only one who ever understood me for who I was – the only person on this earth. And then he went to Eton, and he became so ... distant."

"What did he say?" he asked gently. "Geoffrey." Her eyebrows shot up in alarm as he said it. "I can do *some* detecting."

She smiled briefly, never letting go of him. "It wasn't what he said – it was how he said it. He was surprised I didn't want to go to Town for the Season, just to put myself on the market for someone to scoop me up like a prized animal." She had not, it seemed, lost all of her humor as he listened patiently. "We're both eighteen; what boy marries at eighteen? Students can't even be married. His father didn't marry until he was something near thirty. But girls – we're supposed to be different."

"You mature faster," Audley said. He didn't doubt it was true. "Is your father forcing you to marry?"

"No, the opposite – but I know people *think* things. I have to be a good example to my younger sister. I have to be a proper lady who likes embroidery and painting china. I have to put my hair up." She laughed, but it was a tired and sad laugh. "I got sick of that nonsense. Growing out your hair only to put it up. So I cut it off. No one's looked at me the same since. Except Geoffrey. He said it looked nice."

"I would have to say – I agree with his assessment," he said, entwining their fingers together. Hers were so small and fair compared to his tanned and calloused hands. "And he's the only man you've ever had any affection for?"

"Well," she said, "until recently."

For a time, there was silence, as they sat together staring into their own hands, uneasy in the atmosphere they had created.

"Marry me."

She opened her beautiful green eyes and said, "*No.*"

"I'm serious," he said, pulling her hand against his chest. "I'm fairly sure I *have* to marry you now. Not that I don't wish to."

"*No*, Robert."

"I'm obligated. After we just -"

"I release you from your obligation."

He snorted despite it, and kissed her. "I do love you. I've never met anyone like you."

"That's called infatuation," she said.

She was so perfectly serious and so confident that he didn't doubt her. It would take a strong man to marry Georgiana Bingley. He wondered if this Geoffrey was up to the task. "Then who will the rich and beautiful Miss Bingley marry?"

"Geoffrey Darcy." She saw his frown. "You think I'm deluding myself, but I'm not. Look." She had something around her neck, the locket he had seen in her hands once, but otherwise was normally hidden beneath her clothing somewhere. It was a glass box with two brass points on either end, and she held it like the top was a button. "Robert Audley." She pressed down on the top, which was indeed a switch, but nothing happened. "Now. Who else? The Marquis de Maret?" She pressed it again with a click. Still nothing. "Geoffrey Darcy." This time, when she pressed, the thin wire inside the glass began to rotate, lighting the tiny case with an array of colors that circled for a few seconds before going out.

"What is that?"

"It's magic," she said. "My father bought it in India. He told me that it would only light up when I said the name of one person in the whole world, and only I could make it do that, but the name was a secret I had to discover for myself. I was nine, and I decided to try everyone in the room, as it was Christmas and I had lots of people around. It only worked for one person." She took the chain off and handed it to Audley's waiting hand. "Papa didn't tell me what it meant. I had to figure it out myself. I went to him last year and said, 'That's what it means, right? That it will only light up for my one true love?' And he nodded. He knew all along, the sneaky man."

"And you really think it's magic?" Audley said, inspecting the odd device. There did not seem to be a scientific explanation for it, though certainly, she could know how to trigger it no matter what name she said, or for any reason at all. "I thought you didn't believe in that nonsense."

"I said I don't believe in people turning into wolves on the full moon. I didn't say I didn't believe in any magic *at all*," she corrected. "Try it."

"Georgiana Bingley," he said, and pressed down as he had seen her do. There was a click, but nothing else. "Uhm, Andrea Valjeu." Click. Nothing. "Sophie Murrell." Nothing. "Camille?" Again, nothing. "Maybe it's just not working."

"It just means you haven't found her yet," she said, taking it back from him. "Who's Andrea Valjeu? An old girlfriend?"

"Of sorts. She was my first ... girlfriend." He swallowed. "The kind you pay to be a good friend for a few hours."

She giggled as he blushed. "You can say it, you know."

"Doesn't mean I want to divulge my entire history."

She was still laughing as she put the locket back against her neck and nuzzled into his shoulder. "So – what irrational belief do you have despite all evidence to the contrary? What do you believe in, Inspector Audley?"

"Justice. What an utterly foolish piece of nonsense."

She was smiling. "Still, very noble of you. More noble than believing in a piece of jewelry that lights up."

"It's not the jewelry, it's the part about true love."

"I know *that*."

But she put her arms around him, and there was no more discussion.

CHAPTER 12

The morning became afternoon. Audley watched the sun cross over the trees through the hole in the rock that lit the opposite end of the cave. "Maddox is probably searching everywhere for me. I sent him on an errand with the marquis, but he couldn't possibly take this long, even if he was trying."

"Hardly," Georgiana said from the mat behind him. "But he is your hired samurai. He would never have left you if I hadn't asked him to. After all, how else would I have had any time to talk to you? Though, this was not the sort of chat I intended." She stood up, putting her bonnet back on. "I should probably *eventually* turn up for lessons."

He did not want to leave. He knew – and he knew *she* knew – that when they left this place, like so many lovers' havens, the spell would be broken, and could never be restored. Georgiana had stated plainly enough that she would not marry him, so this would go no further.

"How is your head?"
"Better."

"A shame. If you passed out again, I could keep you here."

He smiled. "I do love you."

Again she said, "I know." This time though, her voice wavered. "Thank you."

Neither of them could bring themselves to say anything more, as they stepped through the wall of water, and back into the daylight.

~~~

They could not be seen together, so Audley returned to the school alone to retrieve his horse, and hurried back to town. He never knew he could be content and yet exhausted at the same time. The only thing that kept him from being happy, aside from the knowledge that the feeling would fade and they would go their separate ways, was his own body, which was ragged from a combination of exertion and injury. He stumbled into the tavern, nearly crashing into Camille before finding Maddox at his table. "I'm sorry – I need to lie down."

"Are you all right? Did something happen?"

No. Yes. "I'm just overtired. I spoke with Lady Littlefield and Miss Bingley, but it is nothing that cannot wait. And you?"

"Nothing that cannot wait. Please," Maddox helped him up to his room, but insisted that he drink and eat something before he was allowed to collapse and finally sleep.

It was still light when he woke, but the light had moved. Blinking, he rose in confusion to find Brian sleeping on a woven mat in the room, his two swords at his side. He must have been exhausted as well. Audley smiled at the sight of the vulnerable warrior and quietly reached for his rucksack, retrieving his watch. It was – nine. *Nine?* It was morning. He had slept for over twelve hours. He must have needed it, because his head was no longer ringing. "Some guard," he muttered, rising to his feet, still wearing the clothing he had collapsed in. "I could sneak up on him and – "

No sooner had his foot moved in the direction of Brian Maddox than was a sword drawn, its blade a threatening inch away from his ankle. Maddox was still prostrate on the floor, but certainly capable of doing damage. He looked up at Audley, blinked, and replaced his sword in its scabbard. "Sorry. You shouldn't wake me like that."

"Now I know," Audley said, a little rattled by the experience. "How did you learn to sleep like that?"

Maddox sat up. "Years and years of experience from sleeping with one eye open."

"How was your visit to the marquis?"

"Fine. Long. You are fortunate that I am a very interesting speaker," Maddox said. "And you? What did you learn?"

"That Miss Bingley knows who the Wolf is. But you already know that, don't you?"

Maddox met his stare, but did not answer.

No sooner were they dressed and downstairs that they were practically assaulted by the barkeep, shoving the daily paper in their hands. This time it was larger, without much more than a headline and an image.

"Two thousand francs for the head of the Wolf," Audley said. "Offered by the marquis to all comers. Should I be insulted that he's worth four times what I am?"

"He's trying to draw the Wolf out."

"Between that and making his escape with his bride, I would say, yes." Audley folded the flier, put it in his notebook, and thanked Anton. "There is someone who I think should be informed of this. Follow me."

Brian bowed. "As always, I am at your service."

~~~

They reached the DuBois estate in under an hour, riding as fast they could. Maddox was actually a more talented rider, which did not surprise Audley in the least, being a city inspector himself. It seemed their arrival was most unexpected, and the flustered footman took their horses to be watered and let them inside to await his master, who was shooting at a flock of birds in the back woods.

Sir DuBois entered, still dressed for the outdoors, and his eyes lit up at the sight of his guests. "Inspector Audley! Sir Maddox! How delightful to see you!"

"Sadly, I turned down my knighthood," Maddox said. "It will be in the third book. And I would be happy to give you a preview, but there is a more pressing matter, and I am only here with the good inspector."

"Yes," Audley said, immediately unfolding the flier and handing it to DuBois. A servant rushed forward with a set of spectacles, and DuBois put them on before reading it carefully, even though there was not much to read below the drawing of a wolf.

"Interesting," was all he said.

"What do you intend to do about it?"

Both DuBois and Maddox looked at Audley in confusion.

"Do about it?" DuBois said. "Why would I do anything? While two thousand francs is a great sum even for me, and I am a bit of a huntsman, I am not out to kill a protective spirit of the land."

"That is what you believe the Wolf to be? A spirit?"

DuBois returned the flier, removing his spectacles. "Metaphorically, Inspector Audley. After all, to my knowledge, he has only killed two men known for attacking women, and set rather harmless traps in the woods to protect the innocent natural wolves there."

"What about Mrs. Bernard?"

"Come on, Inspector. It doesn't take much investigating to realize that the marquis had her killed. She knew all about his abusive habits with his servants. She was killed almost immediately after you appeared and started interviewing the servants, no? You began that first night, the night we played that game in the parlor where I pretended to be dead? How ironically this has all turned out." His tone was partially serious, partially amused. "If he's capable of hiring one bandit– the one who was killed by the Wolf – to attack his former maid, then he's capable of hiring another."

"So you've been following this case?"

"I have little other serious amusement out here in the woods, Inspector," DuBois said. "Not that death is amusing, but a murder investigation is certainly the most interesting thing that has happened here since I acquired this manor. Especially when it is meant to insinuate that the marquis is a werewolf."

"But he is not."

"No, he is not. And neither is the Wolf, I imagine. That sheet describes a man dressed as a wolf." He frowned. "Now, what's all this about? Did you come here to ask me to hunt the Wolf? Because I won't."

"Would you hunt the marquis?"

DuBois was put-off by the comment. "I only hunt animals, Inspector. Not men – at least, not anymore. I am retired from that awful duty." His frown deepened. "Do you mean to imply something? Because if you are in such a hurry, you might as well say it."

Audley did not back down from the challenge. "To be plain, then. The Wolf has been described as someone my height, and we are about the same height – you and I. You are physically capable, you know the marquis well enough to hate him, and as you said, you are an excellent huntsman. You also have the book with the translation for the Japanese symbol that the Wolf left on a wooden cross at Roux's death site – the symbol that means 'wolf.' It's in the French edition that you have. And, you are the only person I've met with any connection at all to Simon Roux. So, if you are so interested in this case, please draw your own conclusions."

"Are you accusing me, Inspector?"

"I am looking for the Wolf, Sir DuBois. I am trying to save his life."

DuBois looked disturbed by the implication, but only said, "Very noble of you, but I must disappoint. I am not the Wolf."

"Prove it."

"How do I disprove a connection that does not exist?" he said, now nervous. "You come to me with an armed man – whom I respect greatly – and you tell me I am the man who dresses up like a wolf and murders people. If you mean to arrest me, you may do so, but I tell you – *I am not the Wolf!* I hunted for him on that day when the woods were full of traps!"

"But you did not kill any wolves on that hunt. You conveniently and harmlessly fell into a trap."

"Why would I fall into my own trap?"

"In order not to arouse suspicion? To throw me off your trail?"

"*There is no trail!*"

"Inspector," Brian said, putting a hand on his shoulder from behind. "There is no trail."

Audley spun around. "*What?*"

"There is no trail here. He is not the Wolf."

"You decide to tell me this now? You know who the Wolf is, don't you?" Audley cried. He didn't understand why his reactions were so strong and emotional. "Why does everyone know except me? You claim to help me, and yet you keep the most important information from me! You are no help at all!"

DuBois paled. "Inspector, I am most sorry, but as I said, I am not the Wolf. Yes, the facts do seem to match up. You may search my whole house if you wish, but it would be a waste of your time."

Audley growled and turned his attention to Maddox, who merely answered calmly, "Georgiana only told me who the Wolf *isn't*."

"Who's Georgiana?" DuBois interrupted.

"Miss Bingley," Audley said, not moving his gaze from his samurai protector. "Why didn't you say something?"

"You didn't *tell me* you were coming here to accuse DuBois of being the Wolf!"

Audley swallowed. This much was true. But if DuBois was not the Wolf, that left ... no one. No one on his lists, anyway. His lists were wrong. He was useless – a terrible inspector. "Sir DuBois," he said with a grave bow. "I apologize for interrupting your day with these foolish accusations. It seems I led myself astray."

To his surprise, DuBois returned the bow courteously. "I am not offended. I suppose I should be, but to be honest, I'm sort of honored that you would think me to be a person I hold in deep respect. When you do find him, Inspector, please ask him if we can be introduced."

This did not completely relieve Audley of his embarrassment, but it helped. He made a quick (but polite) escape and they were barely outside before he said, "Maddox, if you were not so heavily armed, I would throttle you."

"You could have told me what you were doing."

"Before I made a fool of myself, yes." He put his hand over his eyes. "Oh God, I've ruined this whole investigation."

"It has not ended yet, Inspector."

"Is that what you really think? Be honest with me, for once."

Brian put his hands in his robe and said, "We are merely spectators to a larger fight between the Wolf and the marquis. Eventually, one of them will kill the other, and all will be revealed."

"Japaner mysticism?"

"No. Common sense."

Audley did not want to argue with that. He was too busy being furious with himself. They saddled their horses and raced back to town. There was business to be done.

~~~

Audley did have one person left on his list – one person he'd never spoken to. Returning to the town square, he asked for directions to the home of Monsieur Gerard. The man lived not far from the center of town, not a surprise considering his industry. It was a small wooden house, and Audley stepped onto the porch and knocked loudly on the door. Inside, he heard movement, and eventually, the door opened. A bearded man with spectacles said, "Please, sir, I am very busy at the moment."

"So am I," Audley said. "I am Inspector Audley, and I have some questions for you about your paper this morning."

"Oh," Gerard said, clearly terrified of both the imposing figure of a Parisian inspector and the heavily-armed swordsman in robes standing a step behind him. "Uhm, do come in. Excuse me if I work while you talk."

"You are still printing?"

"I have another flier that must go up immediately."

They stepped in as he beckoned them. It was a two-room home, and the main room had been almost entirely overtaken by his large press. There was paper everywhere – in stacks, scattered about, near the press, in the press, stuffed in the bookshelf. Gerard immediately returned to his press. "So, please, Inspector, ask your questions."

He had no time for the simple ones. "I assume you printed this morning's paper at the behest of the marquis."

"Yes."

"And he paid you for it?"

"Twenty francs, yes. Is that illegal?" he asked, his voice reaching a higher, nervous pitch. Gerard seemed, despite his very political and dangerous profession as a gossip reporter, an extremely high-strung man.

"No. I am merely asking. Does he often pay you for such announcements?"

"Not often, no. This is the largest commission he ever gave me."

"And you are still working on it."

"Non. I have something that just came in. I am still setting it. Here, I still have the original." Gerard pulled from his desk a hand-written note that was set up for the purposes of being printed properly as a late edition of the news.

> *The Marquis Is a Murderer!*
> *My Lord,*
> *I have your friends.*
> *Meet me at midnight to reclaim them.*
>
> *You know where.*
> *– The Wolf*

"His friends?" Maddox said, alarmed.

"Monsieur Gerard," Audley said, trying to hide his own rising alarm. "This is a ransom note, not a news report. You cannot print this."

"But I was paid! Fifty francs, to be precise. My largest commission ever."

"By *whom*?"

"*I don't know.*" Gerard backed into his press as Audley stepped forward menacingly. "For God's sake, *I don't know*! He left the note under my door with the money and instructions but an hour ago! I didn't want to question it! The Wolf is a murderer – he would kill me!"

"Why should I believe you? Why should I not have you locked up?"

"You may lock me up, but it will do no good! *I don't know who left the note!*"

Audley had no patience left, but he could not sense that this man was lying. "What were the instructions?"

"Print as many copies as fifty francs would afford and distribute them around town before sundown!"

"Don't you think that's odd? If he's writing a note to the marquis, why doesn't he just deliver it? Must he make his ransom so public?"

"I don't know."

"Maybe it's not the Wolf," Maddox interjected suddenly and calmly. "Maybe it's the marquis, trying to draw the Wolf out. He doesn't know who he is or he would have killed him already. The Wolf has to be wondering the same thing we are wondering – who has been captured. The Wolf is a protector – he will answer this call. The names are just reversed."

It made perfect sense. "And who are the friends of the Wolf?" He paused, and bowed to Monsieur Gerard. "Excuse us, but we must be off."

"May I print? I do not want to upset either one of them."

"Yes, you may print," Audley said. "The damage has already been done."

They had stepped out on the porch and shut the door before Audley said, "Georgiana."

"And Lady Littlefield. What's her name?"

"Heather."

"Who else has the Wolf protected?"

"Sophie, but she is too far from here for the marquis to catch her," Audley said. "We must go to the school immediately."

Maddox did not have to be told twice. They rode harder than they had before, arriving at the school in a matter of minutes. Audley pushed past the woman at the door, and headed straight for the headmaster's office, finding him sitting at his desk, quietly reading his papers as he smoked a pipe. "Where are Miss Bingley and Lady Littlefield?"

"Sir, you have no authority – "

"I have *every authority*!" Audley shouted, and he didn't care that he did. He would draw a pistol on this man if he had to. "While you are on French soil, you will listen to my every command. Now, where are they?"

The headmaster hesitated – visibly. "Lady Littlefield is in her lessons. Miss Bingley is – under the weather and is resting in her dormitory."

"Then I must see her. At once."

"Absolutely not. I cannot allow – "

Before Brian could react, Audley drew his pistol and held it to the headmaster's head. *"Where is Georgiana Bingley?"*

Headmaster Stafford swallowed, trying to maintain some mediocre amount of English dignity as he said, "W – We don't know."

"You *don't know?*" Now Brian was shouting, his hands on his swords.

"That girl is a madwoman! She comes and goes as she pleases! She gets into fights at the tavern in town! The only reason we put up with it is because - ..." He would have trailed off, but the sound of Audley cocking the pistol was enough to get him started again. " – because she would have this place shut down, after the Roux incident. Do you know how powerful her family is?"

"I *am* her family," Brian said. "So yes, I am very aware. How long has she been gone?"

"Two – maybe three days."

Internally, Audley felt a shiver. Georgiana had promised to return to school after he left her yesterday. She hadn't. Which mean she had now been missing for almost a day. "I must see Lady Littlefield. Have her brought to me in their dormitory chambers."

"Sir – "

"NOW."

The headmaster scurried out, yelling at the servants as he went, leaving the two men alone in his office. Audley put his pistol back in his belt and turned to Brian Maddox, only to find him bowing, his head touching the floor.

"Audley-*Keibu*," he begged formally. "Please release me from my obligation to protect you so that I may search for my niece."

"Released," Audley said. "Find her, Mr. Maddox." He hesitated for only a moment before deciding to stammer, "She has a secret place near a waterfall. Follow the streams in the forest until you find it and call out for her."

"I will." Brian wasted no more time and ran out the door.

The headmaster returned, shaking visibly. "Inspector, Mrs. Stafford is the Head of the dormitories, and she will show you to the living quarters of Miss Bingley. Lady Littlefield is being pulled from her lesson at this moment. Are you satisfied?"

"I will be," was Audley's cold warning as he was led deeper into the school than he had ever been by a stern-looking woman all in black. She spoke nothing to him, trying to maintain her own dignity, but he could see she was scared – possibly because a gun had moments ago been aimed at her husband's head. They passed classrooms and a dining hall before arriving in the wing of living quarters.

"Normally men are not allowed in here," she said as she unlocked one of the doors.

"I understand. And I don't care." Audley stepped into a room with two beds at opposite ends. "Please bring Lady Littlefield to me, here."

She bowed with forced compliance and left him. Now alone, he relaxed only slightly with a heavy sigh and looked at both sides of the room. It was not hard to figure out to whom each side belonged. One side was appropriately decorated, he supposed, with a beautiful watercolor of flowers framed on the wall and a jewelry case on the dresser. The other side had some inked drawing of a type of building he had never seen before. Taking a closer look at it, he noticed that it had originally been drawn with a charcoal pencil and then inked and colored later. The building was domed, with pillars on each side and a long blue-colored rectangle in front of it that he assumed was a pool or a lake of some kind. He peered even closer to see the label – "*The Taj Mahal. Agra, India. Charles Bingley, 1817.*"

It was beautiful and bizarre, but he did not have time to give it full appreciation. He slumped onto Georgiana's bed, happy for the rest of a moment but still overly nervous about the situation. She could easily be off doing something for the Wolf – but he suspected otherwise. The marquis was trying to end the story, so-to-speak, and she would have to be a part of it. He looked down at his feet, peering beneath the bed at her selection of shoes and slippers.

There was something to the side that didn't match. He reached down, grabbing the soft foot straps of two sandals unlike anything he had ever seen. They were on wooden stilts, reinforced by metal along the bottom. They had clearly been used well, because they were caked in dirt.

Wooden sandals.

He abandoned all pretenses of not invading her privacy and began going through her dresser. Clothing, notes from schoolwork – a diary. He opened it.

All Japanese – kanji. She knew how to write in Japanese.

He started pulling open drawers and tossing the contents on the bed. Nothing but the things for being a woman here – cloth, ribbons, sewing equipment, bonnets carelessly squished between books – and she had books. She had books in languages he didn't recognize. At last, he saw something unusual and desperately unlatched a small wooden case, revealing an item wrapped in red silk. Unwrapped, he found a bullet – a rifle bullet. Made of silver.

"Inspector Audley?"

From the look of terror on her face, he must have looked like a wild man as he turned to Lady Littlefield while still holding up a rifle bullet. "Where did this come from?"

She curtseyed, and he remembered his manners and bowed. She regained her composure quickly, and was able to answer. "From Georgiana's dresser, I imagine."

"Do you know what it is?"

Lady Littlefield shut the door behind her. "She said she was shot with it. She considers it a good luck charm."

"It's silver."

"I suppose. I don't know what bullets are supposed to be made of, Inspector Audley."

"Lead. Silver bullets are made for hunting werewolves," he said. After a pause he continued, "She's the Wolf, and she's been the Wolf before, hasn't she? It must have been back in England." Thinking out loud, it became clearer. "Of course, when I sent a letter to her uncle about how I was investigating a case of a killer who dressed as a wolf, and my location was so close to her school, he made the obvious conclusion. Why else would the famous Brian Maddox come to the middle of nowhere at top speed?" He played with the bullet, rolling it between his fingers. "He knew all along. He knew when he got the letter. Why didn't I see it?"

"Because a woman couldn't be the Wolf."

Georgiana blended into the background. Just like she did as Lady Littlefield's companion with the marquis. It was perfect. They were all looking for a man – who else would attack men – and win? "But she's so small."

Lady Littlefield said nothing, hiding her eyes.

"She's too short. The Wolf is my height. But if she was wearing -" He picked up he wooden sandals. "If she was wearing these shoes – she would be about my height, wouldn't she?"

"I don't know, sir."

"You've seen her in them, though?"

"Yes."

"Are they her only pair?"

"I don't know, Inspector."

Why didn't he see it? He called the Wolf a man, and she didn't correct him. She was the only other person with a solid connection to Simon Roux –

"Lady Littlefield," Audley said, rushing across the room to her. "What happened between her and Simon Roux?"

"I don't know. I wasn't there."

"What did she *tell you* happened?"

Littlefield sat down on her own bed, setting aside her books. "She said that Simon Roux came upon two of the girls, Sarah and Anna - Miss Ashley and Miss Stevenson. He was riding a horse, had a rifle and a pistol, and he made some lewd comments, and then threatened them both. I don't know what they said." She played with her hands. "Georgiana follows the others when they go into town. It's dangerous, after all, but girls sneak out anyway, so sometimes she trails behind. That time, she did, and she appeared and told him to leave. Then she hit his horse with a rock."

"So she told me. Is there more to the story?"

"Again, I wasn't present, so I don't truly know, but ..." She kept looking away, refusing to meet his eyes. "Sarah told me that the horse didn't run, it just *stopped* charging, and while Mr. Roux was distracted, Georgiana leapt over the horse and tackled him, drawing his own knife and telling him that if he ever came near one of the girls again, she would slit his throat."

This part Georgiana had left out of her own telling, of course – because Simon Roux had gotten his throat slit sometime later. "What about the night he died?"

"She came back very late. Sometimes I don't hear her – I just wake up in the morning and she's there. But that night, I did. Her gown was filthy. I told her to call for water, and she shouted at me –then she apologized. She was shaking."

"Was she armed?"

"No, Inspector."

"Was she injured?"

"No, but there was blood on her face. Not all over – she had tried to wash it off. There were just traces of it."

His heart was racing. "And you thought nothing of this?"

"When I heard he was dead, I knew. There are things she hides from me and things she doesn't. She told me it was in self-defense. She was coming home from wherever she goes, and he came upon her. He was drunk and angry about something, and he remembered her quite well."

"But she did not kill him with the sort of weapon one carries for self-defense."

"She has all kinds of strange weapons. She doesn't keep them here – she had a trunk of them, but she took it somewhere."

The trunk. "Was it red?"

"Was what red?"

"The trunk. Deep red. Almost brown."

"Yes."

He fumed. He had been there – within a foot of the murder weapons – and he had not known it. He told her he needed evidence, but she had it all, locked away in that trunk. "Why didn't anyone tell me?"

"I am sorry, Inspector Audley," she said, and sounded as if she was. "I – had no idea how far this would go. Nor did Georgiana, as she told me a few days ago. She's bullied the marquis, spread rumors about him, fought him, threatened him in person – as the Wolf – and still he will not break the engagement. She has no idea what else to do."

"When was the last time you saw her?"

"Two days ago."

He paced, angry – at himself. Angry for not seeing it. Angry for letting his emotions blind him. She had been right – he had stopped searching for the Wolf when he started chasing Georgiana. He just didn't know they were one and the same – and he probably didn't want to know. How could he love his main suspect? A woman – a tiny girl – who had apparently killed two men and threatened another? He remembered holding her hand in his – how small and gentle it was. Even now –

"She does like you."

You have no idea. "I hope so." He shook his head to refocus. "Lady Littlefield, I have to find her. The marquis has put a price on the Wolf's head."

She gasped.

"Someone paid the local newspaper man to print a note to the marquis from the Wolf, saying the Wolf was holding his friends hostage. Why would she do that?"

"It doesn't sound like her. Do you have a copy?"

He handed her the original.

"This isn't her handwriting!" she said. "This is the marquis's!"

"I thought it might be," he said. "He's doing everything he can to draw her out. I don't know where he intends to meet her, but I have to find out. Her uncle is looking for her, but that might not be enough."

"Let me go with you," she said, rising and grasping him with a gloved hand. "I'm the cause of all this."

"To some extent, yes," Audley said, "but everyone did their part to bring it this far. I cannot allow it to further."

Any further protest by Lady Littlefield was prevented by the sudden entrance of Mrs. Stafford. "Lady Littlefield, the marquis has sent his carriage for you.

He says it is a matter of great urgency." She gave a stern look to Audley.

"I'll escort her," he said quickly. "I'm on my way out anyway."

Maybe she was just happy for him to be gone, but Mrs. Stafford did not interfere as Lady Littlefield put on her bonnet and walked with him back through the hallways at a fairly brisk pace.

Outside, there was a carriage waiting. Durand was there. "My Lady, your carriage awaits." He bowed, and the footmen surrounded them. Audley turned around and noticed the front doors of the school were closed. "And yours, Inspector." The sharp end of a gun pressed sharply between his shoulder blades. "Raise your hands."

"I'm an officer of the law," Audley said as they disarmed him. "This is a hanging crime, Monsieur Durand."

"So is murder, Inspector Audley. And if you will only be patient and play along, the marquis will be good enough to deliver you the head of the Wolf. A good trade, wouldn't you agree?"

So. He and Lady Littlefield were the 'friends' – not of the marquis, but of the Wolf. He intended to use them against her – by any means necessary.

CHAPTER 13

Robert Audley and Heather Littlefield sat across from each other at a wooden table in the woods, surrounded by guards that could only be some of the bandits. Each of them had their hands tied in front of them, and they sat waiting nervously as Monsieur Durand appeared and began to set the table, complete with candelabra. "Your host shall be along shortly."

"You know this is ridiculous," Audley said, "and highly illegal."

"The marquis is aware of these facts, yes."

"If you release us both, I might even be tempted to not press charges on any of the people currently present."

"I'm sorry, Monsieur Inspector, but that is not our concern."

Audley sighed and looked at Lady Littlefield as Durand disappeared. She had stopped crying, but she was shivering as the sky darkened and the air cooled. "Someone untie me so I can give her my coat."

There was no response.

"Lady Littlefield, I'm sorry," he whispered across the table.

"Are they going to kill us?"

"Considering the lengths the marquis is going through to protect his marriage to you, I would say, definitely not," Audley said. That, of course, did not leave him in the equation. If he was a witness to whatever the marquis was enacting, there were certainly no reasons to leave him alive. "I think we are merely spectators." *And hostages.* "You have nothing to fear."

"He's going to kill her!"

"That's not a certainty." Especially if she had Brian Maddox by her side. He would no doubt go to any lengths to protect his niece from her own foolishness. "They've both been readying for this for a long time now, since the death of Simon Roux. It is out of our hands."

"But you're the inspector! How can you just let a crime go by like this?"

With a guilty shiver, he shrugged.

The marquis made his entrance at last, flanked by several of his men. He was dressed perfectly, wearing a red coat, with an exquisite rapier at his side. "I apologize for the inconvenience and my delay. Hello, my darling," he bent over to kiss her. Lady Littlefield tried to squirm away from him, but he pulled her close to plant a kiss on her cheek. "My blushing bride," he said, giving Audley a vicious smile. "Inspector Audley."

"Bastard," he said with all the dignity he would use to address a noble, even pretending to doff his imaginary hat.

"I am attempting the pretense of civility," the marquis said, taking his seat at the head of their table as plates of food were placed in front of them. "Surely, Inspector, you understand the concept of deceit for a greater purpose?"

"I understand when it is used by people to murder others. My job is to stop it."

"I will not comment on your proficiency in your job, Inspector Audley, because you are my guest. And do eat up. We have a long night ahead of us."

Lady Littlefield looked to Audley for assurance, and he nodded. The food was not poisoned – there was no reason for that after all of the attempts to keep them alive, and certainly the marquis would not poison his bride. If it was drugged, he had plenty of ways at his disposal of making sure they were drugged forcibly. Besides, Audley though decisively, he was hungry. "I have never turned down one of your free meals, My Lord, and I don't intend to now." With decreased dexterity and increased awkwardness from having his hands bound, he still managed to spoon the sausage into his mouth. "I must comment on the loveliness of your *red coat*."

"This? Oh, yes. It is new. Just arrived from Paris. I never did manage to discover how Sophie managed to steal my old one without my man discovering her."

"She didn't," Audley said. "The Wolf did."

"So there has been deception on your end, as well."

"I have said once, and I will stand by my words – I am an inspector of the law, and I may conceal any facts I deem relevant to the investigation. As I have made abundantly obvious, I do not answer to you. You would virtually have to imprison me to get me to even listen to your mad ramblings. Oh, how convenient, you already have." He swallowed his food. It was actually quite good. "I assume at least Lady Littlefield's dish is not poisoned, contrary as that would be to your ultimate plan."

"Neither is yours, Inspector Audley," the marquis said. "For the time being, I do need you alive."

Soup was served, which was a bit more difficult to manage than the meats. Lady Littlefield's bonds were cut, but not Audley's.

"You would have done well, Inspector Audley, to simply play your part and hang someone for the crime of the murder of Simon Roux. But you were so intent on finding the real killer – and now I shall have to bring him to you."

"How will he know to come here?" Audley asked. Though it was dark, he recognized the area just outside the den of the wolf pack they had hunted for money last week. There seemed to be supplies stored in the hole leading to the den, and candles sitting on the jutting parts of the rock outside of the cave.

"How does he know everything he knows? Through his network of spies, of course. They would be joining us, but my men are taking care of them as we speak. Who else knows everything in town but the barkeep and his wench?"

Audley leapt up in anger, and even though his hands were still tied, only two men grabbing him from behind prevented him from leaping on the marquis entirely. "If you had Anton and Camille killed – Screw the law, I'll kill you myself!"

The marquis motioned to one of his men (thugs, more accurately), who bashed Audley on the back of the head with something wooden. It was enough to make him faceplant into his soup, but not lose consciousness entirely. It was some time, however, before the ringing went down enough for him to hear over it –

"– hell of a nick to your head, didn't he? Still a tender area? You, please, wipe the inspector's face for him."

His face was roughly wiped off with a very fancy napkin, and he opened his eyes to a somewhat blurry version of the same scene he had been looking at before.

"Michel! Stop!" Lady Littlefield pleaded, and it took Audley's impaired mind a moment to realize she was referring to the marquis. "Please end this madness. I will marry you if you let everyone go! I will not say a word!"

"My dear, it is not so simple," the marquis said luxuriously as Audley tried to force his vision to focus. "I have one person crazy enough to dress up as a beast and make several attempts on my person to stop our marriage, and one legal witness – a detective, no less – who will probably be too concerned about the law and his conscience to keep silent about these events. I have thought on the matter, and unless you can convince both of them otherwise, they will simply have to be removed from the picture." He tried to put his hand over hers, but she moved it away. "Someday, you will understand."

"No, not this," she said. "I will never forgive you."

"Darling, this is not a good way – "

Suddenly the meek Lady Littlefield developed a spine. "You are a murderer, a rapist, and the most vicious man I have ever met, and even if my parents force me to marry you upon hearing all I have to say – "

"– none of which they will believe, it all being so fantastical – "

"– and even if you force yourself on me, because you will have to every time, I will never love you, and I will never respect you, and I will always hate the sight of you!" she screamed. "And if I bear you a child, I will kill it myself!"

Enough to make any man unnerved, the threat brought the marquis out of his self-confident demeanor, and he moved like lightening, striking her from his seat. She did not topple over. Audley's natural response was to come to her aid despite his aching head, but again he was restrained by the marquis's willing and able guards, holding him securely in place as he struggled against them, kicking over his glass as he flailed. "Get your hands off her!"

"Oh, you want me to do the proper Christian thing and wait until marriage?" the marquis said before pulling out a handkerchief and offering it to his fiancée, who had a bloody nose. She looked at him in hatred as she snatched it from him.

"Press softly on the nostrils and it should stop. Does it hurt?"

"Fuck you!"

"Goodness! What are they teaching you in that school of yours?"

"Nothing," she said, "but my companion taught me something about self-respect."

"And where is Miss Bingley?" the marquis said, turning to the still-thrashing Audley. "You should know. You've been following her like a dog after a bone. Very convenient for me."

Less convenient than you think. "When she discovers this, she'll be along. And she won't fall into your trap, Maret. She's smarter than that."

"The words of a man blinded by love. Or mere obsession. You think she would fall for a Parisian inspector? She must have thousands of pounds."

He did not want to discuss his relationship with Georgiana – certainly not in front of Lady Littlefield. "Please set me down."

"I don't particularly see the wisdom of that."

"Or I am going to be sick all over your fine dinner table."

It was not a lie. Between the new head injury, the food, and the physical activity of being grabbed and fighting it, he did feel the need to be sick.

"Gentlemen," the marquis said, after a moment of weighing the situation, "please escort Inspector Audley to an appropriate distance so that he may see to his needs."

Though he was not eager to leave Lady Littlefield alone with the marquis, especially when she was still bleeding, Audley actually did feel ill and knew that, in his condition, he could not free himself from the guards. He was dragged some distance away, behind some of the trees, and there he lost his dinner and probably some of his lunch. They did release him for that, and he sat on the ground with his head in his hands, trying to recover from the dizziness brought on by everything that had happened. He could try to run, but these men had guns, and he had to try to protect Heather Littlefield, even though he had, so far, utterly failed to do that. He stood up and they escorted him back, which he did not fight. He calmly took his seat at the table again, exhausted from the exertion, and was implored to drink some tea to settle his stomach.

"If you continue to put up a fight, I will not hesitate to put something in your drink," the marquis said quite openly.

Audley shook his head and numbly sipped the tea set before him. It had a calming effect, and if the marquis did not press him for questions, he would follow suit. Lady Littlefield still held the handkerchief to her nose, but it was obvious she was barely bleeding. He tried to throw a reassuring glance her way, but he was hardly in the condition to do so.

Then, the howling.

Audley was almost relieved. He had no desire for this macabre dinner to go on. He had long since lost his appetite.

"It seems he is early," the marquis said, rising from his chair with an amused expression as the servants began to clear away the settings and then the table itself. Audley chuckled. "What is so funny, Inspector?"

"Nothing," he said. "Though I think you are in for some surprises tonight, my Lord."

Audley's hands were retied behind his back as he was brought to kneel on the ground next to Lady Littlefield. The servants scattered as the bandits readied their weapons. The lit torches and candles brightened the area and gave it a weird, sort of ritualistic feel.

"She's going to get herself killed," Heather whispered to him.

"You have so little faith in her?"

To this, she managed a weak, frightened smile.

"Can you run?" he said in an even softer voice. "If the time comes?"

"I can try," she said.

"If I give you the signal, go."

"I won't abandon you or Georgiana."

Audley looked at her. She had lost her fear – or maybe it had overwhelmed her to the point where she could no longer acknowledge it. "my Lady – "

"You would do the same for me, Inspector Audley. I won't run from this. I tried, and look what it has caused."

He nodded in silent, painful affirmation.

They did not have long to wait. Before any shots could be fired or any trace of life was seen, from deep within the woods, black with night, an arrow came sailing through the air. It whizzed past the marquis and embedded itself on a nearby tree. The elaborate arrow held only a flag on it – a strip of white cloth.

The marquis pulled it out before his men could say anything, readying his own pistol. "Wolf! Come forward!"

If it was the Wolf, it had lost its Wolf-like qualities. An armored man emerged from the dark entrance to their clearing, wearing an elaborate domed helmet with two brass horns that rose a foot in the air above him. His face was covered in a complex armored mask. The armor seemed to be metal pieces sewn together with colored laces of green, white, red, and black, alternating freely. It made surprisingly little sound when he walked, and he walked with exposed feet with only rope sandals tied around his socks. Despite the extensive disguise, the two swords, one stuffed into his cloth belt and the other hanging from links in his armor, proudly announced who he was. He carried a bow and a brown bag. He stepped fearlessly passed the initial guards, who were stunned by his appearance and the blood-streaked yellow flag that flew behind him by a pole attached to his back.

Still ten feet or so from the marquis, he stopped, put down his bow, and let loose the contents of the bag. Three human heads dropped to the ground. Guns were raised but he did not react.

"These," Brian Maddox said, "you may recognize as the men you sent after Monsieur Anton and Mademoiselle Camille."

The marquis did lean forward a bit to see but did not inspect them closely. He had to visibly try to maintain his composure as he said, "My argument is with the Wolf."

"Assuming it is to be a negotiation, the terms are as follows – the Wolf will fight you without firearms, and you will do the same."

The marquis's hand fell on his blade. "I am prepared for that eventuality."

"No one is to interfere."

"Or?"

"Or the two of us will kill every one of these men," Maddox said. "Sooner or later."

"That is a rather bold statement on your part, Mr. Maddox."

"So is facing an advancing rebel army to save a friend, but I still did it," he replied. "Are the terms accepted?"

"On one condition," the marquis said, stepping forward to meet the armored warrior. "I get to see his face."

"That I can't promise you," the warrior said with a laugh, "but I can ask."

With that, Brian Maddox, Japanese warrior, turned and headed back into the darkness. He left the heads behind.

The marquis made a hasty retreat to where his hostages were being held. He snapped his fingers at the armed man perched up on the cliff over the entrance to the cave. "When the Wolf charges in, shoot it."

"Those were not the terms!" Audley said, which earned him another knock in the head. This almost made him lose his balance, and he kept it only with Heather leaning in to catch him with her shoulder until he could straighten his senses enough to sit up properly again.

"No, they are not," the marquis said. "And you would be wise to –"

Whatever Audley would be wise to do – probably, to silence himself – Audley would never discover. The rifleman did fire, but randomly and awkwardly into the trees as a loud cry came from above, and a blur of grey came down with it. The rifleman screamed as his attacker landed on him and then tossed him at the entrance to the den, so that he landed on his back, his freshly-cut throat still spewing blood. The sound of rifles clicking in the direction of the figure on the mount was audible, but the Wolf held up only a bloodied metal claw with long blades like skewers, with flesh and blood still dangling from it.

"Unless you can dodge bullets," the marquis said, "you are at my mercy, Wolf."

The Wolf growled but did not back down, standing proudly in the spot where the sniper had once sat. How it managed to balance itself on wooden stilt sandals, Audley decided he would never have any idea. The bare feet were tiny, but partially hidden by a layer of fur placed around the ankles.

"I do not know why so many are willing to die for you," the Wolf said in a voice partially muffled by the wolf head mask, and partially disguised by tone, so that it was not recognizably female – or human, "but they all will unless you agree to Maddok-sama's original terms."

There was some murmuring among the men. Many members of this gang had now fallen to the Wolf.

"What's going on?" Heather whispered. "She couldn't possibly win against them."

"She has her uncle, and she may have other resources," Audley whispered back, and then said at full volume, "My Lord, you may have no reason to listen to your own hostage, but you may be wise to take the Wolf up on this offer, before you face a rebellion of a different sort."

The marquis paused before tossing his pistol aside dramatically. He also withdrew another one stashed in his back, and set down the rifle. "No guns." He drew instead his rapier.

"No guns."

"And my men will stay back."

"They won't die for the likes of you anymore, Maret," the Wolf said and picked up something behind it, leaping over the marquis and landing in the clearing with a roll before quickly returning to its feet. The thing she – it, whatever – held was a sword with two small prongs on either side, which was thrown over the shoulder with a strap.

The men did not come nearer. Now face-to-face with him, the Wolf was smaller than the marquis, but still about the height of an average man. *Because of the sandals*, Audley saw now. They gave her another few inches.

"Grant me one small favor, first," the marquis said, not at all in any kind of pleading voice.

The Wolf snarled, shuffling back and forth.

"If I am to die at your hands as you have told me before, I want to face the man, not the beast. Let us leave the superstition behind us."

"If you insist," said the Wolf, dropping its claws first, which it held by rods in her hands. Next was the fur around her ankles, revealing tiny, almost bone-white feet and no appearance of hair – certainly not in this light. That left the lower half only in sandals and breeches cut off just above the knee. With great care – and reverence for the skin – she unfastened the knots tying the wolf's head and hide, and removed the headpiece that covered most of her upper body, setting it aside. Standing up with light of the torches illuminating her, it was Georgiana, bare save for a tunic that went no farther than her elbows, cut-off breeches, and sandals. And, of course, the gigantic sword strapped to her back. She was either already breathing heavily from the exertion, or just seething in hatred, as she turned her eyes briefly to Audley and Heather Littlefield and then back to the marquis. Her face was painted with red paint like some kind of tribesman, with two red slashes starting just above her eyebrows and going down her cheek.

To the marquis's stunned silence she only answered – in her real, womanly voice -, "You were expecting someone else?"

CHAPTER 14

At first no one dared to approach her. Then, perhaps with sheer curiosity, or judging her no longer a threat when revealed to be a member of the weaker sex, one of the bandits did have the gall to approach her, not necessarily with guns blazing, but even his tentative advance didn't get far. Without blinking she pulled something from her pocket and tossed it at him, some kind of small dagger, which pinned him to the tree behind him by his shirt collar. When the others staggered, she drew her blade, handling it with remarkable ease, and the marquis raised his hand for his men to stay back.

"Is this another trick?" the marquis said, raising his own rapier.

"No, my Lord," she said. "No more tricks. At least, not from me." She must have noticed his hesitation. "And if you have any qualms about fighting a woman, I would point out that you already have, twice now."

"What do you want?"

"You know what I want."

"We're beyond the point of talking about marriages, Miss Bingley. We've *all* come too far for that. But a deal can be worked out for your life – and your silence. Would your illustrious family like to know about your nocturnal wanderings?"

She didn't flinch. Instead, she gave a scary, sick sort of laugh. "I think they already know – or else they've forgotten last year. What do you think a girl like me is doing in a proper English seminary, being taught manners and how to dress and how to act and all that nonsense?" She shook her head. "No, Monsieur de Maret – as you said, we've come too far for bargaining." She raised her blade, digging her wooden shoes into the dirt beneath her. "Agreed?"

"Agreed, Wolf."

He came at her first. He was raised a fencer, fighting traditionally, with one hand behind his back, standing mostly sideways and jutting forward. Georgiana fought entirely differently, facing forward before quickly moving out of his way. He realized he was not dealing with an enemy who would move only straight-on like a fencing opponent – quickly enough to block her blade with his to prevent his own quick demise. They stood locked for a moment, as the two blades and their masters tested their strengths against each other before pulling away. The blades themselves were too evenly matched. It would depend on the skill of the fighters.

The marquis was quick to alter his assault, cutting at his side, where she now stood. Instead of blocking with her sword as a traditional swordsman would, she ducked beneath him and swept a foot under his, knocking him to the ground. She jumped on top of him but had to sideswipe off to avoid his rapier cutting off her feet.

She was faster, he was stronger, but they seemed fairly evenly-matched. Audley recalled that they had fought before – and it had clearly been a tie, for him to limp away and her to limp away. At the time, neither had been armed like this, for he had not yet heard of the Wolf having a sword in any of the descriptions.

"Inspector!" Lady Littlefield whispered insistently next to him.

"What is it?" he said without taking his eyes off the fight as the marquis poked, struck, and swung – and missed every time. She was baiting him, and he knew it.

"Do you want me to free your hands?"

Audley leaned back, and noticed she had undone her own bindings, and the guards were too involved in the spectacle to notice. "Yes. How did you do that?"

"She taught me. In case something like this came up. I thought she was being silly at the time – "

"Right, of course." What good was he? He couldn't even escape the rope holding his hands, and the tiny heiress beside him could! She was so deft at it she quickly loosened the knot enough for him to also slip free. "Don't move yet." He glanced at the pistol the marquis had discarded, the closest weapon to him not more than five feet away. But he was distracted by the shuffling and noises of the fight.

The marquis had backed Georgiana to a tree, and her defense was not to block with her sword, but her shoe. She raised her foot and caught his blade in its reinforced metal groove between the two stilts, stamping down so his rapier was lowered. She swung her sword, but he caught her wrist with his other hand.

His hands are too big! He'll crush her! "Georgiana!" Audley cried out without thinking. A guard came forward, only to be cut down from behind as Brian emerged from the woods, joining the two kneeling prisoners. No one got in his way.

"Are you going to help her?" Audley pleaded.

"I tried," Brian said through his mask. "I spent hours trying to talk her out of this. But this is her fight and it must be respected."

"So you would watch her die?" Audley said, keeping his eyes mostly on the fight.

"I don't think she will," Maddox said simply.

Georgiana had broken the crushing hold the marquis had on her wrist, and seemed to be in genuine pain from it, but he had not broken his sword free from beneath her sandal, either. Finally she spit in his face, which sent him back far enough for her to free her other hand and deck him with her fist. The blow landed, and he staggered back, withdrawing, and taking his blade with him, which he flailed in front of him to keep her away. She somersaulted away, hitting him again in the head with her foot while still on her hands, before landing behind and to his right. Their recovery time was the same; both wounded and breathing heavily, they touched blades once again. The marquis moved faster now, his fury growing, while her attacks became more aggressive, with fewer parries and more assaults. The blades met with such force that they seemed to draw sparks of light against the flickering torchlight.

He stabbed again and again for her chest, and every time was rebuffed by either evasion or a straight parry. Each slice of hers, meant to take some significant part of him off instead of stab him, was similarly caught just in time. The marquis suddenly switched his stance – with the intent to throw her off – and swung from above, to come down on her head like she had been trying to do to him.

Fortunately, she caught his thin rapier blade in that groove between her blade and the prong on the handle, and its purpose was revealed as a twist of her wrist snapped the marquis's blade right off, causing it to fall harmlessly to the ground.

The marquis had his back to Audley and the others, so they did not see him draw his tiny gun, only heard the pistol shot and watched as it struck her in the chest. She tried to twist away from it, but the small trickle of blood as she dropped to her knees, clutching her side with her left hand and her sword in her right, indicated that she had not escaped in time.

"Georgiana!" It was hard to tell whose voice it came from first – Audley's, Lady Littlefield's, or Brian Maddox's.

There was no time. Georgiana knelt in front of her opponent, quivering in pain, her head dropped to hide her face. The marquis bent down luxuriously, putting his tiny, formerly-hidden pistol to her head. "And now the life of the Wolf ends."

"Yes," she said, suddenly raising her eyes. "But you're the wolf."

With her right arm, she raised her blade in an upward cut. Its effect did not become apparent until the head of the Marquis de Maret slid neatly and silently off his shoulders, and the hole it left erupted in a gushing fountain of blood.

Audley went for the pistol nearest to him. Brian got Lady Littlefield up as they both raced to the fighters, only to stop short at the sight of the approaching hoards of confused bandits who were watching their leader's limp body slumped backwards onto the ground, next to his head.

"Halt!" Audley shouted, holding up the pistol and swinging it around. "I am Inspector Audley of the City of Paris and the Crown! I have legal authority here!" He had managed to quickly grab their hesitant attention. "Go now, and you will not be prosecuted for any of your doings! Or stay, and be arrested or possibly killed. Honestly, I do not care which. Do you wish to sit in irons for the marquis?"

The answer was apparently not. The men turned and scattered in all directions, some staying to gape for an extra second before doing so.

When the three of them turned to see what the men were staring at, they noticed that Georgiana had stood up and re-sheathed her sword over her shoulder. Her hand was bleeding, but she did not appear in any great pain. Instead she reached under her tunic and unbuckled something. A hidden piece of armor fell to the ground, with a bullet still lodged in it. She stepped away from the body and joined them, her limbs still shaking; her expression numb.

It took every ounce of resistance in Audley's body to not run to her and let her collapse in his arms, as he knew she so dearly wished to do. Brian, removing his facial armor, could not hold her either. It was Heather Littlefield who embraced her, and it was not clear who was sobbing.

"Georgiana," Audley said. "Where are you hurt?"

She separated from Lady Littlefield and held up her hand, which was bleeding, but not badly. He took it in his hands – so small, yet so unmerciful. "The bullet grazed it when I turned," she said. "That was the blood you saw. He only hit my armor, but I wanted him to think he hit me."

He was not sure he heard it all, so distracted by having her hand in his. "Does it hurt?"

"It stings like hell."

"*Jorgi-chan*," Brian said, removing one of his sashes and offering it to Audley to wrap around her wound, "*Yokatta*," (*You did well*) He bowed to her. Tiredly, she returned the stiff bow, not a woman's curtsey.

"*Gomen nasai.*" (*Thank you*) It was with great effort that she straightened up again. Her hair and brow were soaked with sweat, but she was shivering. It was the coldest part of the night, and now that she had stopped moving, the water would be drying on her and cooling her down.

Audley removed his coat and put it around her shoulders. "Here."

Georgiana, despite having accomplished her goal, did not seem to have her full faculties. Maybe it was the victory that stunned her, or the slaughter that it had required. "I – think I've missed some lessons."

"Yes," Heather laughed, her voice also exhausted, but in a different way. "I'll help you catch up."

"What about the marquis?" Audley had to ask. There was, after all, his body, and the additional sniper's body, and three heads.

"*Nanito omoimasuka, Maddox ojisan?*" (*What do you think, Uncle Maddox?*) Georgiana said. "*Ima, kangaerini tsukare sugirudesu.*" (*I'm too tired to think.*)

"*Jibun jishin, ookamiwa karera o tabetara, iindayo!*" (*Personally, I think they should be left to the wolves,*) Brian replied, removing his massive helmet. "But one must honor his enemies."

"English or French will do," Audley said.

Brian went over to the den entrance and rifled through a bag of the marquis's supplies, retrieving two shovels – perhaps intended to bury the Wolf. "Do you remember how we buried Miyoshi? In the book?"

Audley blinked. "I can barely think straight, Mr. Maddox. No, I can't remember."

"Well, take a shovel and follow my example."

Slowly, the two men collected both of the bodies and all of the heads in two separate piles and dug up enough dirt to neatly cover them, at least so they weren't visible, beyond being obvious burial mounds. Georgiana took one of the candles from the cave and put it at the marquis's makeshift grave. Heather silently followed and marked the other one; that of the rifleman meant to kill to the Wolf.

Brian put his hands together, bowed his head and said, *"Namu Amida butsu. Namu Amida butsu. Namu Amida butsu."* Georgiana did the same, silently. Audley had no hat to remove, so he stood quietly beside Heather in silent prayer.

The moment passed, and it grew colder. "Let's go," Georgiana announced, picking up her metal claws and tying them to her cloth belt.

"What about – " Audley felt compelled to mention something. "The wolves will get at them."

"Then let them," she said, "if they'll eat their own."

~~~

The sky was beginning to lighten as they approached the edge of the woods, turning from black to increasingly lighter shades of blue. Maddox made Georgiana open her hand. "The bleeding has stopped, but you still need to wash it as soon as possible."

"You sound like Uncle Maddox."

"Because he's my brother and he's a doctor," he said. "And if he were here, he wouldn't shut up about it."

"I'll go wash it in the stream now," Georgiana said. "Uncle Brian, can you take Heather back to school? It would be easier for her to be there when they wake."

"And you? The inspector will take you home?" he huffed. His disapproval was obvious.

A proper Englishman after all, Audley thought.

"*Anatawa kare o ai shiteimesuka?*" (*Do you love him?*) Brian asked.

"*Anata to nani o surun?*" (*What does it matter to you?*)

"*Taihen kotodayo. Anata wa ore no mei desu.*"(*It matters everything to me. You are my niece.*)

"Don't you love being included in these conversations?" Audley said to Heather Littlefield.

"Absolutely," she said with a soft smile.

"*Jibun no meiyo no mamoru no tame ni anata no tetsudai wa hitsuyouga nai,*" Georgie said. (*I don't need your help defending my honor.*)

Maddox sighed. "You would never listen to reason. Join me for dinner tonight. I should probably leave town before I make myself even more suspicious."

"If they see you like that, I don't think it will be possible," Audley said, referring to his armor. He turned to Georgiana. "I'll help hide some of the ... evidence," he said, gesturing in the direction of the wolf head and hide she was carrying.

"Not exactly your job, Inspector Audley."

"I know. Amazing how odd a little country air can make a city man," he said with a smile, and Brian escorted Lady Littlefield home, his red armor disappearing in the distance. It was too early for anyone to be awake – including them. A heaviness fell on Audley, as if the growing daylight and morning mist was pushing down on his shoulders. He looked at Georgiana and saw the pure exhaustion on her face. All things considered ... "Do you want to wash up?"

She knelt by the stream, and very carefully, and almost systematically, scrubbed the war paint off her face until it was wiped as clean she could get it. She unwrapped her hand and dipped it back in the water, letting it flow over the wound.

Audley undid his cravat, which was at least clean of everything but sweat, and knelt beside her, tenderly taking her hand and rewrapping it. "It doesn't look serious."

"I've had worse. I was lucky."

"How did you know to put armor on?"

She smiled. "I just didn't want to get hit in that spot again. Once was enough. That spot was the only one covered – incredible luck."

"Once?"

"The woods of English are filled with dangerous bandits," Georgiana said, and he believed her. She also didn't seem up to a long story at the moment.

"You are a very lucky woman," Audley said, fighting the urge to run his hand down her arm. "What about – "

"I used ink," she said, referring to what appeared to be blue tribal tattoos – two rings around her wrists and one ring above each ankle. "It was all I could find in blue. It'll take a few weeks to fade."

"So you did do this before."

"The full costume, only once," she said. "When I fought that bandit in England. He wasn't really a bandit. He just acted like one and that was enough." She stood up, but was too shaky, and he instinctively caught and steadied her. "I just need to sit – for a short while."

"So do I," he admitted. He sat down with his back against a tree, still far enough in the forest to not be seen from the road. To his surprise, she hesitated only a moment before leaning back against him, resting her head on his shoulder and letting him put his arms around her.

"Do you mind?" she whispered.

"Not in the least," he said. "But you probably already knew that."

She smiled. He couldn't see it, but he could *feel* it. He looked down at her. "Are your feet cold?"

"To be honest? Freezing." She sat up (to his great displeasure) and pulled over the wolf hide, and removed a dagger from one of its sewn-in pockets, and used it to slice the hide away from the head, making a fur blanket, which she placed over herself. It essentially covered him as well when she leaned back into her established spot. "There."

He just wanted to stay in this position forever. He didn't know why she chose this moment to be tender again and he didn't care. So little of his mind remained awake to think. "I love you."

"I know."

"Does it have to end?"

She snuggled against him. "Not right now."

For the moment, that was enough.

~~~

Robert Audley awoke to full sunlight, shaded only by the tree covering. His neck and back hurt from leaning against a hard tree trunk, his head rang from all of the abuse, and he was soaked from the morning dew. Nonetheless, the warm body in his arms made all of that irrelevant. He was content to stay where he was.

Georgiana, by all appearances, had succeeded in largely curling up beneath the makeshift blanket, insufficient as it was as a reasonably-sized covering. *She's so small*, he thought. He could barely bring himself to imagine the terrifying person who had faced – and slaughtered – the marquis. She was tiny and her skin was so fair, she reminded him of fine china. Yet, she was not so easily broken.

She stirred against him, not in an attempt at separation but in repositioning herself, and he kissed her forehead. Such a delicate and beautiful creature she was, despite her insistence otherwise.

"What time is it?" she mumbled.

"I don't know."

She rifled through his pockets, and retrieved his watch for him. "Ten o'clock. Even Heather will be a bit curious as to where I've been."

"Isn't she always?"

"Well, usually she doesn't see me leave with a man." She raised her head. "I'm supposed to have *some* sense of propriety." Her hair looked a positively brilliant orange against the rays of the sun that hit it when she sat up.

"I am a terrible gentleman for saying so, but I am glad you don't."

She could not hide her grin and turned away, finally pulling out of their embrace and stepping out from under her covers. She stood up with a yawn.

"How do you walk in those things?"

"Very carefully," she said, slinging the sword over her shoulder. "Get up, you lazy man." She offered a hand for him to do so, and he took it, getting back to his feet.

"I seem to be spending more and more time passed out in this forest, thanks to you," he said. "Did you hit me that first time? When I went to investigate the bandit camp and left the note on the cross?"

"Of course. Do you know another person crazy enough to pull such a stunt?" she said as she took the wolf head and hide and pushed them against the base of the tree, covering them with leaves and twigs. "I'll come back to destroy them later."

"Destroy them?"

"The Wolf's job is done," she said. "He disappears back into the forest now, Inspector. That's how these stories are supposed to end."

"Perhaps that's how I should end my report. I suppose I'll have to write one. How do I tell a giant lie?"

"Start with a small one and keep them running until they're a big string, I suppose," she said.

Georgiana began to meander back, but he caught her and pulled her in, kissing her. She didn't fight it, but didn't encourage anything further. "Tell me it was real," he said.

"You'll have to specify, Inspector Audley."

"Robert. My name is Robert."

She grinned. "Robert, you'll have to be more specific."

"You know what I mean. The day in the cave – it wasn't part of anything to do with the Wolf's greater plans. It was because you cared about me, if only for that afternoon, in that place."

She looked away. "Don't make me answer that."

"Yes or no," he said. "Do you love me?"

She said nothing, and he held her hand, which was shaking. He ran his thumb over the ink tattoo. He loved her skin. He loved how it felt. He wanted to savor it – one last time. He waited until she answered, "Yes."

"Why does it hurt you to say it?"

"Why do you think?" she said, almost angrily, but not quite. "Because just like the legend of the marquis and the wolf, this story has to end."

"You will go back for Geoffrey?" he asked, because he had to ask, once and for all. "Does he love you?"

"If I had no affection for you still, I would strike you for that, head injury and all," she said, "Robert."

"Answer me. Please."

"I know he does. He just doesn't have the maturity to acknowledge or express it.

He's not you." She squeezed his hand. "But he's still Geoffrey."

"And your heart belongs to him," he said, with surprisingly little pain in comparison to what he had imagined it would take to say that. "If it turns out he's just no one – "

"Which it won't – "

"– Cut off some vital bits of him and come back to me." He kissed her again, softly on the bridge of her nose, between her eyebrows. "I know it won't happen, but I like to fool myself sometimes. I don't want to see you hurt."

"Everyone gets hurt."

"Not everyone deserves it."

She kissed him. Neither of them cut it off until it became a physical necessity. "It was never an act," she whispered. "Never part of the plan. The Wolf is only a part of me. Not the whole of me."

"That I do realize."

"It's good to know you understand *something*," she said. "Now, for my final act, I have to scare the daylights out of Mr. Stafford. Want to come?"

"I wouldn't miss it for the world."

~~~

"So, Miss Bingley – I find myself pondering the question of what to do with you."

Audley sat in the corner as Georgiana faced the attempted inquisition that was an annoyed Headmaster Stafford. He sat tensely at his desk, his spectacles still on, his expression not wavering. Georgiana did not take a seat but stood across from him, still in the tunic and sandals, with the sword over her shoulder and the ink on her arms and legs. She seemed unfazed – or perhaps just overtired. "Do with me, sir?"

"Obviously we cannot continue to tolerate this behavior. A few absences was one thing, but disappearing for days, only to show up in the company of a man while dressed...like that. And God only knows what you've gotten poor Lady Littlefield into. What if the marquis knew half of this?"

"The marquis is dead."

The statement hung in the air, for her to present and him to debate accepting. It was hard to doubt a woman with a long sword on her back and blood staining her clothing. The headmaster's eyes darted to Audley for help, but he shrugged. Stafford continued, "Inspector Audley, surely you have some interest – "

"I already have this information, Headmaster. Please don't let my presence interrupt you."

"Yes. Hmph," he said, clearing his throat. "So – how am I going to explain all this? Do you think your parents will be happy to hear about your dangerous and highly improper actions, whatever they were?"

"I'm sure my parents would be *very* interested," Georgiana said, her voice an utter calm, almost emotionless. "If I hadn't returned now, this would be the third day I was officially missing. Am I correct? Surely they will be relieved to hear that I am at least alive and well. They must be terrified. My poor Mama …" She didn't flinch as she continued, "That would be, of course, if you notified my father of my disappearance, which any decent headmaster in charge of the safety of his students would have done immediately. They would just be getting the post now, probably. But if you *didn't* notify them, and only *later* decided to tell them for different reasons that their daughter *had* gone missing for three days, they would be very unhappy. They might ask if you had sent out search parties to look for me. They might ask if I've ever gone missing before."

"Miss Bingley – "

"And Lady Littlefield's parents? Mine are aware of my odd behavior, but surely they would also be unhappy to learn that their daughter was so often gone to see the marquis, even sometimes alone, even though he had no mother or sister to greet her. Or that she would often and obviously come home from these visits crying and bruised. Certainly you've not been remiss in your monthly reports in mentioning *that*?" she said. "And I can't even imagine the terror Miss Ashley and Miss Stevenson's parents must be feeling, knowing full well their daughters were assaulted by a known hoodlum and ravager of the local female populace, with only a fellow student to rescue them. Or did that also fail to make it into any reports? Were you too busy discussing their behavior and progress? Is the cost of paper just that high?"

The silence was stunning as Georgiana stood waiting, elevated by her clog shoes and her words, as Stafford mentally tried to scrape together a response. A myriad of emotions passed over his face. He made several false starts, hand gestures that were then cut off, and played with his pen very nervously before he finally set it aside and said, "What do you want?"

"I suppose you'll have to keep up whatever reports you've been sending back to Derbyshire. Disruptive, disobedient, but excellent marks. That sort of nonsense. If you suddenly change it, my parents will be suspicious. But I would like to graduate with a special honor or two. Maybe something about languages. I do know *five* now, if you count Japanese." She paused. "Oh, and no more lessons with Mrs. Halliburton. We've never really gotten along. The other lessons I have every intention of attending, provided you don't try and marry off any other students to abusive local nobility."

Stafford's frown deepened. "Anything else?"

"I don't have to ask you to keep quiet about any goings-on you may hear about. You are already very adept at that. Anything else, Headmaster Stafford? I believe I am late for Logic, but I would like a bath before it."

"No, no, be on your way, Miss Bingley – and the bath will be ready soon."

She curtseyed, which in breeches looked quite ridiculous, but so did everything else about her appearance. Audley stifled a laugh as she showed herself out.

Stafford immediately turned is attention on Audley. "Inspector Audley – "

"I won't say one word – provided you do what she says," Audley said, rising himself. "She's right, you know. You should do a better job of caring for your students. She won't be here to do that next year."

"Thank God she won't be," Stafford muttered as Audley bowed and showed himself to the door.

In the hallway, Georgiana was waiting for him, leaning against the wall in a slackened posture. "So – hadn't you better get on about that missing marquis?"

"I suppose I'll hear all about it when I get in to town, but it's not as if he'll be any deader in a few hours."

She raised her eyes, which softened when they met his gaze. "How long are you going to stay on?"

"As long as it takes to find his body, figure out a way to declare the Wolf dead, and interview enough people to write a report. And then, sadly, I must be off."

"On to the next case." She shook her head. "You should take some time off. Write a novel, like *The Beast of Gévaudan*."

"That book is pure nonsense."

"Precisely. If you tell the real story, Uncle Brian and I will have to flip a coin to see who kills you. But you are an imaginative man. You came up with that clever idea that Sir DuBois was the Wolf, I heard."

"Oh, God, that was so embarrassing! How did I even - ?" He sighed. "What am I going to do without you, Georgiana?"

"Find another lucky girl and marry her."

"But how will I know if it's right without a magic amulet?"

She smiled. "I knew I was in love with him before I knew what the locket meant. Long before."

"Is that supposed to comfort me?"

"I do my best."

He wanted to play with a stray lock of her hair, but they were too short to be strays. This was the hallway of a school – he definitely wasn't going to get past the guards. He just wanted – he wanted to touch her one more time. She grabbed his hand. "Good-bye, Robert."

"Good-bye, Georgiana," he said. "Will I ever see you again?"

She gave him a sly grin. "Perhaps it can be arranged."

~~~

The marquis was missing. Rumor had it, he was dead. Inspector Audley tried not to look distracted and indifferent as he made his way back to the *Verrat*, where

Camille hugged him, almost weeping into his shoulder.

"On the house," Anton said, offering him a glass of whiskey as Audley sat down at the bar. Anton had a bruise on his head but otherwise was unhurt. "What happened to the marquis?"

"I heard he's dead," Audley said. He stared at the drink, wondering if he should have it. He had had very little sleep, still had a headache and a full day of investigative work ahead of him. Then again, it was offered in appreciation for whatever Anton perceived that he'd done; Audley didn't feel as though he'd done much. He swallowed it in one shot. The fire in his throat was strangely soothing, if only to distract him from the pain in his head and the soreness in his back. "Thank you. How are you?"

"I've been better. Been worse, though. Camille got a little hysterical, but she's all right now."

"Where are the bodies?"

"Is that an official question?"

Audley looked up. "No. I am merely curious."

"I've no idea. The Wolf and the Englishman carried them off."

"Did you know it was her? The whole time?"

"Another curious question, Inspector?"

He smiled lazily. "I'm in that sort of mood, yes."

Anton leaned in. "I didn't know. Camille was the one who had the contact and she didn't say. If she'd told me it was a woman, I would have figured it out real fast, I imagine."

"I would have, too," Audley said. "You know what? This case is already ruined, unless I can spin it to my superiors somehow. Another few hours before beginning the search for the missing aristocrat won't matter either way."

"I doubt it."

He nodded, and headed upstairs. To his surprise, his satchel, which he had lost upon his capture the day before, was on the desk. He opened it and retrieved his precious notebook. *How does she - ?* As he opened it, a crème-colored square piece of board fell out. He leaned over to pick it up. *You have been invited to ...*

He smiled after reading it, slid it back in place, and fell asleep on top of the covers, clutching his notebook to his chest.

~~~

"On your way out?"

Brian Maddox was taking a glass of luncheon wine at the bar as servants moved past to carry out his trunk. He was dressed normally again, if there was a thing called dressing normally. Maybe it was all just fashion, but the point was, he was the traveling Englishman once again. Well, aside from the suspiciously heavy walking stick he kept cautiously at his side. "I suppose. In a few hours, anyway. The carriage should arrive sometime after supper."

"I'd be honored to make it into your next book, Mr. Maddox."

"No, no," Brian said. "I'll leave this story in your capable hands, Inspector Audley. Twist it how you like it. Changing names or leaving them out is always preferable. Some people don't want the celebrity."

Audley took a seat across from him. "May I ask you something?"

"What? One last thing you haven't figured out?"

"No, not precisely. How much did Miss Bingley pay you for your services as my bodyguard?"

Brian put down his wineglass. "One *kor* of rice."

"How much is a – *kor*?"

Brian made a loose fist with his hand, as if he were holding a ball. "About that much."

"Wow. You Japan warriors come cheap."

"Indeed."

"So if I got you a *kor* of rice ..."

Brian raised his eyebrows. "My apologies, Inspector Audley, but I am not currently available. And I do not think you are in danger."

"It isn't for me."

It only took the Englishman a brief moment to understand. "In this case, my services are free. However, they aren't very good. You can't very easily protect someone who doesn't think she needs protection."

"But she does."

Brian sighed, putting both hands down on the table. "Some people, their nature is like fire – always moving, always burning energy, always attracting people to their light." He lifted one hand, then the other. "Some people are like water – calm and steady. They flow with their surroundings. My brother and I – well, we're fire and water. It doesn't make us enemies. It just refers to our natures." He put his hands down. "In my first novel, we had two bodyguards. Miyoshi and Mugin. Water and fire. Miyoshi died, but Mugin came with us and stayed in England for a time, until the next boat came along. We didn't know it then, how much he would influence Georgie in that short time. Fire recognizes fire." He picked up his wine. "Another thing I did not mention in the book."

"So what am I?"

Maddox seemed to give him the once-over. "Earth."

"Earth?"

"Full of substance. Tied to something – principles, in your case, no matter how many you might have violated in the past few weeks. It's just a philosophical guess, of course. I never truly understood it, or cared to. But the point is if you see people as forces of nature, then you know that we cannot be forced one way or another out of our habits."

Audley pondered this with a "hmmmm" sound, crossing his arms. "I suppose. Still, keep an extra eye on her, would you? Beyond the one you already seem to be using."

"That I can promise you, Audley-*Keibu*."

Audley stood and they exchanged bows. He was about to turn away when he stopped himself. "Out of curiosity – how would you categorize Geoffrey?"

"Pangs of jealousy? You don't even know the man." Brian smiled. "I won't torture you, even though it's none of your business. Geoffrey is earth."

"Really?"

"It's a good match," Maddox said. "Fire can't burn it, but it can't put fire out."

"I see."

"Someday, you will. Now if I'm not mistaken, I must make quick my escape, and you must spin the biggest web of lies of your career, *Keibu*."

"I learned from the master."

Brian Maddox raised his glass to that.

EPILOGUE

Inspector Robert Audley could not bring himself to return to the forest, even after the passage of time, as it was filled with so many things to distract him from its beauty. Had he never noticed that before? He looked at it as he passed slowly on his horse. Summer had just begun, and the leaves were back and not yet perishing from the heat.

Was it just that it was more distinctive now, after months in Paris's slums, hunting shadows and writing reports? He hadn't missed the country so much when he moved to Paris from Valgones to pursue his career, but he'd been running towards, not away.

He could not enter. It was like violating something sacred, as if his footsteps would ruin it, or at least the memory of it. Not all of the memories were good, but none of them deserved to be marred. Besides, he was only half-finished with his narrative, one that would be about as fictional as his official report but with entirely different inventions.

The manor was no longer vacant. Someone else had moved in – a merchant who had made his fortune with factories that filled Paris with soot. The land renewed instead of laying barren. It was comforting, in a way. But that was not his concern. When he did see someone he recognized, he waved hello but said little else. It was only when he saw Camille scrubbing the pots in a basin outside the *Verrat* that he stopped his horse and tipped his hat.

"Inspector Audley!" Her face, so pale and shrunken when he last saw it, was renewed as well. "What are you doing back out here?"

"Take a lucky guess."

"It's invitation only, Inspector."

"Fortunate then that I have one."

Audley did not tarry long, returning to the road that he had wandered up and down. He could no longer pick out the spot where Simon Roux had died and where he himself had spent a night unconscious. Every ditch beside the forest seemed to look the same. The tall grass had swallowed it.

He de-saddled some distance away from the ceremony, held outdoors to accommodate the guests on their lovely white chairs. He supposed he was underdressed a bit, but not terribly so, once he removed his threadbare riding coat and properly placed his hat on his head.

"Invitation, sir?"

He did not recognize the footman, but he presented it and passed by him without another glance, taking a seat towards the back, where the crowd was more scattered. The girls – the women – had their own seats. No graduation robes. This wasn't a University, but a place to send a daughter who was too wild or too unschooled or just wanted to escape. Maybe a few wanted to legitimately further their studies, but he had his doubts about their numbers being in the majority.

The ceremony was in English. The parents or other guests were sent to retrieve the daughters of the lords and ladies (or extremely wealthy gentlemen). They sat there with their English tall hats and the women with their lace umbrellas as if it were a sunny day just outside London. Perhaps tea would be served.

Headmaster Stafford was in his element, congratulating the students on a job well done (probably meaning the parents on a bill well-paid), and commending them for the seriousness with which they took their studies. Audley couldn't bring himself to listen to this man with any seriousness, and instead watched the crowd, wondering how many of them were peers or knights. He sat among the wealthy of England (or their servants, attending in their stead), and one couple caught his eye. They were easy to spot, because the man's soft blue waistcoat and hat only accentuated his red, almost orange, hair. It was very hard to forget that color, even if his hair was streaked with grey. The woman beside him, her touch gentle as she held his hand, was blond.

The moment he had been waiting for. The special awards were given out – "A special number this year," the headmaster said proudly. Lady Littlefield received an award in exemplary painting. She seemed, even from a distance, like Camille – so rejuvenated by the passage of time. She went up to the small stage eagerly. The man Audley presumed to be her father stood up for her and clapped. Her mother was not obviously present, but not all parents came. Several other girls received awards for languages, and for sewing, and advanced theology. Only two were given two awards.

Georgiana Bingley received three.

She was the very picture of a pretty English lady, all in white with a touch of color from ribbons and a matching bonnet that covered most of her hair – not that there was much to cover. She even walked like her classmates, shyly approaching Headmaster Stafford as she received each certificate. Audley strained himself to take his eyes off Georgiana long enough to observe the headmaster, whose smile when handing those awards to her did not seem particularly genuine. His hands were tense, almost reluctant to give up the slips of paper. She received a double award in language arts and another in philosophy. She smiled at him, but she was too far away for Audley to accurately assess it (and she was such a good actress anyway), for him to tell the truth of it, whether her expression was attempting to rub it in or to just be done with the business. Her parents stood and clapped, her father most enthusiastically. *Fire*, Audley thought instinctively. The mother was obviously *Air*. Since his discussion with Brian Maddox, he had become rather obsessed with the subject, seeking out any book he could find about the elements, and categorizing people. It wasn't particularly helpful in his investigations, but they hadn't handed him an important case until he finally solved the dock strangler case without even being assigned to it. Now back in the department's esteem, he granted himself this small vacation.

After all, he had been *invited*.

After the ceremony, he stood up and clapped with the rest of them, watching as Georgiana was eagerly embraced by her father and then her mother.

"It is not polite to stare, Inspector."

Lady Littlefield had appeared beside him. He bowed to her, and she curtseyed.

"You are alone?"

"My uncle was sent to retrieve me. Not everyone wants to travel to the forest," she said. She had a sort of air of content about her, which was probably unrelated to finishing her year at seminary with honors. "Georgiana sent me to warn you not to mention the word 'wolf' in front of her parents or she'll make you suffer for it. But I would also add that it is good to see you."

He grinned. "Good to see you, too, Lady Littlefield. Where are you off to now, if I may ask?"

"They let us off in time for the London Season, and now that I am an available heiress, I suppose it will be balls and invitations for tea and visits and all of that."

"'All of that?' You seem as though you are looking forward to such a thing."

"I've never been to one – properly. I've been engaged to Maret almost since I was out."

"Enjoy it, my Lady." He knew she would. It was just a feeling, but it was a strong one. They said their good-byes, and Audley wandered around a bit, helping himself to a scone from the refreshment table.

"Are you going to just stand around all day?"

He swallowed as quickly as he could and turned around. Georgiana Bingley was standing behind him. "Mention the Wolf or Uncle Brian being here and you'll never have children," she whispered as her parents approached.

"Good thing I wasn't planning on it," he whispered back, and straightened himself out. He bowed stiffly. "I do not believe we've been introduced. I am Inspector Robert Audley with the Parisian Office."

"Charles Bingley," her father smiled warmly. "And this is my wife, Mrs. Bingley." Appropriate bows and curtseys. "You seem to already know my daughter."

"Yes. I had a brief acquaintance with many of the students here when I was investigating a murder."

"Murder?" Mrs. Bingley said, alarmed.

"Serious business, yes, but the man was not held in much esteem by the community, if you know what I mean. Unfortunately, the case remains unsolved."

"Is that why you are here now?"

"No," Audley said. "I am just passing through. The case was closed by the department for being too costly. Sad, really, that so few people see justice." He glanced briefly at Georgiana. "Some do, though. Usually by circumstance and not my actual work." He coughed. "But I confess – I took a certain interest when I heard your name. I am quite a fan of Mr. Maddox's books."

"I didn't know the second one was available in France," Bingley said. He seemed amused.

"It is by special order. The first one is very popular, even in these parts, I hear. Isn't there supposed to be a third? I'd heard something about that."

"Oh, yes, but once he's finished editing it, I think it'll only be a sort of pamphlet," Bingley said. "Sorry, private joke. My partner is just a very private man. While I can't imagine anything untoward happening during their visit with the Emperor, we still may never know the real story."

Audley smiled at that. "A shame. Well, I won't keep you any longer. It was a pleasure to meet you. Mr. Bingley. Mrs. Bingley. Miss Bingley." He would like to have stalled, but he desperately wanted to read the note Georgiana had slipped into his hand when she snuck up behind him, so he bowed and turned away. It read *Meet me in five minutes behind the carriage with the green colors.*

Resourceful as always. Audley didn't know how she managed it, but she was behind the cart at the appropriate time, sans parents. "Miss Bingley."

"Inspector Audley." She curtseyed. "I'm happy to hear you weren't sacked. I heard you might be after the whole business."

"If inspectors were sacked for every case they didn't solve, we would have a serious lack of them," he said. "I have something for you. I'd forgotten I'd taken it." He pulled out the silver bullet. "Lady Littlefield said you carry it for good luck."

"I used to," she said. "Keep it."

"Really?"

"So you have something to remember me by. That is, if you care to remember me."

"And what will you have to remember me by, Georgiana?"

She kissed him. It was soft, but lingering, as long a moment as they could take with the inadequate cover of the carriage.

"Happy to oblige," he said with a smile. "Good-bye, Georgiana."

"Good-bye, Robert. Take care of yourself – I won't always be there to do it for you."

He still had the broken wooden cross with the kanji on one side and the warning on the other. Now that he knew she'd written it, he could not part with it. It hung on the wall of his apartment. "I'll be more careful next time."

She smiled, a real smile, not forced or circumstantial. It was rare and just for him. It would be a perfect image for the last time he saw her, and this was probably the last time.

Still, he hoped that it wouldn't be.

The End

Historical Notes

There are probably a lot of historical inaccuracies in this book. If that bothered you much, I doubt you would be here. Let's move along.

Bibliography

Artz, Frederick. <u>France Under the Bourbon Restoration, 1814-1830</u>. New York: Russell & Russell, 1963.

Bergeron, Louis. <u>France Under Napoleon</u>. Princeton, N.J.: Princeton University Press, 1981.

De Saint-Amand, Imbert. <u>The Duchess of Angouléme and the Two Restorations</u>. New York: Charles Scribner's Sons, 1892.

Robiquet, Jean. <u>Daily Life in France Under Napoleon</u>. Trans. Violet MacDonald. New York: MacMillan Company, 1963.

Acknowledgments

In no particular order, I would like to acknowledge: Brandy, Mom and Dad, Jane Austen, G-d, Jessica Kupillas Hartung, Cherri Trotter, Brandy's kids, Jeff Gerecke, Diana Finch, Kate McKean, Sourcebooks, Ulysses Press, Hillary King, Yossi Horowitz, Daniel McGee, Brandy's husband, Amazon.com's used book store, Brandy's pets except for the new one who keeps bothering her while she's trying to edit, Deb Werksman, Alex Shwarzstein, Dave Berg, that Salvation Army on 96th that resells books, Talia Goldman, Talia Goldman's mom, Congregation Agudath Israel (but NOT acknowledge the Agudath Israel movement, which is not related and did not contribute to my series), Rabbanite Henkin, Brandy again, Sharon Lathan, Phil Krugman, Abigail Reynolds, my brother Jason, his girlfriend Lindsey, Lindsey's mom, everyone at Austen Authors (authors and fans), Fanfiction.net, Brandy's car, every City College professor I had who was actually good to me, that French werewolf movie with the kung fu Native American, Regina Jeffers, Pepsi but not Coke unless it's Israel Coke and it has real sugar in it,

Diet Coke but not Diet Pepsi because it's horrible, and Brandy.

I may have left some people out.

Preview for Book 7
Young Mr. Darcy in Love

Coming Spring 2013

CHAPTER 1

Anne's Ball

Any man in want of a wife, and thoroughly unacquainted with her father, was seeking only one thing in July of 1825: an invitation to the Pemberley Ball. Anne Jane Darcy, the oldest of the Darcy sisters, was coming out, and not only would the affair be grand, but she was classified by many people as a beauty and her inheritance to be astronomical. However, if they had any inkling of what her father was feeling, every young man with a mother to forward him would have stayed far away.

Aside from his family, everyone at Pemberley steered clear of the master for the entire week approaching the ball. Though he was known well to be a kind and generous master, and that whatever reserve he had could be softened by the presence of his wife or children, that particular week was a variation from the general rule. While Mr. Darcy had little interest in the specifics of the decorations and other plans, he kept a careful eye on the guest list. He was, until the day the invitations went out, marking people off the list with a brisk stroke of his pen.

"Darcy, we're *related* to them," his wife insisted.

"Distantly," he growled.

"It shall be even more distant if you do not invite them."

By mollifying him slowly in the way that only Elizabeth Darcy could, names went back on the list, much to the confusion of the label-maker, so that some people were actually invited.

A further comfort was the return of Geoffrey Darcy from his second year at Cambridge. The upcoming one would be his last. "How's Father?"

"Insane," his mother said. "Stay out of his way."

"I plan to," Geoffrey said with a smile. "Did you hear about George?"

"Through his sister. George is not one to boast in letters, but nonetheless we are very proud of him, if he would ever admit to it himself." Elizabeth shook her head. "A Darcy not admitting to something? Whenever would that come to be?" she said slyly as her husband entered the room.

"What have I done now?"

"Nothing, Father," Geoffrey said. "We were merely complimenting George on his fellowship and chiding him for his lack of communication skills."

"There is no reason to boast about it in a letter," Darcy replied, and in response to their expressions, said, "Why are you laughing?"

There was much to be proud of. George Wickham, newly graduated from his baccalaureate work in Cambridge, had been awarded a fellowship, meaning he could while away the years in the dusty libraries of University as a Fellow if he so chose. They always assumed he would seek further education, though he had not declared in what fashion he would do it, saying only that he was reluctant to go abroad and leave his sister behind. Isabella Wickham was a most eligible lady and heiress, and she was forever dragging him to balls when he was in Town and then forever complaining the next day that all he did was stand in the corner and tell her not to dance with anyone because they were all suspicious – but the Darcys suspected she would not have had it any other way.

Their mother and stepfather, Mr. and Mrs. Bradley, were consumed with their children, all three of them. Isabel nobly tolerated living at home on Gracechurch Street because she loved her little sister Julie, who was now old enough to have talks with, her brother Brandon, and her youngest sister, Maria. She divided her time between Gracechurch Street and Chesterton, where she had a standing invitation with the Maddoxes to be at leisure there, and she was great friends with Emily Maddox, who had gone out last spring.

Alternately Sir, Professor, and Dr. Daniel Maddox lived with his wife in Chesterton. He was now officially retired from the royal service and was the official anatomist professor of Cambridge University, lecturing at Trinity or King's College. When he was not lecturing himself, he was often seen at other lectures. If he had had any part in the granting of George's fellowship, he said nothing. Lady Maddox concerned herself with her daughter, newly available but not quite ready for marriage, and her sons. Frederick would begin Cambridge in the fall, leaving young Danny behind at Eton. Daniel Maddox II was at first picked on for his glasses, but after a few lessons from his Uncle Brian, no one dared to come near him with an awful thought. He was excused from the ball itself, being underage and uninterested. Most of the boys were, even those of age, except maybe Frederick Maddox. The Maddoxes themselves, of course, would be in attendance, along with Brian Maddox and Princess Nadezhda.

Darcy had only regained his ground in the study when a harried servant entered. "Sir Daniel Maddox to see you, sir."

"The doctor? Is he alone?"

"Yes, sir. We don't know quite –"

"– There is nothing to *do* with me," Dr. Maddox said, entering by himself with one hand running along the wall. "Mr. Darcy."

"Dr. Maddox," Darcy said, nodding for the servant to leave as he immediately rose and came to shake the doctor's hand, thereby guiding him to a seat. "It is wonderful to have you back at Pemberley at last. You are truly a –" He trailed off in horror.

"– sight for sore eyes, yes," Dr. Maddox said with a smile, setting his cane against his chest. "Yes, yes, those embarrassing turns of phrase seem to make everyone uncomfortable. But me, it seems."

"Would you like a drink?"

"I am a fan of Pemberley's stock of brandy, thank you."

Darcy got the glass out and poured, handing it to the doctor, who stayed in his chair. It was hard to really read his expression, as his eyes were hidden behind black glasses.

"None for yourself?"

"I am not inclined the night my daughter is entering society."

"Perhaps you should be. It will make the night more bearable," Dr. Maddox said. "The night Emily was presented at court, I was terrified – and proud, mind you. She was very beautiful." It was an unspoken story that Emily had been finally let out mainly because her father's sight was in rapid decline. "I am sure Anne will impress the crowd, as much or little as that pleases you."

"Both, I suppose. But mainly the latter, depending on their intentions," Darcy said, returning to his seat to take up his tea and some notes he had to finish before the evening. "You don't mind if I write? I am very happy to have your company. We have not seen each other since –" He knew he was to say Emily's first Season, but he couldn't bring himself to finish the sentence.

But Dr. Maddox just smiled again. "And there we have it! I think everyone is more upset than I am."

"To be perfectly honest, Maddox, you seem positively jovial."

"To be blind? No," he said. "To have the terrible weight, which has been on my shoulders since I was a boy, of the worry about *going* blind lifted? Yes. No, I will not see my sons or daughter marry, but many parents aren't even present, and I shall be happy for the honor. I simply had no idea how much that fear drove all of my other thoughts. And now it's gone. I have nothing to do but laugh at other people when they say something around me that they think offends me." Dr. Maddox raised his glass before taking another a sip. "As for the other elephant in the room, Danny's condition is considered very stable in comparison to mine. He's worn glasses now for two years with no further degrading and no cataracts. It is the assessment of the head of optometry at the University of St. Andrews, where the medical school has a decent staff beyond their anatomist, that he may just have myopia for the rest of his life, the same way someone is farsighted for the whole of their life. In that, we have been very lucky." He continued, "Speaking of children, Geoffrey seems to be doing well in University, in general and health-wise."

"Yes," Darcy said. "Be careful around him. He reads lips better than he will admit to."

"And my hearing is much improved. So be careful around the both of us, especially if we should decide to team up." Dr. Maddox reached over and found the table, where he set his drink down. "Between the two of us, we should be able to determine every whispered comment about how lovely your daughter looks tonight. And, speaking of which, I shall take no more of your time, Mr. Darcy." He had risen before Darcy could get to him. "I will see you in a few hours, Darcy."

"Doctor."

~~~

Chatton Hall was a madhouse for its own reasons. As the Darcys hosted the Kincaids, the Fitzwilliams, the Townsends, and the Bradleys that were attending, Mr. Bingley was charged with playing host to his sister, his brothers-in-law (as Mr. Hurst was just coming out of mourning for Louisa), children, and relatives.

Accustomed to having many children to get out the door, Charles Bingley (the second) was ready early, and paused in front of the mirror as his manservant ran a lint brush over the coat one last time. "I do believe I've gotten old," he said to Jane as she entered. It was a hard statement to refute. His hair was graying, there were lines in his smile where there had not been previously, and there was the small matter of having two daughters of marriageable age and a son in University with another soon to enter University.

"I failed to notice," Jane said, "as you've hardly been acting the part. The day you retreat to your study with a glass of wine and a book instead of making conversation with your wife, I will declare you old."

"A fair bargain," he said, stepping off the platform and kissing her on the cheek. "How bad is it?"

"Your heir has gone through three outfits now, no one has heard from Brian or Her Highness, and they are still trying to figure out *something* to do with Georgie's hair."

"By the established standards, we are doing well."

"Yes."

"And Lady Littlefield?"

Georgiana's friend from school was paying a visit, and had been invited to the ball. Heather Littlefield seemed a fine young woman, and they were glad to encourage Georgie to have at least one normal friendship. "She is fine," Jane answered. "She is helping with the Georgiana situation."

"So it is a *situation*."

"*Someone* apparently told her to try to put it up."

Bingley wrung his hands. "...And?"

"And then our beloved samurai brother-in-law suggested wax, as that is apparently how the Japanese maintain their hairstyles."

"But that's if – "

"And apparently we did not know the right kind of wax to be used on hair, and it to be – Well, indulge me on one thing."

Bingley smiled. "Anything."

"I want to see the look on your face when you see it."

He could have reacted, but the door was open and Georgie's lady's-maid came rushing in, "Oh Master Bingley, I am so sorry – I didn't want to burn her and we had to get the wax out and Her Highness said she didn't know a way – "

"I'm sure it will be fine," he said, and with one final nudge of his waistcoat, he followed her into Georgiana's chambers, where the already-dressed Lady Littlefield and various female servants curtseyed.

Georgiana rose from her dressing station and curtseyed. "For the record, I wanted to leave it the way it was."

Georgie always had her hair exceptionally short, with the longest locks reaching only her ears, but now it was barely more than shaven. They'd done their best to style what was left, and their efforts were admirable.

"For Sarah's ball, if Darcy ever lets her out, we will cede to your authority," he said and laughed. She did look beautiful – the rest of her certainly was. All of the girls were wearing white now, and nothing but, but it could be tastefully done, with the proper gloves and the unusual locket necklace around her neck. He bowed. "Lady Littlefield." He excused himself to be off to the next disaster and was halted by the passing of a man he hardly knew. "Is that – "

Brian Maddox turned around. "Yes, I do remember how to dress properly," he said, putting a hand on his hip. Brian was, for the first time in recent memory, in proper evening attire, with a tight cravat, matching vest and coat, and even breeches. More importantly, he was swordless – probably. "I promised Darcy."

"I imagine."

"Will you testify to my attire?"

"Testify?"

Brian knocked on the door he had stopped in front of, and it opened, to the protests of some servants inside, and Daniel Maddox stood in the doorframe, one hand clutching it. "Yes?"

"Bingley, tell him."

"What?" Bingley said, distracted by the fact that Dr. Maddox wasn't wearing his glasses. "Oh, yes. Doctor Maddox, your brother is indeed an Englishman again. He looks quite fine."

"Glad to hear it," the doctor said with a smile. What Caroline had said in private was right – his gaze was unsettling. His pupils had settled looking upwards no matter where he might be inclined to look, and his eyes were cloudy from the cataracts, making the irises appear almost red. "Now if we're all done being proud of a man in his fifties of being able to dress himself properly, I'd like to finish getting ready."

"I love you, too, Danny," Brian said, and the doctor smiled and closed the door.

~~~

"Why is it that fathers are more emotional than mothers about sending their daughters out?" Elizabeth Darcy mused as she checked her bonnet once last time. "I am the one who must fret over assuring her a good marriage."

"If we could not use 'daughter' and 'marriage' in the same sentence, I would be very appreciative," Darcy said. "Even by implication. I do recall you were ready to weep when Geoffrey left for Eton." He pulled her in front of him and kissed her gently on the forehead, so as not to disturb either of their carefully prepared outfits. "Besides, Anne will not worry for a good marriage."

"There is more to a marriage than a large inheritance."

"It is a very good start."

The high pitched squealing in the hallway meant his younger girls were having their own start to the festivities. "Papa!"

Darcy gave Elizabeth a nervous smile and opened the door to Cassandra, now twelve. "Yes?"

"Mrs. Annesley says Anne is ready."

"That doesn't mean I am," he said quietly as he followed his daughter down the hallway to his eldest's chambers. There on a stand, surrounded by her two sisters and Isabella Wickham, was Anne Jane Darcy, now seventeen and beautiful. Her brown hair, his shade, was so neatly put up it looked like nothing could take it down without ruining a masterpiece.

"Papa," Anne said. Even on the stand, she was still looking up to him, but not quite so much. "Mrs. Annesley says you shouldn't wear bracelets over gloves, but – "

"But you want to wear your bracelet," Darcy said. "Well, you're a lady now. You may make your own clothing decisions – within reason."

The gold band sat nicely on her white gloves. "Did Grandmama really wear it?"

"To be honest, I have no idea. I found it among my father's personal effects. He may have given it to her and kept it with him after she died, he may have not. Either way, it was meant for someone's darling Anne," he said. Inscribed on the bracelet was, 'To my darling Anne,' and it had been among his father's items in the old d'Arcy mansion in France, so he must have traveled with it, as a keepsake. "You were born just after we discovered it." That seemed so impossibly long ago, and yet he could remember it perfectly.

"Papa! Don't cry."

"I have something in my eye," Darcy said, regaining his demeanor. "I believe your mother wishes to see you, and I've learned not to keep her waiting," he said and kissed his daughter on the cheek as Elizabeth entered, casting him a reassuring glance before turning her attentions to her daughter.

~~~

The evening came despite all the master of Pemberley's wishes that it would not, and Geoffrey Darcy found himself at ease in comparison to the rest of his family. All of the ladies in the house were busy with his mother obsessing over the last minute preparations of Anne's attire, and if there was any truth to Uncle Bingley's jokes (which there usually was), his father was off cleaning the last of his weaponry. The future master of Pemberley rarely made a clothing decision in his life, and when he did it was often terribly done, so he was dressed by his man-servant and that was that. The only one to talk to was George Wickham, who was engrossed in a book in the library. George sat in Mr. Bennet's seat, as Mr. Bennet said he had never cared for balls as a father and now claimed the right of the elderly to avoid them entirely, and was to stay upstairs with the younger children.

Restless, Geoffrey paced a bit while George continued to unintentionally ignore him, played with the fire, and then finally poured himself a glass of brandy.

"Just keep pouring," said Frederick Maddox from behind. The Chatton Hall party was apparently arriving. "I'd better be soused by ten if I'm to make it this whole evening."

"Why? There'll be girls here."

"All of them my relatives," Frederick said, taking his own glass. "Well, not technically. Anyway, cheers." They clinked glasses.

"Congratulations on your graduation."

"Yes, I finally made it through Eton. I surprise even myself sometimes." He smiled with his usual rakish grin. "I wish I could go somewhere other than Cambridge. Just because it's expected. My first year away from home, and my father lives down the street."

"Just don't attend his lectures, and you'll hardly see him," Geoffrey suggested. "Unless you are interested in medicine?"

"God, no."

"I like medicine," George said, announcing his presence rather abruptly to Frederick.

"Lot of good it did you at Oxford."

"I did just fine at Oxford," George said neutrally, not looking up from his book. "I was cum laude when I was dismissed."

"Are we ever going to get that story?"

"It's not polite to ask," said Charles Bingley the Third, entering. "Geoffrey. Frederick. George."

"Want something?" Geoffrey offered.

"Yes." Charles nervously scratched his blond hair, thereby ruining the styling. "Chatton Hall's a madhouse."

"*Chatton Hall?* Have you *seen* my father lately?"

"My father hasn't," Frederick said, and Geoffrey snorted into his glass, Charles colored, and George buried himself in his book.

"I'm damned for laughing at that," Geoffrey said. "And you're double damned for saying it."

"You can't be *double* damned. There isn't a *double* hell. Besides, it's true."

"You're cruel," Charles said.

"What was cruel was being woken by all of the servants screaming at your sister," Frederick countered. "Though it was quite a riot."

"Eliza or Georgie?" Geoffrey said.

"Do you need to ask?"

"Oh," Geoffrey said. "Yes, I heard. I've not seen the evidence."

"Well, you won't. They're making her wear a wig."

Almost on cue, the door opened, and despite the very masculine sanctuary quality of the library, Georgiana Bingley entered, her hair pinned up beautifully for the ball, her dress matching her green eyes in a subtle way with the trimmings. "Charles, whatever it is, stop blushing."

He wrung his hands. "You know I can't help it."

"Fred. George. Geoffrey," she curtseyed, and they bowed to her.

"I do, to be perfectly honest, think your hair looks very nice tonight, cousin," Frederick said. "Odd that it's a completely different shade of red from the normal shade. How did you manage that?"

"Just continue drinking until you pass out, Frederick, for all of us."

"Nice. And I was trying to be polite."

"You were failing," Georgie said.

"It does – look nice," Geoffrey mumbled into his tumbler.

"Thank you," she said in sort of a half-grumble, half-appreciative tone. Frederick just snorted into his glass, Charles squirmed, and George rolled his eyes. In their families, it was impossible to not know that Geoffrey and Georgie were still barely on speaking terms, and that was to be polite.

"Is my sister almost ready?" Geoffrey asked.

"I wouldn't know," she replied, taking a glass of brandy from the table. "I am not going anywhere near four screaming girls, even if they are cousins."

"If I didn't know you better, I would say you have no heart," Frederick said.

"Good thing you do know me, then," she replied, "or I would say you'll be heading to the ball with a black eye."

If Frederick had a response, it was cut off by the bell. The guests were arriving, and that meant the ball was about to begin.

CHAPTER 2

The Dance

Anne Darcy, the first of three very beautiful and very eligible (and very wealthy) daughters of the Darcys of Pemberley, entered society in grand style. Even though it was held at Pemberley and not London, and the guest list was restricted to people Darcy trusted, the ball was still *the* event of the Derbyshire summer. Families with summer houses often ill-used suddenly opened them for the summer. Even the Duke of Devonshire made a rare appearance in this part of his vast empire of English land to see how the other half of Derbyshire was doing.

She was not for lack of dance partners; some were relatives (Charles Bingley the Third, who loved to dance and danced every set) and some not.

"Mama," Anne whispered, "ask Papa to stop glaring at every man who approaches me!"

Her mother laughed. "He's just being a father, dear. There is little to do about it." She added, "Your grandpapa did the same for me. Now ignore him and go dance!"

But her husband had a good ear, and snuck up behind her. "I have trouble imagining Mr. Bennet with a stern look on his face."

"Oh, he did, for me at least." She wasn't invited when Jane went out, of course, but when Elizabeth went out at an assembly, her father was starring daggers into the hearts of any man who approached the then-fifteen Elizabeth Bennet. She didn't recall that so much for her younger sisters, but it had been that way for her.

"He knew what a prize you were," he said with a smile.

"Mr. Darcy, you've now taken your eyes off your daughter for three seconds; she is already *waltzing* with the biggest rake in the county." And when he instinctively had to look, she laughed.

On the other side of the room, Frederick and Geoffrey were spying a pair of ladies who were whispering some distance away. "What are they saying?" Frederick asked.

"They're ... trying to determine which one of us is the Darcy heir," Geoffrey said, focusing on their faces. "And who the other one is, and if he's worth anything. Also, they suspect he may be a fop."

"You made that part up!"

"How do you know?" he said. "All

right, now they're wondering why I'm staring at them. I think we might actually have to dance."

"The blond one's mine," Frederick said. "I'll pay you a sovereign to say I'm Mr. Darcy."

"Not for a quid, Maddox," Geoffrey said, and flagged the house manager Mr. Hawthorn (the MC for the evening) to introduce them. Geoffrey had no desire to dance, and as a student he was not obligated, but this was his sister's debut, and his father demanded at least one dance of him. His partner was a dark-haired girl named Miss Hyde, but he made little conversation and learned little of her, and he politely went back to his corner after the dance to find a scowling George watching his sister make conversation with the son of an earl.

"Tell me what he's saying," George demanded.

Geoffrey turned and focused on the pair in the distance, Izzy and Viscount Something-or-Other. "He's asked her to elope with him tonight, shortly before dinner."

"I'm in no mode for silliness, Darcy."

Geoffrey rolled his eyes. "Fine. He asked her if she preferred the country over life in Town, and she said she had not decided. Am I to be everyone's spy tonight?"

"No. Dr. Maddox is doing his own share."

Dr. Maddox had not retreated like some of the other disabled or aged gentlemen to the card rooms. He took a seat out of the way of the floor as his wife danced with his brother. Brian and Caroline were both partner-less; Princess Nadezhda did not make public appearances unless begged, and certainly not to dance.

"Which one is the cousin?"

"There are two cousins. The Bingleys."

"What, the tradesman at Chatton Hall?"

"Yes. Georgiana and Eliza. I don't know which is which, but they're both out," said the other young man. The two of them were making conversation not far from where Dr. Maddox was motionlessly seated, leaning on his cane. "I heard they have fifty thousand pounds."

"For fifty thousand, I would marry a tradesman's daughter," the other one said. "What about her? The one with red hair?"

"Please. That is obviously a wig."

"No! The other one. In that nice little bodice and yellow ribbons."

"Oh yes. Very lovely. What I wouldn't give for – "

Dr. Maddox said, "That is Emily Maddox."

"Who's she?" said the first man.

"My daughter."

At that point they made no more conversation, at least not within earshot. In fact, he could positively hear them scurry away despite the noise of the dance.

"What are you laughing at?" his wife said, the dance now finished.

"Just enjoying eavesdropping on the brash young men in the crowd."

She brushed her hand over his hair. "Sometimes I think you like being blind."

"It has its moments."

She leaned over and kissed him. "Mr. Darcy has offered to take some time away from following his daughter around with a shotgun to dance a set with me, if that meets your approval."

"Anything that makes you happy meets my approval."

On the opposite side, Jane leaned in to her husband. "Who is Eliza dancing with?"

"I believe that is ... Lord Brougham's son."

"She's danced two dances with him."

"As long as she stops there. And it wasn't the first two."

"Some men like to show their affection by dancing with a woman twice at the first meeting."

Bingley blushed. "Well, he's Lord Brougham's son. It's not the end of the world. Besides, Charles has danced every dance and you haven't said anything."

"Because he dances with anyone. You know he just likes to dance."

"He is his father's son."

"Yes, setting ladies' hearts dangerously aflutter while he's still ineligible."

"Are you going to discourage two of our children from dancing *at a dance* and then also comment on how Georgie hasn't accepted one offer?"

Jane smiled. "I suppose you've caught me on that one."

Georgiana was busy retreating to the corner where George and Geoffrey were standing. "Is this the hiding corner?"

"Only men are allowed to scowl away potential partners," George said.

"Besides, we're ineligible."

"Well, you won't be in a year, unless you're going for a Fellowship, Mr. Darcy. And if you think every girl in this room doesn't know that, you are fooling yourself."

"I assure you, I am aware," he grumbled.

"He's been reading lips all night," George said. "You would be surprised what people will say behind your back. Or just a certain distance away."

"I think I've strained my eyes. I have a splitting headache coming on, and we're still an hour from dinner and possible wine. And many hours from quiet."

"So I suppose we'll all be spoilsports together, then," George said.

Georgiana rolled her eyes. "Unfortunately, my father said I was obligated for one dance, and Charles is *always busy*, the flirt."

"He doesn't talk to them, so it barely counts as flirting," George said.

"If you are under such stringent obligations..." Geoffrey said, "May I have the next dance, Miss Bingley?"

"Are you serious?"

"I am."

Realizing he was, she said, "You may." She curtseyed, he bowed, and she left.

Geoffrey turned to George, who was smirking. "Well, at least it got the only smile out of you that will probably be seen this evening. Do I look all right?"

"How should I know? Ask the man who dressed you."

Geoffrey just gave his jacket a tug and headed to the dance floor. He could have been paying attention to the people who were staring at him, but he was too focused on what he was doing and hoping that she wouldn't notice his hands were shaking when they touched. The dance began. He knew all the steps without thinking, which was quite good, because he wasn't doing a lot of it.

"Your palms are sweating," Georgie said as they crossed.

"How did you know? I'm wearing gloves."

"Because you just confirmed it," she said with a little smirk. She hadn't given him a pleasant little smirk in two years.

Maybe he ought to dance with her more often.

"Are we supposed to converse while dancing?"

"I don't know," he answered. "You've danced more than I have."

"I've never had anything to say."

"Ridiculous," Geoffrey said, though the last turn was a little too fast for him, and he blinked to steady himself. "You always have something to say."

"All right, I've never had anything polite to say."

"Ah, the key difference."

They separated for the last time and took their positions. He bowed to Georgie, but not very well. The dance was too fast for him and he was too distracted. He bowed to her. "Excuse me." And he left the ballroom.

"Did you see that?" Elizabeth said, pulling Darcy away from his current focus on where his daughter was going and whom she was speaking to.

"See what?"

"Geoffrey danced with Georgiana. By choice!"

"That can't be. He only dances when forced," Darcy said. He turned his eyes fully away from his daughter for the first time in the evening, and towards his wife. "My, how he's changed."

~~~

Geoffrey Darcy made his excuses and did not return for the dinner. Darcy had been as careful with the seating arrangements as he had been with everything else, so that Anne was surrounded by family and not overeager bachelors. "I had no idea dancing was so exhausting!" she whispered to her mother.

"Then you haven't done enough of it," Elizabeth said. "But don't tell your father I said that."

Pemberley's food was only the finest, and it brought out the older crowd from the card rooms with exceptional speed. Then there was the white soup followed by the entertainment, which included some lovely playing of the pianoforte by Eliza Bingley, games of whist and casino, and a chance for some gentlemen to smoke on the veranda. It was then that Anne finally had the chance to sneak away, bypassing her sisters, who were eager to talk to her, and open the door to Geoffrey's room.

He was lying on the floor with a pillow under his head, and only a single candle placed high on the shelf lighting the room. He stirred at the light from the hallway and the figure at the door. "What is it?"

"I came to see if you're all right."

"Anne! This is *your* ball."

"And you're *my* brother." She knelt next to him. "Are you going to be all right?"

"In the morning, I'll be fine. It was the last spin that got me. I should have picked a slower dance."

"It would have been more romantic."

"Hush! You're out five hours and suddenly you're all smarmy."

She smiled. "Feel better."

"I will."

"I'll send George up, if you want. He needs the excuse."

"You don't have – " but she was already gone, " – to."

~~~

A few minutes later, Geoffrey was disturbed again from his meditative attempts to stabilize his head. "Sorry. They sent the wrong George," Georgiana Bingley said in the doorframe.

"You're not mad at me?"

"For what?"

"For walking out immediately after dancing. I thought you might think I was running away." He didn't want to say, *again.*

"It's rather easy to tell when your eyes cross," she said. "I shouldn't have pushed you."

"Pushed me? I requested the dance. And I had already met my requirements for the evening."

Georgie looked at her feet. "I should get back to the feast. After all, I must be chaperoned, lest my reputation be marred."

"If anyone thinks less of you as a woman for your perfect behavior as a dancer and your beautiful gown, as well as not being a gossiping chit, I will be very surprised." He added, "And I would be inclined to hit them, but I don't think I can get up right now."

"I'll delay my insults to society and propriety, then. Good night, Geoffrey. Feel better."

"Good night," he said, dreaming even though he was still awake.

~~~

Long after dinner and many card games, the festivities began to wind down and mothers began to reign in their unruly and possibly tipsy sons before they embarrassed themselves, as everyone did at a good ball. As Anne's many new admirers drifted away, back into their carriages and gigs, Darcy began to relax and shared a glass of wine with Bingley while the crowd finished up their card games.

"Well, brother, I think you succeeded in being sufficiently terrifying," Georgiana Kincaid said to Darcy, taking a seat beside him on the settee. "You made my going out party seem almost a delight for you."

"I was just as nervous, I assure you," he said.

"And now, the court presentation," Lord Richard Fitzwilliam said.

"That's hardly anything. Quite brief, actually. And I don't think the king will be paying much attention."

"How is the king?"

Bingley kicked the leg of Dr. Bertrand's chair at the table. "How is His Majesty?"

Dr. Andrew Bertrand, now one of many on the staff of the increasingly fat and ill king of England, Scotland, and Ireland, said, "All I will say is the papers are not lying in their descriptions."

"You're as bad as Maddox!"

"What?" Brian said from over the din. "Whatever it is, I wasn't responsible."

"You weren't," his brother said. "They were talking about me. I treated the king when he was a bit less of a public laughingstock."

"More of a laughingstock and less pathetic!" Mr. Hurst proclaimed between drinks.

"Now, there's some sympathy to be had for a man who is stuck with a horrible wife, has lost his only daughter, and is still responsible for running the most powerful kingdom in the world," Dr. Maddox said. "I would offer up a kingdom *not* to be him and instead be a well-paid physician and professor who is only obligated to teach one lecture a year."

"Hear, hear!" Bingley said, and raised his glass.

~~~

Meanwhile, the relatives of Anne who had no other business at the ball had gathered again on the porch and were passing around a bottle of excellent brandy.

"I thought you didn't start drinking again until your first lecture," Georgie said, joining the three of them with a shawl wrapped around her from the evening breeze.

"It's not all fun and games, you know," Charles defended, however meekly, as he passed her the bottle, which she took a gulp of. "The exams are in Latin. *And* Greek."

"Did they teach you the classics in that fancy seminary of yours?" Frederick said.

"Are you serious? Those are hardly appropriate studies for a lady. Our small minds are not capable of grasping the complexities of dead languages and are more suited to think like living ones, *Maddok-Yarichin.*"

"What did she call me?" Frederick said to Charles.

He shrugged. "I don't know Japanese. I only know it was."

"What good are you, then? I'll have to find someone else. What did you say again?"

"Are you crazy?" Georgiana said. "I'm not repeating it."

"That bad," George said with a smile. "So what did the ladies have to say about us tonight?"

"Mainly they discussed how much you were worth," she said. "Charles, they think you have about ten thousand a year. Frederick, they have no idea, but you're the son of a knight and the second cousin of an earl, so their fathers would approve. George, they couldn't believe how you just stood there silently when there were ladies waiting to dance. How rude!"

He shrugged unapologetically.

"The ladies do seem to have one-track minds," Frederick said, as if he was making a great observation.

"I would say that of men," George said, "but it's a different track."

~~~

At long last, when all of the guests except the very closest of relatives had departed, and many of the ladies had gone to bed, Mr. Bennet hobbled his way downstairs and joined them for a glass of port. "So then ... another thing I never thought I would be present for." He raised his glass to that and sipped.

"To a long life, Mr. Bennet," Darcy said, and they clinked glasses.

"Yes, I may even be so lucky to see all my beautiful grandchildren *marry*," he said just as Darcy was trying to swallow. Darcy choked, of course, and lapsed into a coughing fit before he recovered. "Do be careful with your drink, Mr. Darcy. You never know when life will surprise you."

To be Continued...

About the Author

Marsha Morman didn't have time to write this section. What, you think back copy writes itself?

She lives in New York.

Made in the USA
Lexington, KY
11 July 2013